From the library of
B327 Painting © Roger Cooke

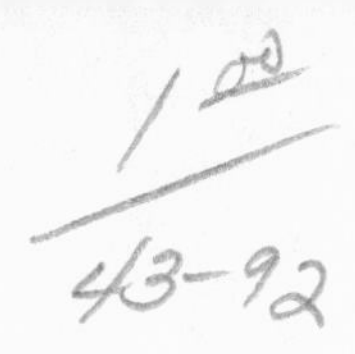

MURDER IN THE WHITE HOUSE

Also by Margaret Truman

WOMEN OF COURAGE
HARRY S. TRUMAN

MURDER IN THE WHITE HOUSE

A NOVEL BY

Margaret Truman

ARBOR HOUSE *New York*

For my husband Clifton Daniel and my sons Cliff, Will, Harrison and Thomas.

 Published in the United States of America by Arbor House Publishing Company and in Canada by Clarke, Irwin & Company, Ltd.

A section of this book first appeared in *Good Housekeeping,* June 1980.

Library of Congress Catalog Card Number: 79-54004

ISBN: 0-87795-245-0

Manufactured in the United States of America

10 9 8 7 6 5 4

ONE

I

Andrews Air Force Base, Tuesday, June 12, 9:00 PM

The radio on the helicopter was tuned to the tower frequency, and the crisp metallic voices said Air Force One was on final approach long before anyone could see it. The little welcoming party—the Vice President, the President's daughter, the President's Special Counsel—climbed down from the helicopter and crossed the ramp under umbrellas held by the Marine attendants. They passed through the knot of media people waiting in the drizzle and stood apart from them, a little closer to the roll of red carpet that would be unrolled to the foot of the steps when Air Force One was on the ground. They joined the media group in staring expectantly at the overcast sky.

Lynne Webster, the President's daughter, found Ron Fairbanks's hand. She squeezed it. One of the television people noticed and nudged the woman beside him. It was nothing odd. Washington knew there was something between the President's daughter and his Special Counsel. The NBC camera zoomed for a moment to the clasped hands, and suddenly hundreds of thousands of people saw. For many it was more interesting than the President's return from Paris, where he had just signed some kind of trade agreement. His daughter was a tall, handsome, brown-haired girl. The nation had watched her mature in three years in the White House: from a gawky adolescent to a young woman gaining self-assurance, poise and presence. Fairbanks was an obscure figure. Everyone had seen his picture in *Time* or somewhere: one of the bright young men who worked for the President; but what he did, exactly, was not clear. Anyway, he was a good-looking young fellow; he made a good picture standing in the rain holding the hand of the President's daughter. They made an appealing couple, a good picture for the home screens and for tomorrow's tabloids.

Air Force One appeared beneath the overcast—a Boeing 747 now—huge, majestic, vaguely eerie in its landing configuration, with flaps down, gear down, long thin beams of light extending from its wings toward the runway. It settled slowly, its movement almost imperceptible, silent, powerful. The honor guard came to attention just as the tires touched the runway with a quick screech, and the airplane rushed past, noisy now, roaring, slowing. It passed the ramp and ran almost to the end of the runway; then slowly it turned and began its slow taxi back to the ramp.

Wind drove the rain momentarily into the faces of the little welcoming party. Fairbanks put a finger to Lynne's cheek and pushed away a strand of her hair that had been blown there and stuck in the glistening rain water. It was an intimate gesture the television cameras missed. He smiled at her, she returned it. They were not lovers, whatever the speculation. Since last fall, when she left for her third year of college, he had seen her only two or three times. Now that she was back at the White House for the summer, he would see her more often. He might become, over the summer, something more than a convenient, quasi-official escort for her—the staff bachelor who was available to accompany her when it was awkward for her to be alone. They might decide if they wanted their relationship to be anything more . . . they were amused, both by the situation and by the speculation it generated. They understood each other. She liked him, he liked her.

The 747 taxied to the ramp, its great engines whining, overpowering the chatter among the media people and the low monotone of the network narrators. Air Force One never failed to awe. Even the bold legend along its body—UNITED STATES OF AMERICA—was awesome by its simplicity. President Webster understood the dramatic value of the big airplane, and he took full advantage of it. He had retired the 707 that had long served as Air Force One and substituted this 747 for it—not without some grumbling from the Congress—probably as much from a sense of its grandeur as from the practical need. The pilots swung its nose around, and the airplane came to a stop only a foot from the stairway that was now nudged up to it.

The airplane sat there in the white glare of floodlights—raindrops sparkling in the unnaturally bright electric light. The engines stopped. Marines rolled out the red carpet to the foot of the stairs. The door opened. The Marine Band struck up Ruffles and Flourishes. The President appeared in the door. Hail to the Chief. He smiled and turned to speak to his wife. She stepped out. They stood for a moment, blinking into the glare of light, both smiling, nodding blindly at the small crowd at the foot of the stairs. Two Secret Service men trotted up the stairs with umbrellas. The President grinned and motioned them away. With his wife's hand in his, he hurried down the stairs.

Robert Lang Webster, President of the United States. He was fifty-five years old and looked maybe a few years younger. They said he had thrived on the presidency; and, although his face was deeply lined, he was gray only at the temples and his hair was thick and dark; he was hard and thin and given to abrupt, decisive movement. He allowed another Secret Service man to drape a raincoat over his shoulders as he stepped up to the microphones and faced the television cameras.

Catherine Steele Webster. She was fifty-four and looked forty. She acknowledged that a New York surgeon had taken some tucks in the flesh around her face and subdued some wrinkles, and she said she would have it done again whenever she thought she needed it. She accepted a raincoat as she sidestepped the microphones and reached out to take Lynne's hands. She stood for a moment, facing Lynne and smiling, then nodded at Ron Fairbanks and winked before she moved to her husband's side. She nudged her husband and muttered something that the CBS microphone, a little closer to her than the others, picked up for the nation—"Let's get on with it, it's raining."

The President beckoned Lynne to come and stand beside him. He kissed her on the cheek.

The Vice President, Allan Torner, began to say something about the President's quest for peace and prosperity and about how the nation had watched what he had done in Paris and now welcomed him home. The President listened to Torner and nodded at him as he spoke, but he was unable—and not at much effort—to conceal his impatience.

"Thank you, Mr. Vice President—Allan," said the President as soon as Torner paused and might be finished. "I appreciate your coming out to meet us. I appreciate the ladies and gentlemen of the print and electronic media, also coming here. This is not a very dramatic homecoming. We made a quick trip to Paris to initial the preliminary trade agreements entered into among many nations in the interest of mutual aid and shared prosperity. It really was not necessary for me to go, as some have pointed out, except that I wanted to demonstrate to the people of the United States and the people of the participating nations of Europe, Asia, and North America—all of whom will be called on to make certain sacrifices to achieve our joint goals—that the President of the United States is wholly committed to the economic program represented by the multilateral agreements. That is why I went. The negotiations are continuing. The initial accomplishment of this agreement will be followed by other accomplishments, other elements of the program. We have charted a difficult course. But we will achieve our goals."

He wiped rainwater from his forehead with the back of his hand, and he could be seen to chuckle quietly as he flipped the water in the direction of the TV cameras. It was somehow the right gesture for the moment, one of the small gestures for which he seemed to have an unconscious but almost infallible instinct. Some of the media people laughed.

The President stepped back from the microphones and glanced at the Secret Service man nearest him: a suggestion the party was ready to be led to the helicopter.

"Mr. President!" The CBS man, Ted O'Malley, was trying to ask a question. "May we ask why the Secretary of State did not go to Paris with you? Is there anything to the rumor he is resigning?"

The President pointed, grinning, at O'Malley. "Hi, Ted!" he yelled. He was away from the microphones, and they were not picking him up. "Don't believe all the rumors you hear," he called over his shoulder as he turned away from the media group and herded his party toward the helicopter. He waved and grinned again at O'Malley before he turned his back and moved decisively away.

The President and Catherine Webster, Lynne, the Vice President, and Ron Fairbanks climbed into the helicopter. The floodlights had been swung away from Air Force One and now glared on the green and white helicopter. The rotor was turning slowly above the helicopter. The red lights on it were blinking. The President's face appeared for a moment in a window. He waved at the media people and the small crowd behind the fence. The rotor swung faster, and the helicopter rose.

The 'copter hovered above the ramp, heavily, gracelessly, and then tipped forward slightly and slid over the ground, away from the ramp and the lights, into the darkness. Two others, just like it, rose and joined it before it gained altitude and left the area of the Air Force base. The other two were helicopter gunships, carrying electronics to detect any threat to the presidential helicopter—from a missile, from an airplane, from a shot fired from the ground—and to take electronic countermeasures, or to fire shots if necessary. The three helicopters flew in formation. The presidential helicopter flew on the left of the formation tonight. Sometimes it flew in the middle, sometimes on the right; an attacker would not know which helicopter carried the President.

Ron Fairbanks disliked the helicopter. No matter it was the President's helicopter, it was always noisy, always shook, and its erratic motion unsettled his stomach. He could never be less than fully conscious that it *was* the presidential helicopter and that he, Ron Fairbanks of Fairfield, California, was aboard with the President of the United States; but it unsettled his stomach just the same. The President was saying something, but it was not directed at him, and he did not try to listen.

The President was talking to Lynne. Fairbanks had noticed before how, at times like this when no one else could claim his attention, the President would focus his attention on Lynne and for a few minutes give himself exclusively to her. It did not happen by chance; he made a point of it. She was his youngest child, and he had been absent during years that were important to her—absent running for the Senate, then being a senator, absent running for President, then being President. At moments like this—and they were always private moments—he would lean toward her and speak quietly but with intensity and animation. And warmth. If the public had seen the genuine, human warmth he showed in these private moments, his public image might have been radically different.

The public image was of an able, tough, decisive man. He inspired confidence. The editorialists and pundits said of him that he was the first President in decades from whom the American people were willing to accept leadership, because he inspired confidence. He was combative. (He had utterly declared war on the Congress—privately he had once referred to the Senate as a "collection of minor-league dipsomaniacs and fugitives from *dementia praecox.*" Publicly, he had called the United Nations General Assembly a circus. He had called a sign-waving, chanting crowd of anti-nuclear power demonstrators "a mob of infants having a public tantrum.") He was almost ruthless at times. When his first Secretary of the Treasury admitted on "Meet the Press" that an income tax rate adjustment the Administration was sponsoring might have an inflationary effect, the President summarily fired him. ("In this Administration everyone sings from the same sheet," he had said.) He was blunt. (He told a summit conference of European heads of government that "the basic foreign policy of the United States is pursuit of the enlightened self-interest of the United States.") The American people loved all of it. He had a high approval rating in the polls.

But he was not shallow. (The remainder of his statement to the European heads of government was that the enlightened self-interest of the United States dictated adherence to the program of multi-lateral trade agreements he had doggedly promoted for three years, and he had been telling them that their own self-interest would be best served if they, too, adhered to that program.) He had courage. (He had anticipated the political furor that would follow his firing of the Secretary of the Treasury and had decided to tough it out.) He could be subtle. (His statement about the anti-nuclear demonstrators was a signal to a hundred other groups of all kinds, who had made a fad of street tantrums, that demonstrations would not influence him to take positions he didn't believe in.) And he was a consummate political manipulator. (Even the Senate he had so colorfully characterized passed most of the legislation he wanted, because he had a thumb, and a dossier, on forty or fifty senators.)

He was powerful. He carried people along with him. His own sense of purpose was real. He was able to communicate much of that sense to the people who worked for him and some of it to the nation. He communicated more of his self-confidence.

He had almost walked away from his appointment with President-elect Webster without seeing him. He had flown from Washington for a two-o'clock appointment with Senator and President-elect Webster in his transition headquarters in the Renaissance Center in Detroit; and when five o'clock came and he knew he would miss his return flight if he waited any longer, he almost walked out and caught a cab back to the airport. He might be only a young lawyer working his way up in a Washington firm, but he had his self-respect, and the apparent rudeness of Webster or of his organization turned him angry. Anyway, the dramatic impact of walking out on an appointment with the President-elect of the United States somehow appealed to him; and it was only the thought of the explanations he would have to make back in Washington that kept him in the bleak temporary reception room, pacing, staring down from fifty floors at the gray waters of the Detroit River through heavy snow swirling on a gusty winter wind . . . .

"Ron . . . good to see you. I appreciate your coming."

It was after five. A secretary had brought him from the headquarters offices to the Detroit Plaza Hotel—still in the Center—

and up to a suite sixty floors above the river. The President-elect, wearing a black cashmere jacket and crisply pressed gray slacks, used his first name immediately, even though they had never met before. Fairbanks had expected a slightly more restrained man.

"Let's get some fresh coffee. That's . . . actually, it's after five. How about a drink? Scotch?"

The President-elect was almost too comfortable. Maybe it was a facile judgment, but Fairbanks felt that Webster did not wear his triumph too well, was somehow pushing it . . . He summoned a secretary to pour Scotch, and while she worked in the corner of the room he made precisely measured small talk: enough to cover the moment, no more. Ron had flown to Detroit in bad weather. Was it as bad in Washington? He had graduated from Stanford Law, hadn't he? He knew Bill Guthrie, didn't he? How was Bill? The secretary delivered two generous Scotches. Webster took a manful swallow from his, leaned back in the corner of his couch.

"Bill Friederich recommends you, without reservation."

Crisp. Abrupt. Fairbanks knew he had been called to Detroit to be offered some kind of job in the Webster Administration; he had no idea what. He knew his old mentor, Justice William G. Friederich of the United States Supreme Court had recommended him. He had clerked for Justice Friederich. It was the thought of having to explain to *him* that had kept Ron from walking out this afternoon.

"Justice Friederich is a friend," said Fairbanks. It was a careful, bland answer. He had determined to keep a wary distance. He did not want a job in the Webster Administration, really. He had come to Detroit out of courtesy to Justice Friederich, and, of course, out of curiosity.

"I'm looking for a few people with a special sense of commitment," Webster said. "There are not many things in this life that are worth a total commitment, and I've known people who made that kind of commitment for nothing very much. But this . . . the presidency for four years. It *is* worth it. I've made the commitment for myself, and I'm looking for people who will make it with me. I'm looking for one hundred percent dedication. You think you could give that to me, Ron?"

Fairbanks looked over his Scotch. "To be altogether frank, I don't think I could. I usually hold back a little something of myself . . . for myself, I guess . . . I don't think I could change that, even if I wanted to." He smiled faintly. "I'm sorry. I don't see any point in lying about it."

Webster smiled too—more broadly. "Well, you're honest," he said wryly.

"I'm a skeptic, I guess something of a cynic," Fairbanks said.

Webster laughed. "Any other disqualifications?"

Fairbanks grinned. "I didn't vote for you."

"I knew that. Bill Friederich told me. He also told me you had your reasons. He said you were circumspect and, if you agreed to work for me, would support me while you were with me. Was he right about that?"

Fairbanks nodded. "I'm rather naive politically," he said.

Webster laughed again. "I hear otherwise."

A door from another room in the suite opened, and Webster's daughter came in. Fairbanks recognized her from her pictures. "Lynne," said Webster. "Pour yourself a drink and sit down. This is Ron Fairbanks. I'm about to offer him a job."

The young woman settled a critical eye on Fairbanks. She was nineteen or twenty, as Fairbanks remembered the press stories about the Webster family: a student, the President-elect's youngest child. She was attractive, not to say beautiful; but Fairbanks thought she looked tired. He remembered reading somewhere too that Lynne Webster had said the campaign had exhausted her.

She did pour herself a drink, and came to stand behind her father, as if waiting for him to dismiss Fairbanks and then she could have a word with him.

"I want you to serve as Special Counsel to the President," Webster said to Fairbanks. . . .

"I didn't expect it," Ron said to Lynne an hour later. He had not expected what followed, either. Webster had said he realized Ron had missed his return flight. He told him there was a room for him there at the Plaza; and then, for a further surprise, he said to Lynne that he could not have dinner with her after all, since Senator Fleming was arriving within the hour, and since Ron was stuck overnight in Detroit, alone, maybe it would be pleasant if they had dinner together.

Here they were, then, in *La Fontaine,* the fine French restaurant in the hotel, sitting opposite each other at a table: the daughter of the President-elect and his new Special Counsel. Lynne was not pleased. She had expected to have dinner with her father, not to be pushed off on a stranger and be compelled to make conversation about such things as her impending move to the White House. She was silent. She dipped her hand in the water in the fountain from which the restaurant took its name—it was immediately beside their table—and said casually that the water was room temperature. People in the restaurant recognized her. They stared. She noticed and was uncomfortable; she stared at her hands. Two Secret Service agents sat at a nearby table too, rarely taking their eyes off her. Lynne glanced around. People were embarrassed to be caught staring and quickly looked away.

"Assault by eyeball," she said.

The waiter lingered over their table, extending the ritual of opening a bottle of white wine so he would have more time to study the daughter of the President-elect, to memorize her features, her clothes, her figure, the better to be able to describe them vividly to friends later. Lynne accepted a glass of wine and held it between her hands, staring into it, frowning.

"There are two things," said Ron slowly, "that being the daughter of the President-elect does not involve."

"Oh? And what are they?"

"First, it involves no obligation on your part to entertain me this evening, simply because your father held me in Detroit so long I missed my plane. Second, it involves no obligation on my part to attempt to entertain you when obviously you are uncomfortable and bored. I suggest I pay for the wine and leave."

She blushed. "I'm . . . I'm sorry—"

"Third thing, no obligation to apologize. We were thrown together, no fault on either side . . . does he do that often?"

"He meant well," she said quickly. "He thought you and I would have things to talk about, things in common. He meant to relieve me of another evening of political talk."

"Well . . ." Ron shrugged, smiled.

"Can you make us some interesting conversation, Mr. Fairbanks?"

"I think so, Miss Webster . . . For starters, you have very good legs . . ."

And from there it went quite well. The daughter of the President-Elect defrosted, though still a bit edgy . . . nervous . . . in a way that made him more curious than he could explain . . .

The White House, Tuesday, June 12, 10:15 PM

Waiting in the Yellow Oval Room were the Secretary of State, the Chairman of the Senate Foreign Relations Committee, the ranking Republican of the Senate Foreign Relations Committee, and the White House Chief of Staff. They had watched on television the return of Air Force One to Andrews, and when the helicopter landed on the lawn they were assembled in the Yellow Oval Room, sipping drinks and munching on chips and nuts.

Senator Kyle Pidgeon, the Republican, flushed and wheezing, held the Secretary of State tight in conversation; and it was only with visible effort that Lansard Blaine was able to break away, cross the room, and shake the hand of the President.

"I'll want you with me downstairs," was all the President said to Blaine. He referred to a meeting in the Oval Office, scheduled for 10:30, when he would report to the other members of the Senate Foreign Relations Committee and to some from the House Foreign Affairs Committee. ("It makes them feel *damned* important to meet with the President in the middle of the night," he had remarked to Lynne as they walked from the helicopter.)

Blaine sipped brandy from a snifter. "Solid front, hmm?" he said. "I heard O'Malley ask you if I'm resigning."

"I'll deal with O'Malley," the President said under his breath—just before he smiled broadly and reached to shake the hand of Senator Pidgeon.

Ron Fairbanks studied the Secretary of State. Blaine had always impressed everyone with his self-assurance, with the reserve and calm he could display under intemperate attack by a senator or a protester or an aggressive interviewer. It was plain tonight, however, that he was ill at ease. Ron watched him slip away from Senator Pidgeon once again and walk purposefully to the steward to order another cognac.

"Are you going to check over the Pillsbury memorandum before you leave for the night?"

Fairbanks' attention was diverted by the question from Fritz Gimbel, the Chief of Staff. "I suppose so," he said to Gimbel. "This is breaking up shortly . . . ?"

Gimbel glanced at his watch. "In eight minutes."

In eight minutes. Yes, in eight minutes precisely if that militaristic little creep had anything to do with it, Fairbanks thought . . . if he left the White House before the Webster Administration left office, it would be because of Gimbel. He was an unpleasant man, invested by the President with a great deal of authority. Small, wearing an ill-fitting gray checked suit, peering about with unfriendly eyes that stared through his austere steel-rimmed glasses, Gimbel orchestrated everything in the White House. In a minute he would order the steward to leave, so stopping the drinking. A few minutes later he would suggest firmly to the President that the meeting in the Oval Office should begin in three minutes if it were to begin on time. Likely, the President would accept the suggestion. Gimbel would hold open the door.

Blaine too disliked Gimbel. Two men could hardly have been more in contrast. Blaine was a preppy, then a Yalie, and he had spent two years at Oxford. Gimbel was from Indiana and had graduated without honors from some small-town Indiana college. Blaine was a scholar of diplomatic history—had come, indeed, to the State Department from a professorship at the University of Michigan, which he had held with distinction for twenty years. Gimbel had gone from college to the Webster Corporation, first as an accountant, then as an administrator, finally as executive assistant to the president—he served Robert L. Webster in the White House almost exactly as he had served him in Detroit. Blaine had a calm, aloof panache. Gimbel was a nervous, abrasive little man.

Blaine and Gimbel had aroused cries of cronyism early in the Webster Administration. Both of them had been personal friends of Robert and Catherine Webster for years. Catherine was a psychiatrist; and, until she moved into the White House as First Lady, she had held a professorship in psychiatric medicine at the University of Michigan. She and Blaine had taken leaves of absence from the Michigan faculty at the same time—Blaine was more of a friend of hers than of her husband, although Webster had retained Blaine as a consultant on foreign affairs during his senatorial campaign and again during his presidential campaign and had expressed both privately and publicly his confidence in Blaine's judgment in matters of foreign relations. Gimbel had served the Webster family as well as the Webster Corporation in Michigan—as a baby sitter sometimes, as a driver, as a runner of errands, as well as a trusted get-things-done man in the executive offices of Webster Corporation.

"Why don't you sit down, Lan?" the President's daughter said to Lansard Blaine. She took hold of his arm. "I'm sure the Senator will surrender you to me."

"Of course," said Senator Pidgeon. He was a little drunk—on the couple of Scotches he had had; that was all it ever took—and he attempted what he supposed was a courtly bow and stepped back two paces.

Blaine allowed Lynne to lead him to a wing chair, where he sat staring into his brandy while she, standing beside the chair, firmly kneaded his shoulders. Blaine did not look up. He accepted a massage from the President's daughter without acknowledging it.

Lynne had a nose that turned up, a pert lively face, a lithe figure (although a little heavy in the bust). Of all the presidential family, the burden of the White House seemed heaviest on her. She seemed to labor under a sense of it: the dignity and burden of it.

Ron Fairbanks watched her rub Blaine's shoulders, looking curiously intent and grim. Ron sipped Irish whisky—Old Bushmills, which they had not served at the White House before Catherine Webster noticed his preference for it and ordered it. He was not jealous of Lynne's somewhat intimate attention to the Secretary of State. He had no claim on her; and, after all, Blaine had been a close friend of her family for many years before he even met her. It *did* annoy him, just the same, to see the way Blaine accepted her ministrations without seeming even to notice, as though it were his due. Ron had seen her do this many times before, and he had seen Blaine receive it just this way.

Lansard Blaine was the author of an estimable two-volume history of American foreign relations, a number of single volumes on specific episodes of that history, and numberless monographs in scholarly journals. He was a rare bird, one editorialist had said: a theoretician who had been given the opportunity to put his theories into practice and had seen them work as well in fact as they did on paper. His skillful, subtle—still almost brutally forceful—intervention between India and Pakistan a year ago had averted a war, conceivably even an atomic war; and a quiet campaign was underway to promote a Nobel Peace Prize for him. He had reason to be satisfied with his tenure as Secretary of State, and the President had reason to be satisfied with it. The rumors of his likely resignation were inexplicable to Ron Fairbanks. Seeing him unlike himself tonight—nervous, withdrawn—gave credence to the rumors. Ron watched him, and wondered . . . .

During the first six months of the Webster Administration, Blaine had hardly spoken to him. Their duties did not throw the Secretary of State and the Special Counsel together very often. Besides, Blaine had been quoted as disdaining lawyers; he was fond of quoting *Henry VI*—"The first thing we do, let's kill all the lawyers." But over coffee and brandy one night, when the President and Catherine Webster had called Blaine and Ron upstairs to relax with them for half an hour at the end of a particularly difficult day, Ron had won Blaine's momentary admiration and at least a small share of friendship from him. "Come," Blaine had said over the cups and snifters—in his very personal way disdainful yet challenging his opposite to overcome his disdain—"what, really, does it require to be a lawyer? What qualities of mind, personality, character? What?" Ron had smiled tolerantly. "To name just one quality," he had said, "I think we might mention tact." The President had guffawed. Catherine Webster had leaned back and laughed. And Blaine . . . Blaine had laughed too and leaned over and slapped Ron's knee. "Damn good, Fairbanks. *Damn* good."

Like almost everyone in politics, Blaine had a public persona and a private personality; and, as was often with people in politics, the private personality was rather less attractive than the public persona. Publicly he was smooth, self-confident, erudite, witty. Privately he was often self-contained, impatient, egoistic. Sometimes he smoked cigars, strong-smelling cigars whose aroma pervaded a dozen rooms. One thing he never was—bland. No one forgot him. No one mistook him for someone else. He defied categorization. Every pundit—and there were many—who tried to settle Blaine into a tiny pigeonhole was sooner or later embarrassed by his error. Ron remembered a luncheon at the Madison Hotel when a *Post* columnist, commenting on the election of an independent as governor of Florida, called it a fluke and compared it to the Bobby Thomson home run that won the National League pennant for the New York Giants in 1951. "Your simile is inapposite," Blaine remarked. "The Bobby Thomson home run was no fluke. Thomson was a great hitter." The newspaperman, a gray-head of many years experience, pulled his pipe from his mouth and smiled on Blaine. "I didn't know you were a baseball expert, professor," he said sarcastically. Blaine shrugged. "Bobby Thomson hit 32 home runs in 1951. And 264 in his career. He is one of the seventy-five or so all-time great home-run hitters." Period. . . .

The White House, Tuesday, June 12, 11:47 PM

In the darkness of his office, Fairbanks saw the light in the button on his telephone before he heard it ring. He had just switched off the lights in the room and was checking the lock on the door to be sure it was secure, when the telephone line lit up and the telephone began to ring. He closed the door and left it blinking and ringing in the darkened office. It was Fritz Gimbel, probably, checking to see if he had read the Pillsbury memorandum—another irritating habit of Gimbel's was to check repeatedly to see if someone were really doing what he had promised to do. Fritz could go to the devil. At this hour he was not going to stay in the office another two minutes to assure Fritz Gimbel he had read the Pillsbury memorandum.

The West Wing was quiet. The meeting in the Oval Office evidently had not lasted long. Ron loosened his tie. His car was parked on Executive Avenue, and he could be home in ten minutes in the light traffic at this time of night. He did not carry a briefcase. He would be back here before eight in the morning, there was no need to take anything home.

"Mr. Fairbanks."

One of the night guards greeted him perfunctorily, and Ron nodded perfunctorily.

Another night man was on duty at the door, as always. But this time the night guard was standing, blocking the door, frowning as Ron walked toward him along the dimly lighted corridor past the closed and locked doors of offices.

"Mr. Fairbanks, I'm sorry; I can't let you out."

There was of course no arguing with these fellows. Most of them were humorless, all of them were armed, and some of them were touchy. This one was named—as he recalled—Swoboda; he was one of the Secret Service men who had been with the President in Chicago when the shot was fired from the hotel roof. "What now?" Ron asked wearily.

"I'll check, sir," said the man. He picked up the telephone.

Ron stood impatiently and watched Swoboda call someone for instructions. He could see the bulge of the pistol under the man's suit jacket. They had ceased to be subtle about the way they guarded the President.

"The President wants to see you, sir. As quickly as possible. In . . . the Lincoln Sitting Room. You're to go to the elevator. Someone will be waiting for you there."

Ron hurried through the West Wing halls. When he reached the Mansion itself he found the doors held open for him. At the elevator, Bill Villiers of the Secret Service was waiting for him.

"What's up?"

The Secret Service man only shook his head. Villiers was ordinarily not a difficult man to talk to; but now he ran the elevator in grim silence.

They went up to the second floor. Villiers led Ron briskly through the long east-west hall. It was silent and deserted until they reached the east end, where Fritz Gimbel stood, talking quietly but with clear tension in his voice, in the center of a knot of Secret Service men. Ron recognized an FBI agent, too. Still without a word, Villiers led him to the door of the Lincoln Sitting Room. He rapped on the door.

The President opened the door. "Come in," he said. He was pallid. His voice was hoarse and somber.

Ron stepped into the room. Two more Secret Service men were there—Wilson and Adonizio—and Dr. Gilchrist. They stood around one of the horsehair-upholstered Victorian chairs, and at first Ron did not see what was on the chair. Then he saw—

Blaine. Not Blaine. The remains of Blaine. The body of the Secretary of State was sitting on the ugly black chair, the head lolling forward and to one side, the chest—the shirtfront and jacket—drenched with blood. Blaine's right hand still clutched a telephone. His left was clenched in his lap, clutching the fabric of his jacket. The blood—so much of it—soaked his trousers, the chair, even the carpet beneath the chair. His throat had been cut. The wound circled his throat just above the glistening red collar, and the blood still oozed from it.

Ron felt the President's grip on his arm. Then he heard his barely audible voice . . . "My God . . . murder in the White House . . ."

The Lincoln Sitting Room, Wednesday, June 13, 2:20 AM

If Woodward and Bernstein were right, Nixon and Kissinger knelt and prayed on the floor of this room the night before Nixon resigned in 1974. Ron Fairbanks had read about that a long time ago. As far as he could recall, that was all that had ever happened in this room. It was a small room, as rooms in the White House went; and it was not a very attractive room—he did not like the heavy Victorian furniture, which he thought gave the room a close, brooding atmosphere. It would have to be re-carpeted now, and the chair replaced. The late Secretary of State Lansard Blaine had bled to death, and clearly not by his own hand.

It was two o'clock before they removed the body. The President had asked Ron to stay while the Secret Service men and the FBI agents—joined for a while by two homicide detectives from the Metropolitan Police—did the mechanical, routine things murder investigators did. They did it all with Blaine's body still slumping—stiffening, Ron supposed—in the chair.

He sat now with the President, and with Gimbel in the room, talking quietly and watching.

Blaine's body began to turn pale. When Ron first saw the body, Blaine had looked alive, as though he might look up and laugh—as though he might put his head back on, so to speak. But after an hour, what sat in the chair was conspicuously a corpse, what remained of a man after the life was gone and much of the blood was drained out of him. The investigators worked around Blaine. They didn't cover him. They took photographs, they dusted for fingerprints, they ran a vacuum all around the room. They worked with a self-conscious, artificial briskness—the pose of official investigators. Ron went out to the bathroom, but he still had to return.

The President watched and said little. Gimbel said almost nothing. The investigators told the President what they learned.

"His throat was cut, sir. Probably with a wire. Probably someone sneaked up behind him, dropped a loop of fine wire over his head, and pulled. The wire was fine enough, and strong enough, to cut through, so he couldn't call out."

"Where's the wire?"

"Gone. Whoever did it could tuck it in his pocket and walk out, easy."

"Why wouldn't a wire that cut his throat have cut the hands of the man who used it?" Ron asked.

It was a Washington homicide detective talking . . . "Maybe he wore gloves, sir. Probably used a handle of some kind. All it would take would be a stick, a long bolt, even a ball-point pen."

"Did you ever see a murder committed that way before?" Ron asked.

"Yes, sir—once. They teach that technique in the military. You can shut up a sentry that way."

Blaine had apparently been talking on the telephone—to whom, would probably be an important question. Someone had come in—or maybe someone had already been there with him. Someone could have gotten behind him if he were not paying attention. Or, maybe someone he knew had stood behind him. Killing him had taken one very determined person only a few seconds.

"Why?" the President said. "*Why?*"

"How strong a man would it take to do it?" Gimbel asked the detective.

The man shook his head. "Not very strong, sir," he said. "It's a pretty easy way to kill someone. It doesn't take much strength or much ingenuity—just the . . . determination to do it."

The President spoke quietly to Ron and to Gimbel. "It had to be someone who could come in here without being challenged by anyone. It had to be someone who could move unchallenged in the White House in the middle of the night."

"Or we've got one incredible lapse of security," said Gimbel.

The President shook his head. "No. It had to be someone who could come to the second floor . . ."

"Another night," said Ron, "that would be a very limited number. Tonight, with your return from Europe . . . some of the senior staff were here . . . some of Blaine's staff too."

"We have got to know *why,*" Gimbel said grimly. "It could have been too damn many people. Until we know *why* . . ."

"White House . . ." muttered the President through clenched teeth. "Someone *inside.* Tomorrow . . . goddamn newspapers, television . . . *inside the White House,* for God's sake . . ."

"We've got to release the story," said Gimbel. "He's been dead three hours . . ."

The President sighed heavily, looked at Ron. "I had some kind of hope that maybe the investigation would come up with something so that when we announced it we could say we knew who did it—or at least we had a suspect. I suppose we'll be criticized for not announcing—"

"Not necessarily," Ron interrupted. "It's accepted investigative procedure to hold the story for a few hours."

The President stood. He seemed suddenly to have shaken off the shock that had subdued him. He nodded decisively toward the door, and Fairbanks and Gimbel followed him out of the Lincoln Sitting Room. The passageway was blocked by a knot of investigators—one scribbling in a small notebook. They jostled each other to make way for the President, but he turned abruptly into the Lincoln Bedroom. He switched on the lights and closed the door.

"Who's in charge of the investigation?" the President asked. He looked around the room, then chose to sit on the edge of the ornately carved Victorian bed.

"Well, it's a Secret Service operation first," said Gimbel. He sat on a chair facing the President. "Of course, the FBI . . . And the Metropolitan Police . . ." He frowned. "Too damn many."

The President nodded.

Ron stood uneasily beside Gimbel, resting a hand on the back of the chair Gimbel had chosen. "It needs a coordinator," he said.

"Right," said the President. "Lansard Blaine is dead, and that's reason enough for a thorough and efficient investigation . . . God, I don't want to sound callous—particularly not tonight—but do you realize what this could do to us?" He shook his head. "The murder of Blaine could bring down this administration. I mean, literally. We could lose every bit of political power we have, every bit of moral authority . . . We could be left with congressional government. And as for reelection . . . This investigation has got to be complete and quick. What's more, it's got to look as good as it is . . . thorough, effective. And there can be *no* suggestion in it anywhere that *anyone* is beyond it. That anyone is being protected. Including me . . ."

"Lyndon Johnson appointed the Chief Justice to head the investigation into the assassination of Kennedy," said Gimbel. "Take a man like Judge Frost. Appoint him coordinator of the investigation—"

"No," said the President emphatically. "I'm not going to pass it to someone outside. It's an executive problem. It belongs here. Unless I'm a real suspect myself, I want to command the investigation personally. But I obviously can't give it all my time . . ."

Gimbel shrugged. "I can handle it for you."

The President looked up at Fairbanks. "I'm thinking of Ron," he said.

Fritz Gimbel looked up over his shoulder at Ron Fairbanks standing behind him. "Ron doesn't . . . have enough designated authority—"

"I'll give it to him," said the President. "I'll give him command over all the investigative agencies involved. I'll give him subpoena power. He'll coordinate the entire investigation through his office. Ron?"

"I think the idea of a single coordinator is fine. Mr. President. I'm not sure, though, that I'm the one who should have that authority—"

"I disagree," said the President. "I was thinking about it . . . in there. You're young. You're a lawyer. You've been around here long enough to know the moves, and you're not politically dependent on me or beholden to me. Hell, you didn't even want the job at first. You and I know each other pretty well, Ron. I think I can trust you, you know what I want."

"You want a tough investigation, with some—"

"Sensitivity," the President finished for him.

Fairbanks shrugged. Murder and sensitivity. An odd couple.

The East Room, Wednesday, June 13, 10:00 AM

It was the first news conference in the East Room, and someone had already suggested it was inappropriate for the President to face television cameras, radio microphones, and a hundred fifty excited reporters there. Ron Fairbanks knew why he had chosen it. To face the world and talk about a murder in the White House, the President needed all the dignity his office and the mansion could provide.

It was a subdued crowd assembled on the chairs brought into the East Room since the decision at eight o'clock to hold the news conference there. The White House News Office had issued the announcement of Blaine's murder at 3:00 AM. Nothing since. The President's morning appointments had been cancelled, but only those he was to meet had been called; the News Office had not even issued a statement that the announced schedule of appointments had been cancelled. Ron Fairbanks had gone home, had a few hours sleep and a bath and returned to the White House at eight—without receiving a single call. He waited now in the Green Room for a word with the President before they entered the East Room together—with a sense that he might be enjoying the last moments of privacy he would know for . . . who knew until when? . . .

In his own West Wing office, in the two hours he had been there this morning, he had only begun to glean the magnitude and complexity of the job he had been given. Curtis Burke, Director of the FBI, had not concealed, during a twenty-minute meeting, his irritation at finding himself subordinated to Ronald Fairbanks in the investigation of the Blaine murder. ("I am curious, frankly, as to what you think your qualifications are." "My principal qualification, frankly, is that my name is in the Executive Order Number 2159.") The Attorney General had been cordial; he offered staff assistance and an office at the Justice Department. Fairbanks had accepted the assignment of two Assistant Attorneys General as his temporary assistants, and he had asked the two to set up a supplementary office for him—as the Attorney General had suggested—at the Justice Department. Fritz Gimbel had come in to pick up pending files and to tell him he could have two secretaries and an additional office in the West Wing. The Secret Service gave him a code name—"Hotshoe"—and put him under protection. Executive Order No. 2159 was signed by the President during the morning, and a signed copy was brought to him. Lynne stopped by—looking shaken; in fact, near trembling—and told him "everything" depended on him. Terrific news. . . .

"LADIES AND GENTLEMEN, THE PRESIDENT OF THE UNITED STATES."

Ron Fairbanks followed the President into the East Room and took a chair at the table where the President stood and faced the microphones. He was the only other person at the table.

"As all of you know," the President said—he spoke somberly and very slowly, gripping the podium as no one had ever seen him do before—"last night . . . about eleven-thirty, Secretary of State Lansard Blaine was found dead . . . in the Lincoln Sitting Room . . . here in the White House. The circumstances of his death compel us to conclude that he was murdered. A very thorough . . . investigation has been underway since the discovery of the body. The Secret Service, the FBI, and the Metropolitan Police have worked all night. At this hour they do not yet have a suspect."

The President's face glistened with sweat. The strain was also obvious in his voice.

"Before I say anything more . . . I want to say that Lansard Blaine was my friend. He was a man of outstanding abilities.

Before he became Secretary of State he had already made an honored name for himself as a student and teacher of American foreign relations. He made an outstanding record as Secretary of State. It is no secret to you that he was under consideration for the Nobel Peace Prize. Personally, I think he should have it. The world has lost an able peacemaker. The nation has lost a great public servant. And I have lost the irreplaceable . . . a friend."

He spoke without notes. His emotion seemed wholly genuine. The news people sat in respectful silence.

"As President—and as a friend of Lansard Blaine—I am determined that we will find out who killed him and why. For that reason I have this morning signed an executive order, creating the office of Special Investigator and giving that office extraordinary powers to direct and coordinate the investigation into the murder of the Secretary of State. I have appointed as Special Investigator the man who is sitting beside me—Ronald Y. Fairbanks." He stopped and for a brief moment stared thoughtfully at Ron. People in the back of the room stood to look over their fellows and identify Fairbanks. "Ron Fairbanks has served in the White House as Special Counsel from the first day of this administration. He is a Californian, an honors graduate of Stanford. He was a law clerk to Justice William Friederich, and he has served in the White House while on leave from the Washington firm of Harrington & Hoy. I have complete confidence in Ron. He will direct and coordinate the work of the Secret Service, the FBI, and any other investigative agency that may become involved in the effort to solve this crime, to bring the killer to justice. I have given him full special powers, to see any file or other evidence, to question anyone, and to issue subpoenas. His instructions are to find out who killed Lansard Blaine and why—*no matter where, or to whom, the investigation may lead.*"

The President paused again, glanced at Fairbanks, then at his watch. "We may be able to answer some questions."

"Mr. President!"

"Mrs. Coughman."

"Mr. President, can you tell us why the Secretary of State was in the Lincoln Sitting Room after eleven o'clock last night?"

"As Secretary of State, Lansard had developed a habit of using the Lincoln Sitting Room occasionally as a private, quiet place where he could make telephone calls and perhaps rest for a few minutes. He often met with me in our private quarters on the second floor, and the Lincoln Sitting Room was convenient for him. He met with me and some members of the Congress last night in the Oval Office, until a few minutes after eleven. I was not aware that he had gone upstairs then, but apparently he had gone up to the room for privacy. He was found with a telephone in his hand. Apparently he was making calls. We haven't yet found out if he was talking to someone on the telephone when he was—"

"Mr. President!"

"Mr. Craig."

"I believe the Secretary of State was divorced and had no children. Is that right?"

"He was divorced many years ago. He had no children. I myself called his former wife last night and informed her of his death, before we issued the official announcement. He had no other immediate family."

"Mr. President."

"Mr. O'Malley."

"Is there any truth to the rumor that the Secretary of State was recently asked to resign?"

"I never asked him to resign. I never suggested he should. He had told me, however, that he was interested in leaving public life and was making some inquiries about another professorship or a position in private business. But that was entirely voluntary on his part."

"Mr. President!"

"Miss Gorman."

"The number of people with access to the second floor, particularly during the night, is quite limited, is it not? Doesn't that lead to a tentative conclusion that this murder was committed by someone fairly highly placed in the White House?"

"All I am going to say in response to that question, Miss Gorman, is that no one, absolutely no one, including myself, is beyond suspicion. And Mr. Fairbanks has plenary authority to investigate *anyone.*"

Special Investigation Office, The West Wing, Wednesday, June 13, 2:00 PM

"It's not exactly your bag, is it?" Jill Keller laughed. "I mean, being chief White House gumshoe."

Ron had asked the Attorney General for her. She was a smart lawyer. Maybe forty years old, a taut-figured blonde, she had worked at the Justice Department for twelve years. He had had occasion to work with her on three or four matters, and he had learned to respect her. He knew she was divorced. He had heard her mention her children. He did not know much more than that about her until this morning when he asked for her and the Attorney General provided a file on her. Now he knew she was a graduate of the University of Virginia, had come first to the Civil Division at the Justice Department, and now worked in the Antitrust Division. The Deputy Assistant Attorney General for whom she worked had been reluctant to spare her for this assignment. She herself had been reluctant to take it, but the Attorney

General had said Fairbanks was to have whom he wanted.

"It's very sensitive, Jill. Politically and every other way." He was sitting behind his desk eating his lunch—a ham sandwich and a Coke. "It's certainly unique and—"

"Are you feeding me the same line that was fed you to get you to take the job?"

"The line is original with me."

She slipped off her spectacles and rubbed her eyes. "I'm apolitical, you know—a career Justice Department lawyer—"

"That's one reason why I asked for you."

"Who else?" she asked.

"Gabe Haddad," he said. "Plus Henry Ritterbush, who works for me here at the White House."

"I don't know him."

"He's not a lawyer. He'll do detail work. He's good at it. He's a Webster loyalist, was an errand-runner in the campaign."

"In other words we don't tell him much."

"In other words we don't tell him everything."

"Well, that's a point with me, Ron," Jill Keller said. She crossed her legs, and her short black skirt rode up—of which at the moment she was oblivious. "*I* won't accept this assignment unless I know everything. I don't want any part of it, I want all of it. If there's going to be anything I'm not trusted to know, tell me now and I'll get out—"

"I'll tell you how I want this investigation run," said Ron. "I want a log kept. Every question, every answer, every phone call, whatever we hear, from whomever we hear it—I want it all written down. I want a complete record of everything we do. I will have access to that log. You will. And Gabe, who's already at work at the State Department. No one else."

"Fritz Gimbel?"

"No. And not the President either." . . .

Gibson Dunn, chief of the White House detail, Secret Service, took a seat on the couch beside Jill Keller. Walter Locke, Special Agent, FBI—in charge of the FBI team assigned to the White House for the Blaine murder investigation—sat in the chair to the right of Ron's desk.

"Gib and I know each other," Fairbanks said to the FBI man. "You and I haven't met before. It's essential that we understand each other, and I don't know any other way for us to do that except to speak frankly. So, frankly speaking, I want you to understand that, for the course of this investigation, you work for me. You don't work for the Director. You work for me, and so does every man assigned to this investigation. You don't report to Curt Burke. You report to me. If Curt wants to know what you are doing, he'll have to ask me. I know Curt's not going to like it, but under Executive Order 2159, if I want Curt Burke to run an errand for me, I have the authority to send him out to run it. I didn't ask for this authority and I'm not very comfortable with it, but I have it and I'm going to use it. I know this sounds arrogant, but I don't know any other way for us to have a quick understanding—"

"I have no problem with it," said the Special Agent. "Director Burke understands I'm on special assignment."

Ron relaxed one degree. "Okay," he said. "Let's hope it doesn't last long. Nothing would make me happier than to wrap this up in two or three days and be able to tell the President he can revoke Executive Order 2159."

"I'm afraid it's not going to be that easy, Mr. Fairbanks," said the Special Agent. "We've had a major effort underway for almost fifteen hours, and we have no leads."

"No fingerprints . . . ? No . . . ?"

The Special Agent shook his head. He was a bulky, broad-shouldered man, strong of chin and jaw, middle-aged, handsome.

"The fingerprints are a jumble. But we found none we could not identify. They are all of people who had valid reasons for being in the Lincoln Sitting Room—custodial staff, the President and Mrs. Webster, the Secretary of State himself . . . We vacuumed the room thoroughly. We've samples of hair, lint . . . all the usual stuff. Nothing suggestive. The preliminary autopsy report contains nothing special. We have questioned staff, the guards on duty . . . Nothing. We don't know who was in the Lincoln Sitting Room with the Secretary. We have no idea."

"Whoever killed him," said Jill Keller, "was on the second floor, entered the room, killed Blaine, walked out, and was noticed by no one. Isn't White House security tighter than that?"

Gibson Dunn answered that question. "Security is by area," he said. "If you're authorized to be in an area, and have entered it, you're not likely to be challenged while you're in it."

"The second floor?" she asked.

"The second floor constitutes a special area," said Dunn. "No matter what your authorization you would be checked before you could enter the second floor. The stairs and elevators are covered tightly. On the second floor, we cover the west end—the family quarters—more tightly than the east end—the Lincoln rooms and the Queen's rooms. Except when official guests are in residence, those rooms are ordinarily deserted at night. Of course, Secretary Blaine *did* often use the Lincoln Sitting Room . . ."

"Still," said Ron, "more than a few people did have access to the second floor last night."

"Right," said Dunn. "We've checked with all the people on duty last night. From ten to twelve last night a dozen people moved in and out of the family quarters—the President and his wife and daughter, the personal staff, Ron here, who escorted the President's daughter from the Yellow Oval Room to her sitting room before he went to his office in the West Wing"—he paused and glanced at Ron with a wry smile—"the Secretary of State himself, Mr. Gimbel, plus the senators who met with the President in the Yellow Oval Room before they went with him to the Oval Office. A snack was carried to Miss Webster's sitting room at 10:42. Mrs. Webster's secretary came to her sitting room at 10:48, and sandwiches and beer were brought to them at 11:04. We know all that. Downstairs, we don't know so much. The senators were in, and some representatives—some of them with staff. They were in the West Wing, mostly, but some of the staff were in the State Rooms, looking around while the meeting continued in the Oval Office. The kitchen staff, the custodial staff, the security staff . . . There were one hell of a lot of people in the White House last night."

"You can tell us that sandwiches and beer were taken to Mrs. Webster at 11:04, but you can't tell us who was in the Lincoln Sitting Room between 10:30 and 11:30," Jill Keller said.

"That's right. We protect the family more thoroughly than we do the house."

"Nevertheless," Ron said through fingers interlaced in front of his mouth and chin, "we have a *relatively* small group of suspects to deal with, don't we? A dozen people?"

"*Two* dozen," Dunn said, "assuming there wasn't a crack in our security."

"All right. As many as *two* dozen could have been on the second floor last night and could have reached the Lincoln Sitting Room for a minute or so and left there without being challenged. That's still at least limited odds for us, isn't it?"

"Motive," said Locke, the FBI man. "The key is motive—"

"Exactly," said Ron. "Who of the two dozen had a motive? *What* was the motive? What was Blaine doing that gave someone reason—real or imagined—to kill him?"

"I suggest two categories," said Jill Keller. "Public and private.

He was killed for a public reason having to do with his conduct as Secretary of State, or for a private reason having nothing to do with his public office."

"Considering the setting," said Dunn, "the public motive seems more likely."

"I agree," said Ron. "But we can't assume anything."

"Where do we go from here, then?" asked Jill. "With all due respect to present company, it seems to me the detectives have done all the detective things, to no avail. Our killer was too smart to leave fingerprints, or samples of his hair, or fingernail parings or whatever. What's next?"

"Gabe Haddad is at the State Department," said Ron, "picking up Blaine's desk calendar and telephone log, and his secretary's. I've ordered the White House telephone supervisor to prepare a list of every telephone call logged to or from the Secretary of State in the past six months. We've ordered copies of his home telephone long-distance bills. We'll continue the check on the people who were in the White House last night. We have to build a file and keep cross-checking it. Somewhere it ought to show an anomaly."

Somewhere.

Special Investigation Office, The West Wing, Wednesday, June 13, 6:00 PM

L. Gabriel Haddad sat on the couch, facing Ron. He was the second Justice Department lawyer Ron had asked be assigned to him. Of Lebanese extraction, he had an olive complexion, piercing dark eyes, and a sharp, prominent nose. He was Ron's age, 34, and a graduate of New York University School of Law. Ron had borrowed him from the Civil Rights Division.

Gabe had brought back from the State Department most of the documents Ron had asked for—the Secretary of State's telephone log, his desk calendar, his appointments book, his secretary's telephone log and calendar. He and Ron had been reading the names when someone from the White House News Office brought in the evening's *Star,* marked with red pen. Ron had read, and now Gabe Haddad was reading, a byline story by Douglas Madison:

> History probably will remember Lansard Putnam Blaine as one of the ablest men ever to serve this nation as Secretary of State. The manner of his death will require the publication of certain facts about his life that might otherwise have remained known only to a few Washington insiders. The fact was, Secretary of State Blaine was a lover of good food, good wine—and complaisant young women.
>
> Especially complaisant young women. Lots of them.
>
> He had been long divorced, and certainly he was entitled to the company of young women. It will be remembered, however, that at the time of his Senate confirmation three years ago a few questions were raised about indiscreet episodes in the past life of Professor Lansard Blaine. It was said in Ann Arbor that Professor Blaine rarely slept alone for long.
>
> The same has been said in Washington.
>
> A regular at Le Bagatelle, where he is remembered for invariably paying his checks with cash, never by credit card, Secretary of State Blaine never dined alone. He dined only rarely in male company. A succession of anonymous and attractive young women shared intimate, hand-holding dinners with him, month after month. It was a point with the Secretary of State, apparently, never to introduce these young women to acquaintances who happened past his table. Since the shy young women were less than *femmes fatales,* they in-

spired little curiosity—only a little wry amusement.

Inquiry at the State Department today, however, produced the identity of one of them. We will not publish her name, but it is commonly understood that a 23-year-old woman in the Information Management Section was a recent Bagatelle companion of the late Secretary of State—more than once—and spent the night, again, more than once, in the Secretary's Watergate apartment.

This is not speculation or rumor—nor is it idle gossip. Secretary Blaine's private and personal life may well not have been the origin of the motive for his murder. We are not suggesting he was killed by a jealous lover or by a woman scorned. The investigators, however, will have to look into this element of the story—unless they come up with the killer very soon . . .

"I heard this story over there," said Gabe Haddad.

"Who is the girl?" asked Ron.

"Her name is Judy Pringle. She's a system designer in the Information Management Section. She didn't come in today. Called in sick."

"Would it be worth talking to her?" Ron asked.

"I suppose we have to."

"I'm already getting to hate this job," Ron said, shaking his head.

"Her name is on his telephone log," said Gabe. "Did you notice? His secretary noted calls from her and calls to her. Apparently she could call right in."

Ron nodded. "Efficient secretary. If she kept—"

"She's smart, and good," said Gabe. "She kept a tight office. She maintained his telephone log and appointments calendar with more thoroughness than he probably knew. Could be a break for us."

"Did you question her?"

"No. She was shaken. We'll have to do it later."

Ron glanced down the final page of the telephone log the secretary had kept for Blaine. "Most of these names are what you would expect," he said. "People who had obvious reason to call the Secretary of State. Some of them—"

"We should check every name on there," Haddad said.

"Which should give our FBI people plenty to keep them busy," said Ron, feeling increasingly uneasy about going through the "effects" of a man, the record of so much of his life. Ghoulish, but, he reminded himself, unavoidable.

The thought didn't wash away the uneasy feeling, though.

The Special Investigation Office, The West Wing, Wednesday, June 13, 9:00 PM

Before he closed the office for the night Ron checked with Honey Taylor, the President's personal and confidential secretary, to see if the President wanted a report before he left. Honey had left for the evening, but her assistant, Claire Bond, said the President had gone up to dinner with his family and had left instructions that he did not want to talk to anyone except in an emergency.

Jill and Gabe had been with him until eight. Gibson Dunn had left only at eight-thirty. Locke, the FBI man, had gone back to the FBI building; but Ron had spoken to him on the telephone and had told him to pick up copies of the Secretary of State's telephone logs and the other documents and to begin checking the listed names. After eight-thirty, Ron had spent half an hour reading a file of clippings sent in by the New Office. He was interrupted once: by a doctor at Bethesda who called to say the final autopsy report would be ready in the morning.

A discreet rap on his door. It was one of the new secretaries temporarily assigned to him by Fritz Gimbel—a young black woman, a Mrs. Walsh if he had heard her name correctly. "There's someone waiting to see you, Mr. Fairbanks. She asked if you were still here and if she could see you."

Ron checked his watch. It had been a long day, but he buttoned his collar and pulled his necktie tight. "Who is it?"

"A Miss Kalisch, sir. She works for Mr. Eiseman."

He shook his head. "I don't know her. Well, I'll see her for a moment. Are you waiting for me to go before you do?"

"Yes, sir."

"Well, thanks. Why don't you go now? I'll only be here a few more minutes."

"Thank you, Mr. Fairbanks."

The Miss Kalisch who had waited to see him was a diminutive young woman who hesitated at the door. Only when he motioned to her did she come in, and only when he indicated a chair facing his desk did she sit down. "I waited for the end of the day to try to see you," she said. "I wanted to see you alone."

He had switched off all the lights in his office but the lamp on his desk, as he often did when he was tired; and the light from the shaded lamp fell on her only from the shoulders down, leaving her face in the shadow. He could see that she wore glasses and that her hair was tied back, otherwise that her face was plain and unblemished; but the light was not enough for him to read her expression. He saw her hands clasped tightly in her lap.

"About the investigation?" he asked.

"Yes."

"Well . . . ?" He tipped back his chair and clasped his hands behind his head. His own face was only half in the light.

"Mr. Blaine . . ." she began in a low voice. "Last night . . . he was talking on the telephone. I read in the papers that he was talking on the telephone when he was killed."

"Go on."

"He was talking to me."

Ron tipped his chair forward again and, leaning over his desk, peered up at her from beneath the shade of the lamp. Her shadowed face was solemn, apprehensive. "Did you hear . . . ?"

She shook her head. "I thought he hung up on me." She lowered her face for a moment and sighed. "I think I heard him die," she whispered.

Ron's immediate reaction was to be skeptical. "Miss . . . uh, Kalisch," he said. "I would like to turn on this Dictaphone and make a tape of our conversation—"

"Before you do . . ." she said with indrawn breath. "I . . . I want to know what you have to make public."

"Since I don't know what you're going to tell me, I don't know what I have to make public."

"Do you know why he was talking to me on the telephone?"

"I'm beginning to have an idea, but I'd rather you told me."

She drew her chair closer to his desk. Her face was in the light. "He was calling me to tell me when he would come home. I was in his apartment. When you have it gone over, you'll find my fingerprints on everything. I slept there last night, even after he was dead, because I didn't know. I thought he had just hung up. He sometimes did when he was interrupted—"

"You were living with him?"

"No. Not really. Not all the time. I . . . It has to come out, doesn't it? There's no way to keep it secret."

Ron shook his head. "I don't know. I can't promise to keep it a secret, and I can't vouch for what someone else will find out and publish."

"I'm divorced, Mr. Fairbanks," she said quietly, grimly. "I have custody of my little daughter, but my ex-husband would like to take her away from me. Lan and I were discreet, but—"

"Lan?"

"Lansard Blaine."

Ron nodded. "Well . . . may I turn on the tape?"

"Yes."

He took a tape cartridge from his center drawer and inserted it in the machine. He switched the Dictaphone to "Conference" and laid the microphone on his desk. "Let's start with your name."

"My name is Marya Kalisch," she said reluctantly.

"It is . . . a little after nine, and this is Wednesday, June 13," said Ron. "Miss Kalisch, will you say for the record that you are talking with me voluntarily and have consented to my making a tape?"

"It is voluntary," she said. "And I have consented."

He heard in her speech the trace of an accent. She adjusted her glasses and clasped her hands in front of her on the edge of his desk.

"Go ahead," he said. "Tell me where you work."

"I work here in the West Wing of the White House," she said. "I am an administrative assistant to Alfred Eiseman, the President's Special Assistant for National Security Affairs. Among other things, I do some translation for Mr. Eiseman. My parents are Russian, and I am fluent in Russian."

"Tell me about your relationship with the Secretary of State."

She sighed, audibly enough that it would be on the tape. "I met him one day about six months ago when he asked me about a word in a translation, whether the Russian word could have been translated in a slightly different sense. We talked. Later he would stop in to say hello when he was in the White House. Then he asked me to dinner. And since about four months ago I have . . . had an intimate relationship with him. He stayed overnight in my apartment a few times. Then I began to go to his."

Ron nibbled the hair on the back of his hand as he listened to her too intimate recital. "How old are you, Miss Kalisch?"

"I am twenty-seven."

"You were in his apartment at the Watergate last night?"

"He called me during the afternoon and told me to go there.

I had—have—a key. I put my child to bed, left her with a babysitter and went to Lan's place about nine o'clock. I prepared a snack in the kitchen and chilled a bottle of wine. That is the way it was with us—late suppers . . . He called about ten to say he would be late, maybe as late as midnight. It wasn't unusual. I watched television while I waited. He called again . . . the call that was interrupted. He said he had been in a meeting with the President and was ready now to leave the White House. He asked me what I was wearing—I mean, was I wearing something . . . intimate? I said I was. Then I heard him . . . I suppose you could say, sort of, grunt. Then the line went dead."

She was carefully controlled, not without rigid effort. Ron wondered if her control would come through on the tape. "What time was this?" he asked.

She shook her head. "The eleven o'clock news was still on, on television. The late movie had not begun."

"You say he sometimes hung up on you without a word when interrupted while he was talking to you?"

"Yes. Maybe last night . . . maybe someone came in. Maybe he just hung up. Maybe I didn't hear . . ."

"How long between this grunt and when the line went dead?"

She shook her head again, biting her lower lip. "A long time," she whispered. "They say . . . I heard he was strangled with some wire or something. Probably he grunted, or choked or . . . oh, God . . . I don't know . . . but that probably was the sound I heard . . . then I guess whoever killed him hung up . . ." She was crying now.

Ron watched her closely. "I'll turn off the Dictaphone," he said quietly.

She wept for a minute, then sucked in her breath and wiped her eyes with the back of her hand.

Ron glanced around the shadowed office. "I have to ask

you . . ." he said. "About the relationship. Did you love him?"

"Yes . . ." she whispered. ". . . and no." She drew in a breath and found her voice. "I am not a fool, Mr. Fairbanks. You have to be realistic. I had a sense of being a little part of history. I knew there were others. The newspaper says there was another even . . . even recently. Maybe I was only one of . . . at the same time." She swallowed. "I didn't know about that, but I knew I had no claim on him. I knew there had been others and would be still others. I knew what he wanted. I was willing to give him what he wanted, for what I got in return."

"What did he want?"

She lifted her chin a bit and spoke more crisply. "A fresh, young . . . vigorous woman. One who would be available whenever he wanted her. One who wouldn't argue with him or make demands on him. One he could drop when he got tired of her. I understood all that. That's my realism. In return I . . . He was a fine man . . . kind, thoughtful, generous. He talked with me about his duties. I shared some little part of the history he was making. I told myself it would end, and I told myself I would remember it and treasure the memory all my life."

"You have a security clearance, don't you?" Ron asked, following a sudden random thought.

"Yes. But not for diplomatic and political secrets."

"Did he talk to you about resigning?"

"Yes. He said he was tired of Washington and thought he might return to the campus or find a place with some company."

"When did he say that?"

"Oh, he said it two or three times in the last two weeks."

"Was he serious?"

"Yes. I thought so."

Ron turned to another thought. "You say he was generous. In spirit? Materially?"

"Both ways. I have some lovely gifts I'll remember him by."

"Expensive gifts?"

"I think so."

"Could you give me a list?"

"Must I?"

"I'll need it," Ron said firmly. He stood. "I'll try to protect your reputation. I'll need the list, and there will be more questions—"

"When they find my fingerprints . . . ?"

"I'm sure they already have. And when they report it to me, I will keep it confidential that you lived part-time in the Secretary of State's apartment—if I can." . . .

Ron recalled now a weekend at Shangri-La. (Eisenhower had changed the name to Camp David, and Webster had changed it back again.) It was during the second summer of the Administration. Webster never retreated to Shangri-La to brood, or for intense meetings with his inner circle; he went there to relax in the company of people he liked. It had been a well-noted measure of Ron's relationship withthe First Family that he was invited to the weekend mini-vacations in the Maryland mountains. Blaine was invited too. Gimbel was not.

This was in August. It had been intolerably hot and damp in Washington ever since June. The government had slowed down, literally, because of the heat, the sweat, the fatigue. At Shangri-La it was hot, but here the heat was at least dryer, and windy; and drinking long cool drinks in the shade of the trees, the presidential party could loosen some and regain a sense of perspective.

President Webster was no athlete. He swam lazily in the cool water of the big pool, but he kept away from the tennis courts, from the volleyball games, from the joggers on the trails through the woods. No dedicated walker like Truman, or frantic jogger like Carter. Ron did the same. The sweaty camaraderie of the lockerroom was alien territory to him. He swam, sat by the pool, sipped gin-and-tonics, and caught some needed shut-eye.

Blaine jogged. Blaine played tennis. Blaine encouraged Lynne to do likewise. She played a decent game of tennis; he was too old to beat her. Catherine Webster also played tennis, but she was no competition for Blaine.

Blaine had brought with him to Shangri-La this particular weekend a young woman, an associate professor of far eastern history at Northwestern University. She had been his student a few years previously. An attractive, golden-tanned blonde, she would have been a beauty except for being somewhat overweight. Ostensibly she was spending the weekend with Blaine to brief him on some recent developments in Taiwanese party politics. In fact, she was sleeping with him, slipping from her cottage to his after midnight and slipping back at dawn, pretending that no one knew. She was overwhelmed by the good fortune—actually, Blaine's good favor—that had brought her to Shangri-La to spend a weekend in the company of the President of the United States. She was conspicuously and—as Lynne put it—disgustingly grateful.

"Another touch, professor?" the President said to her. Her name was Barbara Galena, but the President had begun to call her "professor" immediately after being introduced to her on Friday afternoon. She was already slurring her words and suppressing giggles with difficulty, and it seemed to amuse him to offer her another drink.

"Thank you, Mr. President, I believe I will . . . just a small one, though . . ." She looked at him over the tops of her sunglasses and grinned. She wore a bright red maillot swimsuit, stretched tight over her generous figure; and when she got up from her lounge-chair to accept another bloody mary from the President, parts of her noticeably shifted inside the tight thin fabric.

Catherine Webster, also in a maillot—hers violet—watched the President serve the drink and Barbara Galena accept it. She glanced at Ron. He had decided that Catherine, left to her own inclinations, would be a quiet, introspective observer, would understand better than anyone else what was happening and who worked from what motives, and would offer her husband only occasional terse words of advice. It was the President who could not endure a lonely or a quiet moment, who urged her forward to shake hands, to chat, to know names, to smile—to "politic." When he chose to be a public man, she held herself apart as long as possible. Now she couldn't.

The President, stretched out on a padded loungechair with his telephone and the bar within reach, had sipped gin half this Sunday afternoon, as he had done Saturday afternoon, and was thoroughly relaxed. He wore a pair of swimmer's trunks—white with red-and-blue stripes—and a dark blue baseball cap with the presidential seal on the front. He talked easily. He was holding court, in fact.

Lynne and Blaine were on the tennis court. Senator Syndall and his wife were napping in their cottage. Admiral Mead and his wife were off somewhere jogging.

"Congress is a pain in the backside," the President was saying to the professor. "It's a pain in the backside of every President. On the other hand, what would I do if I could do anything I wanted to, professor? Did you ever wonder? Scary idea, isn't it?"

Barbara Galena smiled. "I have confidence in you, Mr. President."

"I am flattered," he said. "I am also frightened. You're an educated woman, professor. If you have confidence in me, what does the electorate have? It's a mistake ever to have confidence. You should watch the man you entrust with vast power, every minute. Never trust him. Never have confidence. That's my point. If it weren't for the Congress frustrating me, what would I do? The idea that I could do anything I want is a very scary . . . albeit at times damn attractive . . . notion—"

"I know it scares the hell out of me," Catherine Webster said as she got up, stepped to the side of the pool and jumped in. She swam away from the conversation.

"Scare you, Ron?" the President asked.

Ron shrugged. "I'm petrified, sir."

"*He* didn't even vote for me," the President said to Barbara Galena.

The young woman glanced incredulously at Ron. A nervous grin flickered on and off her face.

"Ah well . . ." said the President, and lifted his glass to take a swallow from his gin-and-tonic.

The professor rolled off her chair and stood at the edge of the pool, dipping a foot in to test the temperature. She stood with her back to Ron and the President, and Ron wondered if it had not suddenly occurred to her that she had just been made a conversational plaything, and maybe had been throughout the weekend. He did not like that role for anybody. He went to her side, dipping his own toes in the water as if he, too, wanted to test. He looked at her . . . her face was hard, troubled.

"I really didn't vote for him," he said.

She looked at him. "Really?"

He nodded.

She smiled, as though relieved.

Ron looked past her to the President. He was watching them, obviously curious about what this exchange was. His fingers drummed the arm of his chair. He seemed anxious to pick up the conversation and wanted his listeners back.

But his telephone rang.

The President listened intently to someone on the line, grunting umm-hmms, nodding as if the someone could see, glancing toward the tennis court, frowning. After two or three minutes he hung up and called out, "Blaine. Problem."

Lansard Blaine, with a quick small show of reluctance, put his racket down on the bench at the court and walked toward the pool. Lynne picked up some balls before she followed him. Blaine was dressed in tennis whites, with a sweat band around his forehead. Lynne, following him twenty paces behind, was wearing her white two-piece bathing suit. She carried a towel and wiped off the perspiration as she came.

The President sighed as Blaine reached the pool. "Goddamn Zaire's invaded goddamn Zambia," he said. "Two or three army divisions across the border, some paratroops dropped on the airport at Lusaka. Looks like a full-scale operation."

"Their own?"

"Apparently. No report that it's otherwise."

Blaine shrugged. "Then good luck, I guess."

The President nodded. "I guess."

"The British . . . ?" Blaine asked.

"Yelling their heads off, of course. They want an emergency meeting of the U.N. Security Council."

"We have to support them on that."

"And keep a close watch to be sure it's only a local operation," the President said.

"Right. Support the British in the Security Council. Call home our ambassadors for consultation. Deplore. That's it. I'll call the Department—"

"Not so quick," the President said. "We need to make it look like we've wrung hands over it for a while." He felt less cynical than he sounded, but the sense of a giant's impotence to *do* anything about such actions led him to affect the facade.

Blaine nodded, understanding. He reached for the Scotch bottle on the President's bar, poured two drinks, one for Lynne.

Catherine had lifted herself out of the pool and was sitting on the edge, warming her legs on the concrete. "Well?"

"Well," Blaine said, "it's another case of a small country being swallowed by a bigger neighbor. Let's hope it doesn't escalate into something more . . ."

Barbara Galena still stood at the edge of the pool beside Ron. She had turned and was staring at the President and Blaine. "Isn't all this a little cynical?" she asked Ron quietly.

"What else do you think they can do? I mean really do?"

"Even he," she said, nodding toward the President, "says he wants it to look like they wrung their hands over it." She shook her head.

Blaine had not heard what she said to Ron but he'd noticed her talking and had guessed. He came now to the edge of the pool. "A lesson in what it's really like, right Barb?" he said.

"I'll keep my promise not to tell anything I've seen or heard here this weekend," she said, "but—"

"But when you're sixty years old and departmental chairman, and he's dead"—he glanced toward the President—"you'll write for *Foreign Policy Review,* or for the *Journal of the American Historical Society* about the Sunday afternoon at Shangri-La when you watched President Robert Webster and Secretary of State Lansard Blaine allow a small African country to be taken over by its neighbor because they didn't care. Right?"

"Maybe I will . . ."

Blaine nodded. "I'm sure of it . . . Well, you used to play a fair game of tennis. Any more?"

Ron winced. It was unfair to her. For whatever reason, she had gained weight, and it seemed fairly obvious she could not play "a fair game of tennis" any more. She shook her head, looking pained.

"You do two things exceptionally well, Barb," Blaine said coolly. "Judging the facts of *realpolitik* in central Africa is not one of them."

"Just what do I do well, in your estimation?"

"One," said Blaine, "you are, with perhaps an exception or two, the hardest-working and best student of far eastern diplomatic history I ever knew, and you probably know more about Taiwanese politics than most politicians on Taiwan. Two . . ." He stopped and grinned. "Your other talent I'll leave to Ron to speculate on," and he turned abruptly, walked toward Lynne and motioned toward the tenniscourt.

Barbara Galena looked up at Ron, her mouth tight.

"Let's take a swim," Ron said quietly, wishing that ability and compassion were not such apparent strangers in Secretary of State Lansard Blaine.

The Special Investigation Office, The Justice Department, Thursday, June 14, 10:00 AM

The Attorney General had assigned an office. Jill Keller had recruited two secretaries and appropriated some furniture and equipment. Gabe Haddad had been to the State Department early and had returned to the Justice Department, bringing with him Judith Pringle, the young woman said to have been intimately associated with Lansard Blaine.

"I want to avoid embarrassing you," said Fairbanks. He sat behind the scarred desk appropriated from the GSA, in a chair with one broken spring, looking at Judith Pringle across a desk littered with boxes and files. He fiddled with the controls on a dictating machine also hastily appropriated. "If your name is published, it won't be because *we* published it."

"It's been done already," the young woman said miserably. "Everybody knows who the *Star* meant."

"Everybody at the State Department?"

"Yes."

He was impressed with how much she was like Marya Kalisch. He had a file on her, provided this morning by the FBI. She had a degree in mathematics from the University of Tennessee. She had worked briefly for IBM and had come three years ago to the State Department as a systems analyst and designer . . . a young woman with ability and a career, yet mousy in appearance and with a quiet manner, a young woman who had been, no doubt, surprised and flattered by the attentions of the distinctly suave Secretary of State of the United States. She had dark brown hair, blue eyes, regular features—nothing exactly memorable. She was wearing a cream-white pants suit, and she was clearly nervous.

"Is what they said about you in the *Star* true?" Ron asked.

"What part of it?"

"That you had an intimate relationship with Lansard Blaine."

"What if I refuse to say?" She spoke with the soft, southern accent of Tennessee.

"We can stop the interview right now until you get a lawyer," Ron said. "He'll tell you that I have the authority to ask you questions and require you to answer."

She frowned and sucked in her lower lip.

He was not moving well. Not yet. He had dinner last night at eleven, in a hurry, nothing very good, and he'd not slept well and this morning his stomach was queasy and his head hurt as if he'd drunk too much the night before . . . He'd worn a dark blue suit this morning, it was almost a uniform with him, but now his blue and white striped shirt was limp in the June heat and damp. He had loosened his collar and tie. A cup of coffee, turning cold, and a half-eaten Danish sat among the litter on his desk. He carried a pair of half glasses in the inside pocket of his jacket—he almost never put them on when anyone could see; in fact, he never put them on at all except when squinting was painful. Hell, he was thirty-four and too young to be wearing reading glasses. Now he pulled them out and pressed them into place astride his nose. He peered at her file.

"I propose to switch on this dictator," he said. "I need to make a tape of what we say. If you don't want to, I'll have to arrange for a subpoena and take your testimony with a reporter making the record—"

"I have nothin' to hide."

"Good, so please let's get on with it."

He switched on the recorder, and she told him her name, how old she was—twenty-nine—and what she did at the Department of State. "Mr. Blaine spoke to me one day when he came in our section. I was sort of surprised. He was, after all, the Secretary of State. Then he seemed to be saying something to me all the time. I kept reading in the papers about him—and hearing his name every night when I watched the TV news—and when he called me and asked me up to his office and then asked me if I'd have dinner with him, I was—"

"Flattered." They were all so damned flattered . . .

"Yes. And I suppose more than that."

"When?"

"I've been . . . I guess I have to say it, I *did* see him . . . for about a year."

"Tell me about it. How would you describe the relationship? A love affair?"

Judy Pringle frowned. "I would . . . like to call it that," she said in a voice close to breaking. She shook her head. "It wasn't that, I guess. Not really."

"A sexual relationship?"

She nodded.

Ron sighed. He did not want to cause pain for this young woman but he felt he had too little time for subtlety. "Why you, Judy?"

She lowered her eyes. "Because I was willing, I suppose. I mean . . . with *him!* He was so great, the things he did . . . he was making world *peace.* I . . . I would have done about anything for him. And I did, too—just about . . ."

"Did he take you to Le Lion d'Or?"

She nodded.

Ron glanced around the shabby room. "Do you know anything about his death?" he asked casually.

She shook her head. "No, *nothing.* I swear it."

"When did you see him last?"

She drew in a long breath. "I was with him Sunday afternoon."

"Where?"

"In his apartment, at the Watergate."

"How long?"

She sighed. "All afternoon. We had champagne and caviar and paté. That's the way it was with him. No . . . quickies. He was a wonderful lover, I've never known anyone like him—"

"Did he talk to you? Confide in you?"

She nodded—but without conviction. "He didn't talk about his official life, his work for the government. He talked about his ex-wife and about his personal life . . . I was surprised at how much he told me."

"Such as?"

"About his . . . preferences. About his experiences. Unless he was a liar—and I don't believe he was—he'd certainly been, well, around. Which isn't surprising, considering who he was and where he traveled."

"Could he back his words with performance?" Ron asked bluntly.

"Yes." Her voice was very low.

"Did he say anything about resigning?"

She shook her head. "As Secretary of State? No. It was the biggest thing in his life, what he'd always wanted. He was *proud* of being Secretary of State. He was a proud man, a *great* man."

"Did he spend much money?"

"On me? Expensive dinners. Wine . . . *one bottle,* forty years old, a hundred dollars! Checks at the Bagatelle . . . He gave me some lovely . . . lingerie—"

She paused abruptly. "Oh my God . . . that *stuff* . . . it's all in a drawer in his apartment . . ."

The State Department, Office of the Secretary of State, Thursday, June 14, 11:30 AM

"It was Dr. Blaine's. It does not belong to the government," said Mary Burdine. She was Blaine's secretary, the only person Ron Fairbanks had ever heard call Blaine by his academic title. She was talking about a Louise Nevelson wood sculpture mounted on the office wall.

"Do you have any idea what he paid for it?" Ron asked.

"No, sir."

It seemed inappropriate to sit behind Blaine's desk. Ron sat on the couch. Jill Keller sat beside him. They faced Mary Burdine, who sat in a chair—a woman in her fifties, gray, sitting stiffly erect, conveying, maybe unintentionally, an air of building hostility. She had ordered coffee brought in, and all three of them had cups in their hands.

He had already covered all the inevitable questions . . . No, she had never heard the Secretary of State threatened; no, he had not seemed nervous or worried the day of his death; no, he had not told her he was considering resigning. She knew nothing that suggested any reason at all for his death.

"All I'm turning up so far," said Ron, "is one young woman after another who seems to have had a love affair with him. What do you know about his personal life?"

"Mr. Fairbanks," said the woman primly, "I was Dr. Blaine's secretary. I made it a point not to know anything about his personal life."

"But if a Judith Pringle called, you put the call through."

"Yes, sir."

"And if a Marya Kalisch called, you put the call through."

"Yes, sir."

"Why?"

"Because he told me to," she said crisply.

"Well, who did you think they were?"

"That was none of my business."

"Unfortunately, Mrs. Burdine, it's become *my* business. What about the others?"

She stared for a moment at the carpet, shook her head. "I can give you a list," she said quietly.

"About how many names will be on it?"

She looked up. "Five or six."

"All current?"

"*No,* sir. Consecutive."

Mary Burdine had allowed herself a small smile, and Ron returned it and hoped the meeting would now be less a confrontation. "Do you know who they are?" he asked. "I mean, the two I've mentioned are career women with the government. Are they all?"

Mary Burdine sipped her coffee. "Mr. Fairbanks," she said,

"when I first had occasion to see that Dr. Blaine was having, shall we say, an intimate relationship with a young woman, I was most sympathetic. He was, after all, a divorced man, and the girl, the first one I noticed, was a nice girl who worked at the French embassy . . . she was an American but she worked at the French embassy. He had what I suppose you might say was a pretty intense relationship with her . . . I thought he might even marry her. He sent her flowers. He took her to South Carolina with him one weekend on a holiday. Then I discovered he had another one, and after a while he dropped the first. It was, well, a pattern. He was discreet about it, though, and they didn't make scenes when he dropped them—or if they did they didn't do it publicly. I . . . never quite understood this side of him . . ."

Jill Keller spoke. "It's my impression he was not very secretive about it. He took them to Le Lion d'Or, for example. They went to his apartment."

"But it was a *small* element of his life, after all," Mary Burdine said. Let's not forget that. He *was* Secretary of State. He had relatively little time for a personal life of any kind. The newspapers talk about his taking girls to Le Lion d'Or for dinner. How many times could he have done it? How many evenings was he actually free to have dinner there? The stories exaggerate, I *assure* you . . ."

The White House News Office, The West Wing, Thursday, June 14, 1:00 PM

Sitting at a red and black NEXIS terminal, Ron touched the keys and called up newspaper stories from all over the United States. They appeared on a television screen, and he frowned as he read. "Look at this," he said to Jill Keller. "New York . . ."

People who live in the Watergate apartment complex in Washington probably wish history would keep its distance. The name of their home became a synonym for political chicanery in 1973 and 1974. Now it seems likely to become a synonym for erotic fun and games—even for harem-keeping—by high ranked public officials.

The death of Secretary of State Lansard P. Blaine has blown the cover he maintained over his personal life, and we learn now, after his untimely and tragic death, that the Secretary of State all but sustained a harem in his Watergate apartment. Indeed, on the very night he died, a young woman spent the night in his apartment—to which he never returned. It was only in the cold gray hours of dawn that she gave up her wait—or maybe she woke up—and left the Secretary's luxury apartment.

She was, it seems, one of many, including professionals, though the Secretary's tastes were said to be catholic.

A White House source insists that President Webster had no knowledge of his Secretary of State's personal life. It has become known, however, that—except for the enhanced opportunities afforded him by his high public office—Secretary Blaine was continuing a lifestyle established many years ago.

Ron touched a key, and a newspaper story from Chicago began to appear on the screen . . .

Among the persons being questioned by investigators working on the Blaine murder are a number of young women said to have been intimately involved in the personal life of the late Secretary of State. A White House source has confirmed that at least two young women have been identified as having had keys to the

Secretary's Watergate apartment. It is understood that there are others.

One theory is that Secretary of State Blaine was not murdered for any reason involving his official duties, but as the consequence of some emotional conflict arising out of his complex personal life.

"Look here," said Ron. "The wire story . . ."

The investigation into the death of Secretary of State Lansard Blaine has been complicated by revelations that he was intimately involved with a number of young women in Washington, some of whom at least stayed overnight in his Watergate apartment. Although investigators have not revealed the identities of any of the women involved, it is understood that at least one is a civil service career worker employed at the State Department and one is rumored to be a sometime prostitute.

Lunch for Ron, for Jill Keller, and for Gabe Haddad—fruit salad, sandwiches, Cokes—was brought to Ron's office. His jacket tossed over a chair, Ron in his shirtsleeves leaned back in his reclining chair and propped his feet on the corner of his desk. "I'm assuming none of us has talked to reporters," he said. "None of *us* are 'White House source.' So who the hell is?"

"You'll never find out," said Gabe Haddad. "No President ever did, and I don't think you're any more likely to."

"Well, it's clear someone's talking," Ron insisted. "And whoever it is," he said, picking up a ham salad sandwich, "could be our killer—"

"Oh, come on now, Sherlock Holmes," Jill protested.

"Well, it's not so farfetched, really . . . Blaine didn't become a sexual acrobat last week or last month. He was at it from the time he came to Washington, and, as they say, probably before. And he wasn't too secretive about it. Still, the media apparently never found out, though it's the kind of thing they thrive on. Then suddenly, within hours after he's dead, they all know it. I doubt that his Watergate neighbors called the papers and blew the whistle. The women involved didn't call. Someone *here* did. Someone leaked it, made a point of leaking it. Why? To divert attention from whatever, whomever—"

"A smokescreen," Jill said.

Ron nodded. "To confuse, to obscure, blur the lines."

Gabe Haddad shrugged. "So all we have to do is third-degree a reporter until he tells us who fed him the story. Right?"

Ron nodded again. "All we have to do is make a reporter reveal his confidential source."

"And after we're black and blue and covered with lumps," said Jill, "we'll have nothing more than a suggestion that supports your theory and no hard evidence. All we can do is just refuse to take the bait, to be distracted."

"Right. If I'm right," Ron said, "Blaine probably wasn't killed by a jealous lover or a woman scorned, as they say. It was someone who would like us to think he was . . ."

"But is our killer that naive?" Gabe asked. "I mean, to think he could throw us off this way?"

"Probably not," Ron said. "But it's worth something to him to make a confusion."

Gabe Haddad shook his head solemnly. "Too bad, I was looking forward to interviewing Blaine's girlfriends."

"Don't worry," said Ron. "We'll interview them . . . every one of them. My theory *could* be all wet. And besides, the ladies had big ears, and it seems the Secretary was less than discreet in filling them. It seems he left secret diplomacy at the office."

III

The Special Investigation Office, The West Wing, Thursday, June 14, 2:45 PM

"We'll fly to Detroit," said Lynne. She was telling Ron that she and her parents would go back to Michigan the next day to attend the funeral of Lansard Blaine. "Then out to Ann Arbor. We'll be back here early in the evening, as I understand it."

"I'm not going, of course," said Ron.

"Well . . . my father told me to tell you to come with us if you want to. I . . . I'd appreciate it if you came."

"I'd like to, Lynne, I'd like to be with you, you know that . . ."

She wore no makeup, her eyes were swollen, and she spoke in a subdued, almost trembling voice. Was it possible that *she* had been one of Blaine's young women too . . . ? He put the notion aside, but it was there—to be, he realized, followed up if necessary. The shock she felt at the sudden death of Blaine would, of course, be deepened if she'd been intimate with him . . . He looked at her . . . she was not like Marya Kalisch or Judy Pringle. She was a damn sight prettier, and younger. The whole world was still open to her, she was receptive and fresh and—

"Do you have any idea who killed him?" she asked, breaking into his thoughts.

"Afraid not. It looks like a long by-the-numbers investigation.

"I'm sorry it's fallen in your lap," she said.

He shrugged. "It's not exactly my kind of thing."

"My father has complete confidence in you—"

"I appreciate that . . . and try to relax, Lynne. You look a little beat yourself. Just leave it to supersleuth."

He said it with a straight face, and then they both allowed themselves a smile and a moment's letdown from the tension.

"This is not finished, you understand." The FBI man Walter Locke scowled over a list in his hand, marking out typographical errors with a Cross pencil. "There's still a lot of work yet to be done—"

"I understand that," Ron said. "And I appreciate your coming up with what you have as quickly as you have."

"We've got his home telephone bills from the Watergate apartment, our copies of the telephone logs and appointment books from his State Department office. We used the past four months as a preliminary basis. Later we'll have to go back more months, but using the past four months we have a list of two hundred eighteen names. Of those we can positively identify all but twenty-seven. They're all people he obviously had business with."

"Do you include Judy Pringle and Marya Kalisch in the twenty-seven or the hundred ninety-one?" Gabe Haddad asked.

"We include them in the twenty-seven," he said. "We know who they are, but their business with the Secretary of State is not apparent."

"What in the world do you mean by 'positive identification' then?" Gabe asked.

"We mean we know who the person is and why, probably, he talked to the Secretary of State. Among the twenty-seven are some people we know but we don't know—aren't certain—why they had telephone conversations with the Secretary of State. For example, here's the name Diego Lopez-Ortiz. He's the ambassador from Costa Rica. It seems apparent that he would have business with the Secretary of State and reason to receive a call from him. We've listed him among the hundred ninety-one. On the other hand, on April 24 he received a call from Barbara Lund, and later that day he returned her call. Barbara Lund is a dancer at a place called The Blue Lagoon, which is where he called her. We know who she is, but we're not certain why he called her. Oh, sure, I know, with all the stories going around now we *think* we know why he called her, but we could be wrong. Diplomacy works in strange ways, I hear. Anyway, that's why she's in the twenty-seven."

"Do the names suggest anything?" Jill Keller asked.

"We might be curious about the number of times some of the names occur," said Locke. "For example, during the four months before his death the Secretary of State made or received fourteen calls from an Inoguchi Osanaga. Osanaga is the accredited correspondent for the Honshu Shinbum. We know who he is, but why did the Secretary talk to him so often?"

"Are there any names you can't identify at all?" asked Gabe.

"Several. Of course we've only begun to look. We identified the ones we know so far simply by checking the telephone book and other available references. But there's one that's especially interesting—a man named Philippe Grand called Blaine repeatedly over the past four months. Blaine always returned his calls. No one knows who he is."

"Have you asked Mary Burdine, Blaine's secretary?" Ron put in.

"Yes. She doesn't know who Grand is."

"Does she know who Osanaga is?"

Locke nodded. "But she doesn't know why Blaine received calls from him and made calls to him."

"What about the home phone?" Jill asked.

"He didn't keep a home telephone log, of course," said Locke. "We have the long-distance bill and are working on that with the telephone company. There's a name that appears on the State Department logs and also on the apartment telephone bill we have no explanation for either. We've identified the man—Jeremy Johnson is United States sales manager for Great Britain-Hawley-Burnsby Motors, Limited. Blaine called him at his home in Virginia, from the Watergate apartment, half a dozen times in the last four months. Besides that, his name is on the logs as having called Blaine or having received calls from Blaine at his Washington office some eighteen times during the same period. The FBI has a dossier on Johnson. I've ordered a copy be delivered here. It's on its way."

"Why do you have a dossier on Jeremy Johnson?" asked Gabe Haddad.

"I'd rather you read the file yourself. I don't want to draw conclusions, but it's hard to understand why the Secretary of State would have so many contacts with a man who came to our attention as a possible money launderer."

"Clarify *that,*" Ron said.

"Let the file do it. It speaks for itself."

"I'm worried about something we haven't even talked about," Ron said to Jill Keller and Gabe Haddad when they were again alone in his office.

He was sitting behind his desk, Coke can within reach, in shirtsleeves, feet on the corner of his desk. Jill had settled into a corner of his couch, had kicked off her shoes, and sat now with her legs stretched out on the couch. Only Gabe had not shed his jacket as yet, and he sat in the chair facing Ron, frowning over a page of handwritten notes.

Ron went on . . . "He spent a lot of money, have you noticed? He lived at the Watergate—which isn't cheap. He ate at Le Bagatelle and places like it—all not cheap. He bought art. (You remember the Louise Nevelson in his office is his, not Uncle Sam's.) I expect we'll find more expensive things in the apartment. He wore expensive clothes. He gave Judy Pringle and Marya Kalisch expensive gifts—as we'll probably find he did for others. The Secretary of State earns $80,000 a year. A professor of history is paid considerably less. Where did all the money come from?"

"Corruption in the Webster Administration?" asked Jill lazily.

"I hope not," Ron said. "I'd like to see this case resolved without damage to the President—"

"I've read the autopsy report," Gabe said. "Word for word. Gruesome damn thing. We need to interview the pathologists. Personally I don't see anything in it except what we expected—that Blaine's throat was cut and he strangled and bled to death. There's one thing I'd like to know more about, though. Why did the contents of his stomach and intestines include distinct traces of dextroamphetamine?"

"How much alcohol was in him?" Jill asked.

"Point zero eight percent," said Gabe. "He was sober enough to drive a car. I expect, though, he was feeling pretty good."

"What's dextroamphetamine?" Ron asked.

"A mood lifter," said Jill. "An upper, as they used to say."

"He'd had sex within the preceding eight hours," Gabe said as matter of factly as he could manage. "Since we know it wasn't with Judy Pringle or Marya Kalisch, we have to wonder who it was . . ."

"I want a minute-by-minute of his last twenty-four hours," said Ron. *Everything* . . ."

A courier delivered the FBI file on Jeremy Johnson. Ron called the British Embassy and asked Christopher McLeod to have dinner with him at Dominique's while Jill and Gabe scanned the Johnson file.

"Spooks," Jill said. "Sneaks. They know a lot about this man, and there's nothing in here to so much as suggest he's a criminal. It makes me wonder what they have on *me.*"

"Spare me the editorial," Ron said. "What's it say?"

" 'Johnson, Jeremy Richard. Stirrup Lane, Alexandria, Virginia. Vice President and North American representative, Great Britain-Hawley-Burnsby Motors, Limited.' " She stopped reading and summarized. "Londoner, red-brick university. An engineer. Spent some time in Africa, some in India. Seems to have gotten around all the colonies. Divorced, father of three. Ah . . . married and divorced a second time. Et cetera, et cetera, et cetera. Now, looking at some of the other junk in here . . . He frequents the gambling casinos in the Bahamas and Las Vegas, where he's known and where his room and board are invariably given him free of charge."

"Standard procedure for a high roller," Gabe put in.

"Yes. He has virtually unlimited credit at the casinos. On the other hand he brings cash and takes away cash, sometimes in large quantities. That's what the FBI is interested in. That's why they think maybe he launders money."

"Is there any mention of Blaine in the file?" Ron asked.

"Yes, as a matter of fact. Jeremy Johnson gives parties—large and small, all expensive. He's not a registered representative of a foreign government but has taken the trouble—and gone to the expense—to entertain prominent members of Congress and some members of the Administration. Including Secretary of State Lansard P. Blaine . . ."

Dominique's, Thursday, June 14, 8:00 PM

Ron had particularly chosen Dominque's for his dinner meeting with Christopher McLeod because of its small, private niches—favorites by couples looking for intimacy. He knew Christopher would prefer to meet him inconspicuously; and he knew that Christopher appreciated good food and wine. At the last moment, just before he had left the office, on impulse he had invited Jill to come with him. He had asked her to bring a pad and be prepared to make a few notes of the dinner conversation, but his invitation had been on an impulse that had nothing to do with taking notes.

McLeod was late.

Jill ordered Glenlivet on the rocks, and Ron went along. In the light of the candle they toasted each other quietly and for minutes sipped thoughtfully and said nothing.

"Are you going to marry Lynne Webster?" Jill asked.

Ron only shook his head.

"The newspapers think you are."

"It makes copy."

"I saw you holding her hand on television."

"I'll hold yours." He put his hand over hers on the table. "I'm basically just an affectionate guy. I also react to attractive women."

"But not enough to marry them?"

He smiled. "Not enough to marry them just because they let me hold their hands."

"You'd make a fetching couple."

He closed his hand around hers. "Why don't you drop the subject, Jill?"

She lifted her glass. "This job you let Webster talk you into, it will make you or break you, you know. You don't get two jobs like this. Just one. To make or break."

"Which do you think it will be?"

Her eyes followed her glass back to the table and stayed there, fixed on the Scotch and ice. "I happen to think it's more likely to break you. If you don't find out who killed Blaine, they'll say you were either stupid or covered up for somebody. If you do, probably it will destroy somebody Webster doesn't want destroyed, and he won't appreciate it. Neither will the Democratic party." She shook her head. "Between the proverbial rock and a hard place."

"Why'd you agree to come work with me then?"

"I'm career civil service. Whatever happens, I'll go back where I was. Whatever happens, I'll never get up to where you are. I'll go back to Justice. Whatever happens, I'll pick up where I left off . . . He's thrown you to the wolves, you know."

"Webster?"

"Sure. The President's bright young man, likely son-in-law. If things don't work out and he has to sacrifice someone, he'll sacrifice you—with great reluctance and crocodile tears. The bright young man who held his daughter's hand on television . . . the public will figure he's really suffered, the ladies in plastic curlers will weep real tears."

"Your cynicism isn't very attractive."

"Neither is his—"

The waiter asked if they wanted another round of drinks, and Ron nodded, grateful for the interruption.

And then—"Sorry to be so tardy," said Christopher McLeod brightly, bustling up to their table. "Taxis. Traffic. You know. Well! Will you introduce me?"

"This is Jill Keller, Chris. Jill's a Justice Department lawyer assigned to the Blaine investigation. Jill, Christopher McLeod, a career diplomat who does something or other at the U.K. Embassy. Lies for his country, I suspect. Isn't that the definition?"

"I wish it were," said McLeod gaily. "That would make it all so simple." He smiled at the waiter. "Whisky," he said. "Ah, same as they're having."

McLeod was a slight, bespectacled, graying young man whose appearance was older than his age. He was, as Ron knew, only thirty-six, but he looked over fifty if not older—florid, wispy, lined. He wore a gray suit, white shirt, bow tie. He had served in Washington for eight years, and Ron had met him before the Webster Administration came to power—by applying to the Embassy for the quick resolution of a client's problem in the days when he was practicing law.

"I saw your name in the morning papers," McLeod said to Jill. "Let me think . . . how did it say? '. . . an exceptionally capable lady lawyer . . .' Right? Journalists! Sickening fellows."

"I've been called worse," said Jill.

"I'm afraid I have as well," said McLeod.

"We're one drink ahead of you."

"I shall catch up. Well! All must be in an uproar at the White House. And you, picked to put it all to rights! I was amazed when I saw your name."

"So was I."

"The two of you. Detectives. I am afraid this dinner is part of the official inquiry. Am I right? What could I know about the murder of Lansard Blaine?"

"Let's don't spoil a nice dinner," said Ron. "Let's talk about Blaine first and get it out of the way."

"Ah, well . . . I assume you have questions."

Ron nodded. "This is just a line of inquiry, there's no accusation in it."

McLeod smiled. He smiled a lot.

"The North American sales manager for Great Britain-Hawley-Burnsby Motors, Limited is a Jeremy Johnson. You know him?"

"Yes, I've met him. Actually I know *of* him."

"Tell me."

McLeod shrugged, raised his eyebrows. "Not *my* sort of chap, if you know what I mean. Hail fellow well met. A drinking man. Raconteur. Devotee of the table—the gaming table, that is. Something of a . . . ladies man, if you'll forgive me. Also a boor, if I may say so."

"Officially," Ron said, "he's in this country as North American sales manager for a British company. What does he really do?"

"Oh, I think he represents his company," said McLeod. "Hawley-Burnsby ships a few cars into the States, you know."

"So he's just a car salesman?"

"Well . . . may I ask why you ask?"

"Give me a couple more questions before I tell you?"

McLeod shrugged, looked up and nodded at the waiter who served his drink. "Ah," he said after he had sipped. "Glenlivet. Good whisky. As to your questions, I may invoke diplomatic immunity, but go right ahead."

"Do you have any reason to think Johnson may be involved in any sort of criminal activity?"

McLeod raised his eyebrows. "In London he consorts with the gambling crowd. What that signifies, I don't really know. He gambles here. Whether it simply means he's fond of gambling, or in some way is involved in nefarious schemes of theirs, I have no way of knowing. I should be surprised if he's involved in anything illicit in any large way, though. He's too much the drinker, the talker. I doubt they'd trust him."

"I ask because his name appears often on the Secretary of State's telephone log. Also, Blaine made long-distance calls to

Johnson at his home in Alexandria, Virginia. I'd like to know why."

"I can suggest a reason why Johnson would call Blaine," McLeod said, "but I can't imagine why Blaine would call Johnson."

"Why?"

"Well, as you know, the President just returned from Paris, where he and the President of France and the Prime Minister initialled the protocols for the multi-lateral trade agreement. The new trade arrangements, as you also know, abandon—philosophically, at least—the old liberal idea of free trade and take the world backward a long step toward mercantilism. That's my judgment, at least—that it's a step backward. My government, of course, does not agree and has entered enthusiastically into the Webster talks. At any rate the multi-lateral agreements, when they go into effect, will recognize the right of each participating nation to erect protective barriers around specified protected industries. In the case of the United States, one of the protected industries will be the automobile industry. I need hardly tell you what that will do to Great Britain-Hawley-Burnsby Motors, Limited. In effect it will shut them out of the American market. Jeremy Johnson is by no means the only representative of a foreign industry lobbying to defeat the multi-lateral trade agreements. Indeed, there's a gaggle of your chaps in London trying to persuade Her Majesty's Government to abandon the talks and the rush to the treaty. Johnson's an embarrassment to us. He entertains senators. He lobbies shamelessly. I'm not aware that he had conversations with the Secretary of State, but I'm not surprised that he had."

"As you suggested," said Jill, "that would explain his calls to Blaine, but not Blaine's calls to him."

"I suppose the circumstances do suggest an explanation," said McLeod, "but I'll not be the one to give it . . ."

"I can't help but wonder," McLeod said after two whiskies and they'd ordered their dinner, "if there weren't a bit of disagreement between President Webster and Secretary Blaine over the multi-lateral trade agreements. Blaine was, after all, a student of international relations. His writings suggest, I think, the traditional liberal's commitment to free trade. Webster's policy has shocked a lot of old liberal consciences, and I wonder if Blaine's might not have been among them. I notice, too, that Webster negotiated the trade agreements himself, along with close aides, not through the Secretary of State—not, indeed, through the State Department. There were rumors of Blaine's pending resignation. I wonder—"

"So do we," Ron interrupted, "but right now we're focused on his death, and I can't believe any kind of policy difference with the President had anything to do with that—"

"Oh, of course not," McLeod said hastily. "Please don't take my little digression to suggest anything sinister."

"The Webster Administration's commitment to protection for the automobile industry is not sinister at all," Jill said. "It's perfectly rational, perfectly cynical. Robert Webster made his personal fortune in the automobile industry, and he's going to help his friends in that industry any way he can."

"Carburetters, as I recall," said McLeod. " 'Carburetors,' I believe you call them."

"And fuel-injection systems," said Ron. "Half the cars in the country run on Webster fuel systems of one kind or another."

"Yes, a hard-headed industrialist, your President. It's hard to imagine how an academic fellow like Blaine could have gotten along with him."

"It's hard to imagine how a Prime Minister like Harwood gets along with the Queen," remarked Jill dryly.

"Ah. Very good," said McLeod. "Very good."

Ron shoved his empty whisky glass across the thick white tablecloth toward McLeod. "There's a lot of money at stake in those trade agreements. Fortunes are going to be lost—and made. How many dollars do you suppose it's worth to certain people to have barriers put up against the importing of British, German and Japanese cars?"

"Yes, of course," said McLeod. "And perhaps somewhere in that tangle you might discover your motive for the murder of Secretary Blaine."

"If he was opposed to the agreements," said Jill, "he was subtle about it—"

"Subtle, yes," said Ron, "but it was known he wasn't enthusiastic. Privately, in conversations with the President, he may have been fighting hard against the agreements. Someone may have known that. Someone in a position to profit from the adoption and ratification of the agreements would have had a damn powerful motive to get rid of Blaine."

"Whole multi-national industries are going to live and die by what's agreed to, or isn't. Nations have gone to war for less than's at stake for many of them in these agreements. One man's murder would be, in their view, a good piece of business if it got them what they wanted. . . ."

Seven months before, in Chicago, a man named Hooper had fired a shot at the President from the roof of a hotel. His motive had been almost lost in the rush to judge him insane and inconsequential.

Ron had been with the President that morning. The President had asked him to make the early-morning trip from Washington so they could use the hours on the plane to review the draft of a speech the President wanted to make about law reform and expediting criminal procedures. The President had given a talk at a breakfast meeting at the Merchandise Mart in support of the multi-lateral trade agreements. He had a short meeting scheduled in mid-morning with a group trying to raise funds to pay off the debt of the Illinois campaign committee. When they left the Merchandise Mart in the limousine, rain was falling on snow and ice. The mayor was in the car and wanted to talk, but the President was distracted by the sight of Chicagoans struggling against the weather and the conversation was fragmented and strained. The car slid twice, once until its front wheels came to a stop against a curb.

"You must have the worst weather in the United States," the President said to the mayor just as the car pulled to a stop in front of the building where the campaign-fund group was waiting. Sensing that the comment had an abrasive sound, he added, "Maybe we can get the Congress to vote you two extra months of sunshine."

The President and the mayor stepped out on the sidewalk. A Secret Service man was handing the President a coat, and Ron was just emerging from the car, when the shot was fired. The President was in almost no danger. The bullet struck the building behind him, four feet above his head; and the Secret Service man grabbed him instantly and wrestled him to the icy sidewalk in the shelter of the door and fender of the big car. Another man grabbed the mayor and threw him back into the car, knocking Ron to the floor.

Ron had not heard the shot. He had not seen the bullet whack against the stone facade of the building, chipping out a hole the size of an egg. On the floor under the mayor he could see nothing, but he heard furious bursts of automatic-weapons fire. He thought the presidential limousine was under attack by a heavily armed group. He was properly scared.

Actually, the automatic weapons were fired by the Secret Service. The man who had fired at the President had remained standing on the roof of the hotel across the street, eight stories up. The Secret Service had spotted him, aiming his pistol at the limousine, and they had cut him down before he could fire a second shot.

Before Ron and the mayor could disentangle themselves and get up, the Secret Service men shoved the President into the backseat with them and slammed the door. The car lurched forward, and the motorcade sped away in a howl of sirens. They returned to the airport, and the President boarded Air Force One.

The "incident" was over.

At the airport the President asked Ron to return to the city with the Mayor of Chicago and the Secret Service contingent that would remain for the initial investigation. Ron would have no part in the investigation, but the President wanted a personal representative to stay in Chicago for at least twenty-four hours to see how the follow-up was handled and to report personally and confidentially.

Ron stayed. He saw what they did. He reported to the President.

He was even obliged to view the ghastly remains of Donald Hooper. He was present when they searched his luggage: everything personal of his that was in Chicago. He was present when a Secret Service agent telephoned the man's wife and told her her husband had attempted to assassinate the President and had been killed. He watched and listened for the required twenty-four hours, then hurried back to Washington.

Hooper, they said, was mentally deranged. He had fired at the President with a .357 magnum revolver, a weapon with which he had no experience and which was unsuited at best for a long-range shot. He had acted on an impulse apparently formed no more than 48 hours in advance and had traveled to Chicago from

Wichita with the newly purchased pistol in his luggage. He had talked of suicide in recent weeks, it was reported from Wichita. He must have been, everyone concluded, insane.

Ron thought otherwise. Hooper was employed by a Wichita corporation that manufactured a line of 35 mm single-lens reflex cameras under the name Digiflex: a high-quality, high-price line, matching excellent optics with sophisticated electronics. The line was new, but it had begun to compete successfully in many markets withthe Japanese lines that had long dominated the high-price camera market. Hooper was a high-school graduate who had educated himself to be a skilled technician for Digiflex. Under the multi-lateral trade agreements proposed, this kind of camera was assigned to the Japanese. Japanese cameras were to have tariff concessions—in return for, among other things, similar concessions for American-built cars. Digiflex faced economic disaster. Hooper faced unemployment.

Hooper was a prospective victim of the multi-lateral trade agreements. The jobs of tens of thousands of other Americans might be made more secure by the agreements, and the overall prosperity of the country might be improved; but for this American and his company the proposed agreements would be a disaster.

No one covered up the fact that Hooper might have tried to kill the President out of frustration with the consequences of the trade-agreement proposals. It was just too easy to reach another conclusion. But Ron suspected he saw in this one man a manifestation of the kind of intense disruptions and conflicts the agreements were going to create. They would trade some people's prosperity for that of others—for the greater good of the greatest number, some of the Administration loyalists would put it.

Donald Hooper, he felt, had decided otherwise. And it was not unreasonable to suspect he was not alone.

Jill Keller's Apartment, Friday, June 15, 12:15 AM

Ron, shirtsleeves rolled up, tie and collar loosened, sat alone on Jill's couch, idly swirling the Scotch in a glass and frowning over his thoughts.

She returned. "Everything's okay," she said. She had heard a sound in her children's bedroom and had gone in to check them. "I'm sorry I had to come home," she said. "It was a good evening in every sense, but—"

"I have no right to complain."

"The babysitter—"

"No *problem,* Jill. It was time for Chris to be on his way, anyhow."

She sat beside him on the couch and picked up her own glass of Scotch.

"Do you remember what I told you?" he asked. "I mean, when you said you had to know everything, that you wouldn't work for me if you weren't told everything. Remember, I said I wanted to make a record of every interview, every thought."

"I remember."

He rubbed his mouth with the back of his hand. "I'm going to talk right now. I'm going to tell you what I'm thinking. And I'm not going to make a record. This is just speculation. It's just something that has to be brought out. I'm not sure we even need to tell Gabe."

"Well . . .?"

"There was talk the President had asked Blaine to resign. The rumor was denied, but it persisted. Marya Kalisch says he told her he was thinking of resigning. He—"

"The President told the press conference Blaine had spoken to him about resigning."

"Yes, but he insisted it would have been voluntary. Anyway . . . there was . . . I'm sure I saw it, there was real *tension,* something was wrong. I know the Websters pretty well, I think. I knew Blaine. I'd seen them together many times. The other night, the night when Blaine was killed, there was something unspoken between them, some"—he shook his head—"*tension.* I even saw it between Blaine and Mrs. Webster. They were great friends but—"

"Is this just a feeling, or did you see something specific?"

He shook his head. "The President and Blaine . . . there was always a degree of what I suppose you could call competition between them. Blaine was, after all, Mrs. Webster's friend from the University of Michigan faculty, and the President, I always supposed, made Blaine his adviser and Secretary of State because he respected his judgment, not because he liked him all that much. You had to wonder if he didn't suspect his wife's friendship with Blaine was maybe a little too close. He called Blaine *professor* sometimes, and it wasn't exactly in an affectionate way . . . you could hear in his voice that he was putting Blaine in his place . . . a subordinate, an academic abruptly elevated to a position of power. And Blaine . . . Blaine tended to show some contempt for anyone he didn't consider his intellectual equal, which pretty much included everybody. You couldn't think the two of them liked each other very much if you saw them together. I always thought maybe the President considered Blaine the way I did . . . I often wanted to tell him to go to hell . . . I think he and I might have at least gotten on better after something like that cleared the air between us—"

"Tuesday night . . . ?" Jill prompted.

"The facade was down. Blaine was uneasy. It was as if he had somehow overstepped his bounds and been called down for it.

And the President, I thought, was maybe a little pleased for having called him down and having settled something between them."

"Speculation," Jill said, and sipped her Scotch.

Ron shook his head firmly. "The tension was *there.* It was *palpable.* Maybe it had something to do with Lynne. Mrs. Webster didn't seem to like the way she was rubbing Blaine's shoulders . . . although come to think of it I'd seen her do it before . . ."

"Do you suppose Blaine had made a pass at Lynne?"

"Well, I could see the way the President and Mrs. Webster watched Blaine let Lynne massage his shoulders. They didn't like it. They'd not minded before, but they clearly did now . . ."

"Do you think anyone else was aware of this . . . tension?"

"Gimbel. No one else."

"Well, do you really think it possible the President killed Blaine, or somehow conspired in it?"

Ron tipped his glass and gulped the last of his drink. "No. No, I don't think that. And I'm not just being loyal—"

"Ron . . ." she said quietly. "You've got to protect yourself. I've said this before and now I'll say it again . . . it's possible he may have set you up to take a fall for him—"

"If I just had some hard *evidence* . . ." He pressed his forehead with his clenched fist. "Right now all we've got is theories . . . suspicions . . . no *evidence* to back any of them. We're no damn closer to knowing who killed Blaine than we were Wednesday morning." He stopped, his face creased with deep lines. "I can't seem to—"

"Ron . . ."

"If we could just . . . can't you see? If—"

"Ron. It's after midnight, you're exhausted . . ."

"Oh, right . . . I'm sorry, I'll go—"

"No, not what I meant." She put her hand on his shoulder and pulled him toward her. "Come here. Put your head down. *Relax,* for God's sake."

Awkwardly, a little embarrassed, he put his head down on her breasts, where she guided him. He closed his eyes but felt her hand moving and opened his eyes to see that she was unbuttoning her blouse. She pressed his head down so that his cheek was against one of her full, soft breasts.

"Ron," she whispered, "you have another day to face tomorrow, and another one after that . . . you've got to take care of yourself too. You don't have to leave here tonight, but if you want to, just sleep a little now and I'll wake you up."

He reached for her hand.

"Thank you, lady. You are, to coin a phrase, just what the doctor ordered."

IV

Ronald Fairbanks's Apartment, Friday, June 15, 8:30 AM

Ron let Johnson's telephone ring, suspecting he was at home but in bed. He sat with the telephone in his left hand, pressed to his ear; with his right he sipped from a glass of orange juice. He would let it ring twenty times. The Washington *Post* lay on his breakfast table. He had made coffee and had a croissant, warmed slightly in his microwave oven, with good English marmalade. He sat there in a short black-and-white silk robe and a pair of shorts. Ten rings, or twelve. If Jeremy Johnson didn't answer he would call Locke and have him put a couple of agents out to find him.

"Hullo?" A dulled voice exhaled.

"Jeremy Johnson?"

"Yes. Who's this?"

"My name is Ronald Fairbanks. I'm Special Counsel to the President, and I'm in charge of the Blaine murder investigation."

"Hullo, Jamie, or Georgia, or whoever it is. It ain't funny, you know. You've woke me up in the middle of the night practically, for naught. Goo-by, and be a good chap and don't ring me again."

"This is serious, Mr. Johnson. I need to talk to you."

"Wha'd you say your name was?" His cockney accent was thick.

"Ron repeated it, and his position with the President.

"Really?"

"Yes, really."

"I don't believe it."

"Let me suggest you try—"

"All right, all right, you're the special . . . whatever. Investigation of the murder of Blaine, you say."

"Yes."

"Well, what do I know about that?"

"I'd like to find out."

"Nothing."

"I need to see you just the same. This morning."

"Out of the question. I'm not coming into town this morning—"

"I can have you *brought* in."

"How's that?"

"I can have you picked up and brought in."

"Wha'? By the police?"

"By the FBI."

"Now, see here! What is this? Maybe I'd better talk to my counselor first."

"Well, that's your right. You can bring him with you. But I want to see you in my office at the Justice Department this morning—"

"This *morning?* It's . . ."

"It's eight-thirty. Let's say eleven?"

"What's your name again, one more time?"

"Fairbanks. Ronald Fairbanks."

"Bloody fancy name, that. All right *Ronald* . . . see you at bloody eleven."

Special Investigation Office, The Justice Department, Friday, June 15, 10:30 AM

"I've got another one here you'd better know about," Walter Locke was saying.

"You worry me," Ron said. "I wonder what you have in those files on me."

"Well, you work for the government . . . or did the Secretary of State . . ."

"A lot of personal stuff," Ron said. "I don't know if—"

"It may help us find out who killed him. Remember that."

Ron glanced at Jill Keller, who sat to one side, taking in this sparring between Ron and the Special Agent. They were talking about the women in Blaine's life. Ron had been surprised to learn how much the FBI did in fact know about Blaine's personal life, and it troubled him that the FBI should know so much. He put aside his feelings for now. He had no other choice . . . "All right, who else?" he asked.

"A woman named Martha Kingsley. She's the wife of a naval officer. We have a separate file on her . . . separate from the file on Blaine. She worked once as an aide to Senator Killbane, which is why the file was open. There's reason to think—it can't be proved—that she once used confidential information from the files of the Armed Services Committee, gave it to a defense contractor, probably for money. There *was* a leak, and she's the most likely source of it. She moves around. Her husband is on sea duty much of the time, and when he's away—sometimes even when he's not—she is seen in the company of members of Congress, members of the Administration, prominent lobbyists, wealthy men . . . She's an exceptionally good-looking woman. She's Washington-wise. If she slept with the Secretary of State, she got some advantage from it, you may be sure."

"Do you know he slept with her?" Jill asked.

"We know he visited her apartment," said Locke. "At night."

"You know too much for my comfort," said Ron.

"We don't know anything about you that need make you uncomfortable," said Locke, this time smiling openly.

"You've looked."

"I've looked."

"If you read history," said Ron with a shrug, "you know that the files of any police organization, anywhere, contain a lot of . . . gossip."

"You can't keep it out," said Locke.

Johnson was late. He said he had reached the Justice Department building by eleven, but he swore no one knew where Fairbanks had an office—and some swore he had none, had no connection with the Department—and it had taken half an hour to find the Special Investigation Office.

"I require information, not punctuality," said Ron. "Let me introduce Mrs. Keller. She's a lawyer with the Justice Department, assigned to temporary duty with me."

"It's right Christian of you not to complain about my bein' late," Jeremy Johnson said.

He glanced around the shabby temporary office, sat down. He was a young man, maybe thirty-one or -two, tall, broad-shouldered and roughly handsome. His thick sandy hair hung errant across his forehead. His jaw was broad and strong, and his face was flushed. He had brought the butt of a cigarette in his hand, and as soon as he was seated he crushed it out and took another from a pack. The aroma of whisky was discernible on his breath.

"You knew Lansard Blaine," Ron said. He did not intend to give Johnson a chance to balance himself. "How did you come to know him?"

Johnson shrugged. "Ah . . . well, I represent my company in the States, I see a lot of people. I met your Secretary of State at some party somewhere—I don't remember where. We struck up an acquaintance." He shrugged again. Ron noted that his East End accent had diminished.

"Did you know him well?"

"No, not very well. He was, after all, your Secretary of State."

"Did you know him socially or in business?"

Johnson took a drag on his cigarette. "A bit of each, I guess."

"Talk to him often?"

"Not often."

"You live on Stirrup Lane in Alexandria. I called you at home this morning. I took your home telephone number off the telephone bill for Lansard Blaine's Watergate apartment. He called you at home, from his apartment, six times in the past four months. How many times did you call him?"

Johnson crushed his cigarette between his lips. "I find that 'ard to believe—"

"Your name also occurs in the State Department telephone log eighteen times for the same period."

Johnson nodded. His face was red. "I believe I should ask," he said, "whether you're suggesting I had anythin' to do with the death of Lansard Blaine? Because if you are, I want to talk to—"

"He was killed in the White House."

"*Never* been in the White House."

"I believe it. So you didn't kill Blaine . . . but you can help us find out who did—"

"I don't know anythin' that's got to do with his being murdered—"

"Did you ever pay a girl to sleep with him?"

Johnson glanced at Jill. "Yes." He said it quietly.

"Buy him liquor, meals . . . entertainment?"

Johnson nodded. "I represent a company with important business interests in this country. I wine and dine a lot of people—"

"We know. Why Blaine?"

Johnson sighed. "The bloody multi-lateral trade agreements, of course. They'll destroy my comp'ny—or could."

"You wanted Blaine to do what for you?"

Johnson shrugged. "To make us an exception. If he couldn't kill the damned agreements outright maybe he could have got us out of them anyway. Your President . . . well, you know, he set up the agreements to take care of his friends in Detroit, at the expense of European and Japanese companies like mine."

It was plain to Ron that Johnson only played at being the Cockney fool, that in fact he was a shrewd operator who used his East-End accent (turned off and on at will) for all the advantage he could gain from it. He was, on the other hand, frightened by this investigation. Keeping him off balance with questions was a useful tactic . . .

"Winning an exception for British automobile manufacturers would be worth millions, wouldn't it?" Jill said.

"I'd say so."

"So you spend your company's money," Ron said. "You're not a registered representative of a foreign government, though, are you?"

Johnson grinned. "Representative of my government? Hardly. That's the last thing in the world I am—"

"Blaine," Ron said, "was murdered, as you may recall. Millions of dollars—"

"Wait a minute 'ere—"

"If Lansard Blaine was worth millions to you, alive, then he was worth as much to someone else dead. Or, if he was on the other side, then he was worth all that to you dead. It depends on whether or not you're telling me the truth about where your real interests lay—"

"Blaine," Johnson said "was *against* the damn trade agreements your President wants . . . 'E could've been *our* salvation."

"Spell it out."

"By convincin' Webster—who knows *nothin'* about foreign relations . . ."

"Was Blaine going to do what you wanted?"

"He was against the damn treaties, he was on our side."

Ron glanced at Jill. "What did it cost you to get him there?"

Johnson drew a deep breath. " 'E believed we were right," he said more weakly.

"And?"

Johnson let out his deep breath. "And we paid him. So you see" —he rushed—"it would have done *us* no good to kill him. 'E was on *our* side. 'E was against the damn treaties."

"You paid him *what,* Johnson?"

Johnson shrugged. *"Money.* What more?"

"You're saying you bribed the Secretary of State . . ."

"Bribe . . ." He rolled the word around on his tongue. "Bribe . . . well, that there presupposes a *quid pro quo,* does it not? I'm not sure we ever got our money's worth—but, yas, goddammit, we paid him. We paid your precious Secretary of State to push our side of the argument with the President. We knew his relationship was a whole lot more than just Secretary. He was a personal friend of Webster, of long standing . . . he could argue our side of the thing the way no other man could, and we paid him to do it. We paid him a lot of money. We promised him more if he won the case. Yas, we did. But we didn't kill him, he was workin' on our side of the case, on our payroll, as you might say."

"How did you pay—?"

"Girls, wine, food, but all that was a pittance. *Cash,* like I told you . . . your Secretary of State sold his influence for cash. You mean to tell me you didn't know that? We paid him cash money a hundred thousand dollars. We were ready to pay a lot more. You still think we killed him? He was worth at least the hundred thou' to us, alive . . . why would we want to kill him? We owned a share of him and we paid a good price for our share. Kill him? Whoever did it, a piece of what they killed was bought and paid for by *us* . . ."

Special Investigation Office, The West Wing, Friday, June 15, 2:00 PM

Lieutenant General Robert Hurd was Director of the CIA. He sat on the couch in Ron's office with an open briefcase in front of him—he had unlocked the briefcase with a large key—and lifted out several thick files. He was thin, long-jawed, gray, with the crisp yet faintly seedy appearance of a career military officer. His brown suit fit him ill. His shoes were scuffed. He spoke in short sentences, with an economy of words.

"These files are the ones you requested. They're classified top secret. I hope you can review them and let me take them back this afternoon."

Ron was surprised that Hurd himself had come. He had asked the CIA what it had on three people: Jeremy Johnson, Inoguchi Osanaga, and Philippe Grand. He'd not anticipated that the director would come to the White House with the files.

"Osanaga is no journalist," General Hurd said, looking into the file he had opened, then peering up at Ron over his half-glasses.

"He represents certain Japanese manufacturing companies as a lobbyist."

"Automobile manufacturers?"

"Yes."

"Johnson, the same?"

"Essentially. Also, he's a sort of playboy."

"Philippe Grand?"

"We've nothing on him, never heard of him."

"I'm going to ask you to check three more people for me," Ron said. "Judith Pringle, Marya Kalisch, and Martha Kingsley."

Hurd nodded.

"You know who they are?"

The general nodded again.

"Do you see the drift of the investigation?" Ron asked.

"It's out of my sphere—"

"Off the record, of course," Ron said.

"Everything's off the record," the general said dryly.

"Off the record, the investigation produces some reason to believe Blaine was taking bribes from foreign businesses—"

"The Agency, of course, hasn't conducted an investigation of the Secretary of State. To do so would violate the definition of the Agency's function—"

"But you *have* investigated Johnson and Osanaga," Ron said. "Does Blaine—"

"His name does not come up in their files."

"What do you have to suggest that foreign businesses standing to lose from the signing and ratification of the multi-lateral trade agreements are illegally spending money to defeat the agreements?"

"They're doing it in other countries. Japanese businessmen may force the Japanese government out of office. They've formed an alliance with labor unions. Conservatives and socialists find themselves on the same side . . . it's bread and butter. They want their stuff to get into the U.S. . . ."

"Does the President know what they're doing?"

The general nodded. "We've reported to him."

"Do you have any reason to think one of the young women I mentioned—Pringle, Kalisch, Kingsley—is in any way involved in the effort to defeat the agreements in the United States?"

"I've no information that suggests it."

"Do you have anything on them at all?"

"I'll have to check, as you asked me to. I'd never heard of Pringle until yesterday. I know Marya Kalisch. She works for Alfred Eiseman and I've had occasion to read translations she's done. As for Martha Kingsley, her name has come up in several connections. She is known."

"I'll give you a receipt for these files," Ron said. "I'll keep them securely locked up and you can have them back in a day or so . . . after I've had a chance to look through them."

The Director of the CIA didn't like it one damn bit, having to back off to a damned lawyer half his age. But back off was the drill at the moment, and the general was a survivor. He wasn't altogether sorry, though, to see Fairbanks up a tree, obviously fishing . . . and to hell with the mixed metaphor . . . "Whatever you say, Mr. Fairbanks. And *good luck* . . ."

British Embassy, Office of the Ambassador, Friday, June 15, 4:45 PM

"It was short notice," Ron said as he sat down.

"Under the circumstances . . ." Sir John Bedilion smiled engagingly.

Christopher McLeod had arranged the appointment on a telephone call from Ron. He took a chair to one side, eyeing the

Ambassador. Sir John Bedilion, a man of sixty with a liver-spotted bald head, seated himself in the tall leather chair behind his writing table.

"Whatever we say will be confidential," Ron said.

The Ambassador momentarily closed his small hazel eyes, nodded.

"I regret I have to ask you some questions I know will be embarrassing," Ron went on. "I might even say, Sir John, that I ask them of you personally, not officially. I feel I can trust you. I am also conscious that I'm imposing on you."

His acquaintance with Sir John Bedilion predated his joining the White House staff. As a young lawyer he had been assigned by his firm to resolve for Lady Sarah Bedilion a contretemps over the price of a watch she had bought in a New York jewelry store.

"Let's not worry about that," the Ambassador said. He took a cigarette from a silver box on his table, lit it with the tiny flame that appeared on top of a massive silver lighter. "You don't smoke, as I recall."

"No, thank you."

"I watched a part of the funeral on the television."

"We're grateful to the Queen for sending the Earl," Ron said.

"Frankly, so am I. As much as I respected Secretary of State Blaine, I'm pleased to have been relieved from going to his funeral . . . well, you have yourself quite a job, don't you?"

"I'm afraid I do."

"How can I help?"

"I've begun to suspect it was near-common knowledge, among insiders, at least, that Blaine was susceptible to improper influences . . . I've reason to think he took bribes."

"Indeed? And what makes you think *I* might know if he did or not?"

"I'm not suggesting you have any exclusive knowledge," Ron

said. "I'm asking you because I'm frankly reluctant to ask people who might be in a more obvious position to know."

"It would be most undiplomatic"—he allowed himself a smile —"of me to discuss the subject with you at all."

"I know that."

"Suppose I say I think possibly he did take bribes. What then?"

"Then I'll know from someone I trust," Ron said. "I'll have to find the evidence for it somewhere else."

"And this is important to your investigation into his murder?"

"Very."

Sir John Bedilion glanced at Christopher McLeod. He frowned over his cigarette and took a shallow, thoughtful puff. "Very well," he said. "I think your suspicion is well-founded. Lansard Blaine was a bold, clever man. He mostly covered his tracks quite shrewdly, and he managed to do what he did all but under the noses of the Washington press corps, which would have eaten him alive with great relish if they had found him out. Indeed, I have myself marveled at their naiveté—as much as, to be blunt, I marvel at yours and at the President's if he remains ignorant. But then, one does tend to give the professionals in the art of propriety the benefit of the doubt. To be discreet is presumably our stock-in-trade . . . which, of course, is a useful cover for indiscretion."

Ron enjoyed the man's style. "Sir, could you please be a bit less diplomatic?"

The Ambassador drew again on his cigarette. "I've no direct personal knowledge, of course, but I have *understood,* shall we say, for quite some time, that Secretary of State Blaine put out subtle, and some not-so-subtle, hints to certain people from time to time suggesting that he might accept inducements . . . I'm certain that certain *governments* responded to his hints . . . others he may have received from individuals—"

"Such as Jeremy Johnson," Christopher McLeod put in.

Sir John frowned. "Yes. Such as Jeremy Johnson."

"And what did he do in return for these inducements?" Ron went on.

"Well, there's a good deal of mystery about that. In a democracy the secretary of state or foreign minister doesn't normally make many significant decisions. He influences the making of policy more than making it himself. And he shades policy in the execution. But he rarely has occasion, or the power, directly to make a major decision. That's one reason, perhaps, why so many missed what Blaine was doing—plus that it was rather subtle."

Ron shook his head. "Unbelievable . . ."

"Remember," the Ambassador said, "that Blaine was a lifetime student of diplomatic history. He would have known very well what most people have forgotten: that there was a day when diplomacy was carried out on this very basis, day-to-day, year after year. The clever Talleyrand was a prime example. History tells us he took millions in bribes—some of those millions for services he never performed and never intended to. He was not alone. Bismarck kept what he called his 'reptile fund'—money he used to bribe newspapers."

"And Asian governments . . ." Ron said.

"Yes. To this day. Americans tend to be a bit naive about things like this. Lansard Blaine was not a typical American. He was also anything but naive."

"He was a professor most of his life," McLeod said. "Academics can be damned righteous sometimes about their noble calling and about how little society respects and rewards it. That may have provided him a basis for rationalization—"

"Do you know of a specific instance of his taking a bribe?" Ron asked.

"I'm afraid I do," the Ambassador said. "I won't tell you who offered it to him and how I found out. I'd have to breach a confidence to do that. I will tell you, though, that a man I know, the representative of a certain government, offered Secretary of State Blaine ten thousand dollars to obtain an American visa for one of his nationals. The visa, which had been held up five years, was issued immediately, and Blaine took the money." Sir John paused. "The man who got the visa paid a hundred thousand dollars for it. Blaine only got ten, although the man presumed he got it all."

"The diplomat pocketed the rest, I suppose," Ron said.

"No, not all. Some of it had to be spent to cover the transaction, money paid here and there."

"But what a risk—"

"I've another story that I can't vouch for . . . Blaine was paid money, I don't know how much, to delay the negotiation of the international agreement on construction standards for ships to carry liquefied natural gas. He accepted the money and didn't delay the negotiations at all . . . at least there's no evidence that he did anything to delay them. The story is that he did not even promise he would try, he simply took the money, promised nothing and, indeed, did nothing. He may have been Talleyrand reincarnated."

Ron shook his head. "The man we thought might win a Nobel Prize . . ."

Sir John shrugged. "Why not? He was an effective diplomat. He probably was responsible, more than any other man in the world, for averting war between India and Pakistan—which could have been an extremely destructive war. He was bold and shrewd, as I said before. He was intelligent and knowledgeable and . . ." —Sir John smiled—"he had considerable style, no question. He took his *inducements* with panache. He was, in fact, a great man in many ways—"

"And the ways in which he was not may well have gotten him murdered," Ron said grimly.

Sir John looked at him, his expression altogether diplomatic. "Perhaps . . ."

The Oval Office, Friday, June 15, 7:05 PM

The retiring president of the Inter-American Development Bank had kept his six-thirty appointment and had met with the President immediately after the President's return from Michigan and the funeral of Lansard Blaine. It was a courtesy call, which had ended short of the thirty minutes allotted to it, and the President had summoned Fritz Gimbel to the Oval Office at six-forty-five. Ron Fairbanks had the seven o'clock appointment, and Gimbel was still with the President when Ron was admitted to the office. Ron would have preferred not to report to the President with Gimbel there, but after a few minutes it became apparent that the President meant to hear his report without dismissing Gimbel. Ron had no choice.

The President had left a stack of files on his desk—apparently what he and Gimbel had been discussing—and had sat on one of the couches near the fireplace. He had ordered drinks, and their conversation remained casual until the butler brought the tray. Gimbel smoked. He was one of the few people who would smoke a cigarette in the presence of the President, who had made it plain to the White House staff that he did not like it.

"I'm pleased you haven't generated any more flack than you have," President Webster said to Ron. "You'll have to talk to the media people, though . . . sooner or later."

"I've nothing much to tell them—"

"Then make up something," Gimbel said.

Gimbel's tone brought no reaction from the President. He'd said of Gimbel many months ago, in Ron's hearing, that though Gimbel was an exceptionally able man in many areas he had absolutely no sense of public relations. The man was blunt, all edges.

"Maybe a press conference . . ." the President said. "Maybe tomorrow—"

"I've no idea who killed Blaine," Ron said, blunt as Gimbel.

"Well, do you feel you're making any progress?" Webster asked.

"I've learned a lot about Blaine . . ."

The President drew a deep breath. "Such as?"

Ron glanced at Gimbel, then spoke directly to the President. "The way he lived . . . the way he spent money. The stories about the women he slept with are true. He—"

"Does any of this have anything to do with his death?" the President broke in.

"Probably. He spent more than he earned. Much more. It's obvious, and anyone who does any accounting on it is going to figure that out. The problem is, I don't know precisely where the money came from. But it's pretty clear that he took bribes—"

Gimbel grunted in disgust. "Fairbanks, you—"

"Do you think that has anything to do with his death," the President interrupted Gimbel.

Ron nodded. "I think it's likely. And whether it did nor not, the investigation—either our investigation or one by some reporter—is going to bring it out. I think we have to be prepared to deal with it."

Ron noticed that the President and Gimbel exchanged glances. "I have to ask you something, sir. Blaine was opposed to the trade agreements, wasn't he?"

"Yes."

"Why?"

The President frowned and once again glanced at Gimbel. "The classic liberal . . . free trade. All that. The usual arguments."

"Suppose I told you," Ron said carefully, "that Blaine received a hundred thousand dollars from an overseas industrial corporation to exert his influence with you to abandon the multi-lateral trade negotiations, or at the very least to exempt what this corporation makes. Suppose also I told you he was to receive a great deal more if he succeeded in so influencing you."

" '*Suppose,*' " snapped Gimbel. "Dammit, Fairbanks, let's not suppose. *Did* Blaine get a hundred thousand or *didn't* he?"

"I've some evidence of it—not enough to prove it, but enough to make it seem very likely."

Gimbel shook his head.

"I'm not entirely surprised," the President said. He stood and walked across the room to the windows behind his desk. He parted the curtains between the gold drapes and looked out on the cloudless, golden June evening. "I'd begun to suspect something like that."

"I wonder how widespread the suspicion is," Ron said.

"I don't know," he said quietly.

"How did you come to suspect?"

The President let the curtains fall together and sat behind his desk. "He knew my policy about international trade . . . that I was committed to a departure. He knew my mind was made up. Still, he continued to argue, and toward the end of the arguments became more and more vehement, until they weren't arguments at all, close to just angry harangues. He stopped being rational on the subject—Lansard Blaine, who had always been the *most* rational of men . . ."

"Some people stand to make and some people stand to lose millions through the trade agreements," Ron said.

The President nodded. "It balances out equitably among nations but not necessarily among industries and certainly not among individual corporations. German and British and Japanese automobile manufacturers . . . but our automobile industry will be strengthened and will survive, and it's *essential* to our economy."

"Did Blaine argue for an exemption for automobiles?"

"For a partial exemption." The President abstractly tugged at the fringe on the presidential flag to straighten it. "Is that who you think bribed him? Automobile—?"

"Great Britain-Hawley-Burnsby."

"God!" The President shook his head unhappily. "And others?"

"Probably. I haven't found out yet."

"And you think," said Gimbel, interjecting a louder, more impatient voice into the conversation, "that the people who may have paid him bribes are the ones who may have killed him?" He got up, took up the President's glass of Scotch and carried it to him at his desk. "It could be a lot of people then. The investigation widens considerably, doesn't it?"

"Not necessarily," Ron said. "In fact, it narrows it. How many people with access to the White House at night are also involved in potentially vast profits or losses from the trade agreements?"

"Profits?" the President said.

"Well, someone who stood to profit from the trade agreements may have killed Blaine to shut up an influential voice against them . . ."

The President got up to stand behind his desk. "I think you're on the right track, Ron. People who try to bribe . . . you follow me? They're capable of other crimes. And you're right, there's profit and loss involved in these trade agreements. People working for foreign governments, or for foreign business corporations . . . concentrate on them."

"Well, there's still a problem in the theory, Mr. President. Whoever killed Blaine had access to the second floor of the White House after eleven at night."

"Someone who could pay Blaine a hundred thousand to try to talk me out of the trade agreements could also buy someone with that access . . . household staff . . . even a Secret Service man . . . Concentrate on that, Ron. Concentrate on that."

"I will, sir. I'm not sure we'll find our murderer that way but . . ."

"What else, Ron? What else do you have in mind?"

Ron shook his head. "Nothing else, Mr. President, not really—"

"Spit it out, Ron."

"All right." Ron glanced at Gimbel. "I found it out too easily. I mean, that Blaine was taking money. Someone else must have known, it opens up all kinds of possibilities—"

"Even that the President might have killed him, right?" said the President. "Or that he conspired in it. Even that, hmm?"

"I'm hardly thinking of you, sir."

"Concentrate as I told you. If that doesn't produce anything, then look where you think you have to. I told you there is no limit on this investigation. Look where you have to, Ron. *Everybody's* a suspect."

He nodded vigorously, as though to convince all—including himself—of his sincerity.

The Blue Lagoon, Friday, June 15, 10:45 PM

Barbara Lund smoked a joint of marijuana and sipped only occasionally from the bourbon and soda Ron had bought for her. She sat at their table—with Ron and Gabe Haddad—in her stage costume: fringed white bra top, matching fringed briefs. She laughed at the suggestion she knew anything about the murder of Lansard Blaine.

"Hey, fellas," she said languidly, "I hardly knew the man." She used her left hand to brush her long bleached blonde hair back from her bare shoulder. "I mean, what he was to me and I was to him didn't have anything to do with politics."

"How do you suppose I found out you knew him at all?" Ron asked.

"I'd like to know."

"The FBI told me."

Her smile vanished. "FBI . . . ? How'd they know, what'd they know?"

"They know you spent the night in his apartment several times."

"Why? Why'd they know that?"

"They were keeping a tab on him, not on you," Ron said. "That make you feel better?"

She nodded. "It makes me feel better. Y' know, I'm just a Kentucky girl come to the big city to make a little money. No reason the FBI'd have any interest in me."

She was, as Ron judged, about thirty years old. She had a small, dark blue tattoo on the inside of her right thigh just below the fringe of her briefs; below the tattoo on her leg was a larger dark red bruise. She was tall, fleshy—a big woman. She talked hard. Her face was pretty; it had a delicacy and innocence incongruous with the rest of her.

"How did you meet Blaine?" Gabe Haddad said.

"Here, he came in here one night."

"And you hustled a drink from the Secretary of State, and that was the beginning of a beautiful friendship?"

"I don't care what you believe."

"We can have you brought in to talk to us."

Barbara Lund was not frightened. "But you'd rather come in here and get a look at me," she said.

"Okay, where did you meet Lansard Blaine?" Gabe persisted, secretly admiring her starch.

She glanced from him to Ron, back again to Gabe. "You really have to know, huh?"

Gabe nodded. "We really do."

"I was at a party, I was the entertainment. He was there."

"Whose party? Where?"

"In a suite at the Mayflower. Some English character gave it. I don't remember his name."

"Jeremy Johnson?" Gabe asked.

"Yeah, I think that was it . . . hey, you guys know everything, don't you?"

"The circle closes a little," Ron said to Gabe.

"Johnson hired you to entertain Blaine, correct?" Gabe said to her.

"He hired me to entertain at a party."

"Just dancing?"

She sighed. "Come on."

"Johnson hired you for Blaine," said Gabe.

"Whatever you say . . . Listen, I got to put on a show. You want me to come back afterwards?"

"Yes," Ron said. "We'll buy you another drink."

"Thanks, big spender."

A girl had just left the stage—a raised square platform in the center of the room. Barbara Lund stepped up on the platform. She stood in the center for a moment under bright pink lights, all but ignored by the twenty-five or thirty people at the tables around the platform. She called a word to someone behind the bar and the music began again. She danced.

Ron watched. It was a sad performance. The men at the tables stared dully. They did not change their expressions when she took off the fringed top. They did not change when she slipped down the briefs. She danced through four records. Between the records she stood nude in the middle of the stage. Waiting. No one applauded. She wiped her forehead with the back of her hand and waited until the music started again. When she took up her bra and briefs off the stage railing and stepped down to the floor, a few actually clapped. Big spenders.

She returned to the table where Ron and Gabe waited for her, tossed the bra on the table and bent forward and pulled on the briefs before she sat down. She picked up the drink she had only sipped before and gulped it down. She snapped her fingers at a waitress, pointed at her empty glass. Finally she picked up the fringed white bra and put it on again.

"Jeremy Johnson's an operator," she said quietly to Ron and Gabe. "I've worked for him a few times." She looked down at her hands on the table. "I'm a hooker," she said, looking up into Ron's face, then into Gabe's. "I don't want my mother to know it, but I'm not ashamed of it and I'm not telling you anything you haven't figured out. It was business with me and Blaine. Johnson paid me to be with Blaine . . . three, maybe four times. Then Blaine paid me himself. He liked me."

"He had more girls than one man could handle," Ron said, "and he didn't have to pay them. Why did he pay you, do you suppose?"

She shrugged. "He never came in here. He never saw me

. . . dance. I put on my act in his apartment for him. I guess it sort of interested him. Everybody asks, but he talked to me about it a lot. He was interested. Maybe it turned him on, the idea. One time he asked me to dance for some friends of his. I don't know who they were. I did it. In his apartment. And so forth. So what's that got to do with his being murdered?"

"When did you see him last?" Gabe asked.

"A month ago, I think."

"I want the names of anyone else you saw at parties Johnson gave for Blaine," Ron said. "If you have to think about it and write them down for me—"

"Honey, c'mon. People don't *introduce* me. I didn't know who Blaine was the first night. I mean, I did the whole thing and didn't know who he was. Look, I'm a nude dancer in a crummy joint, and I'm a prostitute. I mean, not knowing who anybody is, is part of my game. Besides, who'd introduce me? At parties the boys that carry off the dirty dishes got more standing than I've got, even if I do make ten times their money. Honey, Barbara's part of the damn *furniture.*"

Apartment of Commander and Mrs. George Kingsley, Saturday, June 16, 10:15 AM

Martha Kingsley knew he was coming—on the telephone she had said she had been wondering how long it would take the chief investigator of the murder to get to her—but she opened her apartment door wearing a bra, a half-slip, no shoes or slippers, and, inviting him to her kitchen to sit down at her kitchen table for a cup of coffee, she did not pick up a robe. The coffee was ready. She offered him a croissant with English marmalade.

He accepted. "Are you moving?" he asked. The apartment was

crowded with taped boxes, the shelves were empty, nails stuck out of bare walls from which pictures had been removed.

"Don't you know?" She stood at the kitchen counter spooning marmalade from a jar into a small dish. She was an exceptionally attractive dark-haired, brown-eyed young woman—beautiful was not too strong a word for her. "My husband has been assigned to the U.S. Embassy in Paris. We're moving there next week."

"Did Lansard Blaine arrange that for you?" Ron asked bluntly.

She looked away from her marmalade to him and smiled. "Knowing him didn't hurt," she said.

"I don't have to ask you what your relationship with Blaine was," Ron said. "The FBI has filled me in on that."

She smiled again. "The FBI tells you I stayed all night in his apartment and that he stayed all night here—both more than once. What we were doing, the FBI does *not* know, let me remind you. We might have been working on his stamp collection."

"Did he have a stamp collection?"

"No."

He sat at her round glass-topped table and watched her prepare a tray of coffee cups, cream and sugar, butter and marmalade, croissants. Barefoot, in her half-slip and brassiere, she was confident and comfortable—if anything, amused by the contrast between herself and him in his proper dark blue suit, striped shirt, necktie.

The FBI had furnished him a dossier. Maiden name, Koczinski. Native Washingtonian (rare), twenty-nine years old. She had worked as a secretary at the law firm of McIntyre & Drake, later as secretary-aide to Representative William Horner—working her way through George Washington University, from which she graduated with a degree in English literature. After graduation, public relations writer for Air Transport Association. Married for three years to Commander George Kingsley, Annapolis graduate, career naval officer.

The FBI dossier was assembled because of her association, not just with Lansard Blaine, but with a variety of prominent people. Her marriage seemed never to have interrupted her active and varied social life. While her husband was away from Washington, on sea duty or otherwise, Martha continued to travel a circuit of cocktail parties, dinners, out-of-town weekends, concerts, and shows with senators, congressmen, diplomats, judges, lobbyists, wealthy businessmen. A report in the dossier described an evening and night spent on a yacht with the press attaché of the Soviet Embassy and a visiting associate editor of *Izvestia*—the same week when she spent a night in the apartment of Secretary of State Blaine. It was this coincidence and several others like it that had moved the FBI to open a file on her.

Martha Kingsley put the tray on the table, then the coffee pot. She sat down and poured. "It's a tragedy about Blaine," she said. "He was a rare man."

"The FBI seems to think you're a rare woman," Ron said.

She broke a croissant. "Don't be unsubtle, Mr. Fairbanks. Or too subtle. Anyway, what could the FBI know about rare women?"

She had her point, Ron thought. "When did you last see Blaine?"

"Two or three weeks ago."

"What was the occasion?"

She smiled. "I spent the night with him in his apartment."

"Blaine had a variety of young women available to him, as I think you must have known, and you had your other male friends. So why you and Blaine or the night together? What was the nature of the relationship beyond sex?"

"It was highly personal. We *liked* each other."

"Let me explain something to you," Ron said. "Discovering the nature of the relationship between you and Blaine is part of the investigation into his death. It may have no relationship to his death. I hope it doesn't. But I'm going to find out. If necessary I'll block your husband's transfer to Paris and keep you in Washington until I find out."

She flushed with anger. "Do you have that kind of power, Mr. Fairbanks?"

"Yes." He wasn't at ease saying it.

"Well, then . . . just what do you want to know about my relationship with Lansard Blaine?"

"Look, Mrs. Kingsley, I don't like the role of inquisitor, holding a secret-police dossier on a person and confronting you with that kind of advantage. Believe it or not, I'm opposed to it. But I've got a job, I have the FBI file on you, and it's complete with detail—"

"Voyeurs . . ."

"Maybe. At any rate I have a good deal of information about you and I've drawn some conclusions. The file says, to be frank, that you sleep in a lot of beds. The way I read it, though, I don't think you do it without motive. You didn't sleep with Blaine just because he was Secretary of State. That made a big impression on a lot of little girls but I don't think it did on you. So, why, Martha Kingsley? Why Blaine?"

She sighed. "How well did you know him? He was a Renaissance man, Mr. Fairbanks. It could have been . . . I could have fallen in love with him. I really could have—"

"He didn't slow you down," Ron said.

She winced. "That's hard talk."

"At the time when you were sleeping with Blaine you were sleeping with a variety of other men," Ron said. "I'm not quite prepared to accept that you were in love with Blaine."

"I didn't say I was in love with him. I said he was worth it."

"Well, then?"

She held her coffee cup in front of her in both hands. She had regained her composure. She smiled. "Your FBI file really doesn't suggest why I slept with Blaine? It doesn't suggest why I entertain —or am entertained by—a variety, as you put it, of men? Really, Mr. Fairbanks, isn't there a word in there?" She sighed again, this time with impatience. "Prostitute, Mr. Fairbanks," she snapped. "Prostitute."

"No," he said quickly, "no, it doesn't say that. And I didn't draw that conclusion either."

She laughed quietly. "I'm a very expensive, very high class call girl, Mr. Fairbanks. I'll slip in the bedroom for an hour with you right now, if you like, for, say, a hundred dollars. Or I'll spend a night with you for a minimum of five hundred. I am employed by people to entertain them. Sometimes I am employed by people to entertain other people. How could you and the FBI miss that?"

"Paris . . . ?"

"That's my retirement."

"Your husband knows?"

She shrugged. "He's a good but naive man. He knows, but he doesn't know everything. He's also lazy and willing to let his wife procure a good job for him. He's also charming, and he doesn't get in my way."

Ron poured himself more coffee. "That explains why you . . . It doesn't explain why Blaine . . . Are you telling me he paid you?"

She nodded. "He did, or someone else did, every time."

"That's hard to believe."

"Why? Because he had his little girls any time he wanted them? If you're that naive, Mr. Fairbanks, I can see why it's hard for you to understand. Look, I demand, and get, five hundred dollars minimum for spending a night with a man. There are plenty of young women in Washington, just as good-looking as I am, who will do the same for fifty or a hundred. I have two or three appointments a week at five hundred each. Don't you really know why? It's not because I'm better in the sack, I'll tell you that. Any of them can do anything I do. Lansard Blaine and I . . . well, let me explain it this way. Do you remember the story about Louis XV? One of his mistresses died, and he wept—he wept, a man who could have his pick of any woman at court or the little girls in the Deer Park. He wept, and he said, 'Who now will tell me the truth?' I do what I do in the classic tradition, Mr. Fairbanks. I'm a professional listener, a professional sympathizer, a professional propper-up of sagging egos. Lan was a satyr, but he didn't have a wife. I'm not sure he had a friend. I spent many quiet hours with him, talking about all kinds of things. I could hold up my end of a conversation with him. Many people couldn't. We talked. Sometimes we didn't even talk when he was tired or troubled. The sex part of it wasn't very much, usually. He never omitted it, but it was not the major part of our relationship. He certainly could and did have that cheaper."

Ron wasn't too sure he believed all this, and said so.

"Suit yourself."

He watched her for a moment as she spread orange marmalade on a piece of croissant and nibbled at it, looking away from him, looking out the window at the single leafy limb that intruded between her window and the white-painted brick wall of the neighboring building.

"When did you meet him?"

"A year or so ago," she said, still looking out the window.

"How did you meet him?"

She glanced at him but looked out again. "I was employed to entertain him."

"By whom?"

She shook her head.

"Sorry, but I have to know."

She sighed shortly. "I was paid by the Spanish Embassy."

"After that?"

"They paid me once more. After that Lan paid me himself."

"Did he ever suggest a different relationship?"

"He was Secretary of State. I was, am, a call girl, which is known to a great many people, even if the FBI seems to have overlooked it." She shook her head. "There was no way we could have a relationship other than . . . occupational."

"Even so, your relationship was very confidential," Ron said. "Do you have *any* idea who killed him, or why?"

"No," she said quietly. "I have no idea."

"We believe he took bribes. In fact, you say he accepted a gift of your services."

Martha Kingsley frowned. "Lansard Blaine," she said intently, "was a *very* complex man, Mr. Fairbanks. It's difficult to apply simplistic rules of right and wrong to him. I'm afraid he did play a dangerous game. I heard some hints about it."

"If what you've told me is true," Ron said, "you spent more hours in intimate conversation with him than probably anyone else in Washington. I'm going to have to review all of that conversation with you. Before you leave for Paris we'll need to have another talk, longer than this one and on the record. I want you to think about it. Reconstruct some of the talk. You may know more than you think. We need to know. Think, Mrs. Kingsley. You're a bright lady. Think very hard . . ."

She looked at him for a moment, then slowly nodded.

Special Investigation Office, The West Wing, Saturday, June 16, 2:00 PM

At 1:00 PM Ron gave a briefing to the newswires, TV networks and reporters from the newspapers who had people on duty at the White House on Saturday afternoon. He had chosen early Saturday afternoon as a time when not many would be available, a time when the networks and newspaper offices had slowed down for a lazy, late-spring, weekend afternoon. He told the reporters little . . . he had no solid leads as yet about who had murdered Blaine. The briefing over, he had returned to his office before some of the more aggressive reporters, hastily summoned from their homes, arrived at the White House. They were denied the opportunity to question him.

In his office at 2:00 he received a call from the Navy, a call arranged for 2:00 o'clock by a demand he'd made on the duty officer before noon. Captain Frederick Elmendorfer, Special Counsel to the Secretary of the Navy, had returned from Alexandria to check some files and call Fairbanks.

"Frankly, Mr. Fairbanks," Captain Elmendorfer said—his voice was hard and resentful—"you put the Secretary on a spot."

"Frankly, captain, I don't give a damn. I'm asking you to read me the contents of a file. If what's in the file puts someone on a spot, then maybe someone has made a mistake. I don't care about that. I don't mean to make an issue of it but I intend to know what's in that file if I have to call the Secretary off the golfcourse and back to his office this afternoon to read it to me."

"It's highly confidential—" He'd fallen back on his last line of defense.

"Not to the President, and I'm acting for the President."

A sigh. "Okay, Mr. Fairbanks . . ."

"Commander George Kingsley, what's the file got?"

"Graduated from Annapolis Class of '68, he's served in Panama, the Mediterranean, most of the time at sea. Nothing much on his record, actually. No bad reports. He's second officer on the *Spruance*—or was until he was assigned recently to the United States Embassy in Paris."

"Is there anything in his education or record that suggests embassy duty?"

"No. And nothing that suggests he's not qualified for it either."

"Does he speak French?"

"The file doesn't say so."

"Is it customary to assign officers to diplomatic duty in countries where one of the major languages is spoken if they can't speak that language?"

"No, sir."

"Who appointed him?"

A pause. "The Secretary."

"Personally?"

"Yes, sir."

"On whose recommendation?"

A longer pause. "Secretary Blaine's . . ."

"He was assigned by the Secretary of the Navy on the recommendation of the Secretary of State?"

"Yes, sir."

"I want that file, captain. Have it sent by messenger to my office this afternoon."

Jill, who had been sitting on the couch listening all during the conversation, grinned and shook her head. "You talk pretty tough, Mr. Chief Investigator."

"A pose," Ron said. "Sometimes you need it with the career people."

"Don't forget you're talking to a career civil-service employee."

"I'm sorry . . . I just don't think I could make a career there."

Her grin turned bitter. "Maybe you had a choice." . . .

He had, indeed. When he graduated from Stanford Law he had offers from both California and New York firms, in addition to the offer of a clerkship with Justice Friederich. These offers had come to him in recognition of his promise as an exceptionally able young lawyer. His personality had been shaped by the recognition he had always had as a bright young man who would go far in whatever career he chose. He had been shaped, too, by the acknowledged envy of his peers.

But Jill's point was valid. He had had a choice. He still had a choice. He had told President-elect Webster that he would not, probably wasn't able to, commit himself without reservation. He had a choice.

Service in the White House, though, had amended his sense of himself. The President thought well of him, respected him as a young lawyer. Still, being a bright young lawyer on the White House staff did not afford him power or even much influence. His perspective changed. As he approached the point where ability like his might realize its potential, suddenly the doors did not any longer open so easily, and being the bright young lawyer did not count for so much.

Only once had he exerted any influence on a major policy decision . . . He was in the Oval Office the day the Aeroflot Ilyushin crashed on the approach to Kennedy Airport . . . specifically, he was there when the angry Soviet message arrived. The President and Catherine Webster had purchased a beachhouse on the Texas Gulf coast, and Ron was in the Oval Office with them and with the Texas real estate agent, acting as their counsel at the signing of the documents. The papers had been signed and exchanged when the telephone rang. The President abruptly asked the Texan to leave, saying he had a little problem on his hands. When Ron and Catherine got up to leave too the President motioned them to sit down again. He turned on the telephone speaker, and Catherine and Ron listened to the conversation between the President and Deputy Secretary of State William Ahern.

The Aeroflot plane had crashed into the Atlantic on the approach to Kennedy about five miles off the coast at approximately 11:00 that morning. The President knew it had crashed. He had mentioned it to Ron when he first came into the Oval Office. What he had not known was that Soviet U.N. Ambassador Konstantin Dobrodomov had been a passenger on the Ilyushin and had been killed with several members of his staff. What the President also had not known was that two United States Air Force jet fighters had flown close to the Ilyushin only a minute or two before it crashed.

The angry Russian note, delivered to the State Department within two hours of the crash, charged that the two fighters had buzzed the Ilyushin, that it had been forced to take violent evasive action to avoid a mid-air collision and that the maneuver had damaged it and caused the crash. The note demanded investigation by a U.N. commission empowered to issue subpoenas within the United States. The note also demanded that the United States keep clear of the wreckage and that it allow a Russian salvage task force to enter the territorial waters of the United States to recover the wreckage and the bodies.

Deputy Secretary Ahern had already talked to the Air Force. The two fighters had flown within half a mile of the Aeroflot Ilyushin. One pilot, Major Donald Hummell, was an Air Force veteran of many years' experience. The other, Lieutenant Nancy Wilkinson, was flying only her second patrol after finishing her training. The major insisted that neither he nor the lieutenant had buzzed the Ilyushin. The lieutenant had told her commanding officer she thought she might have flown too close.

There was background. Eleven weeks before, the Vietnamese had suddenly arrested, charged as spies and executed more than two hundred Russian engineers, technicians and advisers. Since then the Soviet Union, as part of its protest and retaliation, had systematically harassed Vietnamese airline flights—ironically, Ilyushin jets they had themselves sold the Vietnamese—in several parts of the world. Aeroflot pilots crowded Vietnamese flights on the approaches to major airports . . . a dangerous game, and it had nearly become a fatal one when three weeks ago an Aeroflot Ilyushin on approach to Kennedy had departed from its assigned approach course fifty miles out, intending to fly close to and harass a Vietnamese Ilyushin arriving at Kennedy on a scheduled flight from Paris. The Aeroflot Ilyushin had flown into airspace assigned to a TWA 747, almost causing a mid-air collision. After that incident the President had authorized the Air Force to intercept Aeroflot flights and, as he put it, to herd them into Kennedy. Air Force pilots, angry at the threat represented by huge civilian jets wandering off assigned courses, had herded some Aeroflot flights with enthusiasm. . . . It was not impossible that the two jet fighters this morning had contributed to the crash.

Secretary of State Blaine was in London. Deputy Secretary Ahern spoke with the President for half an hour: a mechanically hollow voice on the telephone speaker. When he had finished, the President told him to come to the White House. They would meet with someone from Defense, with Eiseman, the Special Assistant for National Security Affairs, and they would ring up Blaine in London.

But it would be an hour before that meeting could convene, and—as Ron knew—it was not the President's way to put aside a problem like this until a meeting assembled. He was not surprised when the President began to pace the Oval Office and talk. He knew the President had wanted him and Catherine to stay so he could talk—as much to himself as to them, but still to talk with someone listening. This President, he had observed, did not function alone; he functioned in company. He bore his responsibility alone, as any President had to, but he worked best when other people were around him, listening, watching . . .

He would tell the Russians to go to hell, he said. They had created a hazard and now were complaining that they were its first victims. Of course he could not allow a U.N. commission to go poking around inside the United States in violation of our sovereignty. The goddamned Russians, he said, were obsessed with turmoil and tension, because they thought they could profit from it.

Catherine Webster sat quietly. Her eyes were on Ron almost as they were on her husband. He had learned to see her as a complex and subtle personality who communicated with such subtlety sometimes that only a few people sensed what she was saying. Blaine, probably, was one who understood her. As they sat there now, Ron read her eyes, the lift of her head. If he read right she was sending him an invitation to work together . . . they should help the President together . . .

Sometimes she was content to be a sounding board, sometimes not. This time she wasn't. She shook her head. That was all. She shook her head, and he stopped. "Huh?" he said, surprised.

"If you think they want to profit from tension and turmoil, then your course of action is to prevent tension and turmoil," she said.

He stopped. His spring unwound. This was why he needed people around him: to stop him. He sat down, facing Catherine and Ron from a wingchair. "How?"

"Talk-talk," said Catherine. "Talk-talk. Diplomatic obfuscation. Tell them you can't *imagine* how their airplane got on the bottom of the ocean; it's as big a surprise to us as it must be to them. And we're going to do everything we can to find out what happened. Don't tell them we won't allow a U.N. investigation. Don't tell them we won't allow their salvage ships in our waters. Let them find out. Slowly."

"Well . . ."

"May I make a suggestion, Mr. President?"

"Sure, Ron."

"How about getting a naval vessel over that wreckage . . . if we know where it is. With a radiation counter. They're so anxious that we not look at the wreckage, it makes you wonder what was in that plane."

"Good idea," the President said.

"Then maybe get some divers down there to take a look. We don't have to tell the Russians we have divers looking. Just do it."

The President nodded.

Encouraged, Ron went on. "As far as the U.N. investigatory commission is concerned, we might suggest its jurisdiction be expanded to cover all air-traffic-control violations by Aeroflot planes over the past several weeks. They'd like to question our two pilots. Okay, we'd like to question several of theirs. The Vietnamese would like to know if anyone in the Soviet government has issued orders to Aeroflot pilots to harass Vietnamese flights. Obviously, the investigators can't confine themselves to questioning pilots. They'll have to question people higher up. And so on."

"And if they accept the proposition?"

"I don't think they will," Ron said. "They don't want anyone, U.N. or anyone else, poking around in their closets."

"What about the salvage operation?"

"We'll cooperate with them. We can do it better in our own waters but we'll allow some of their people to work on the salvage ships and observe what we do."

Catherine Webster was smiling at Ron. He had—he guessed—followed her cue.

Within a few days he saw President Webster put his suggestions into effect. It was never acknowledged, and the opportunity had not so far come again. But it might . . .

Or, rather, it had—with this strange and baffling investigation . . .

Sakura, Silver Spring, Maryland, Saturday, June 16, 9:00 PM

Given their choice of sitting at tables or on the floor in the handsome, quiet Japanese restaurant, Ron and Lynne had chosen to sit on the floor, on cushions, facing a low table. The restaurant had arranged privacy for the President's daughter by giving her and Ron one of the small rooms to themselves. Now they sat alone, talking, drinking, and nibbling at their appetizer while their diminutive waitress bustled in and out, bringing and taking, anticipating, serving with elaborately courteous attention.

Lynne had suggested that his appointment as special investigator, which had intervened since they had agreed to this dinner date, had been so demanding a job all week that she really did not expect him to spend the evening with her. He told her the anticipation of this evening had been all that had kept him going all week. She had not argued the point further, and they had left the White House at eight. He had driven her out here in his Datsun, with her Secret Service detail following in an inconspicuous Chevrolet. The Secret Service had checked out the room and were hovering about the premises somewhere.

"Detroit . . ." Lynne said. "Here in the east I find myself

defending it all the time, but actually it's a good city with a lot to recommend it—"

"You didn't actually live there," Ron said.

"No, but it was our city, where we went for things only found in a city."

"Will you go back there?"

She shook her head. "I don't suppose so."

His sense of her vulnerability had been strongly reinforced this evening. She was not tough like her mother and father, and Blaine's death had apparently shocked and hurt her more than it had them. Her eyes looked deeper tonight. Her voice was softer. He had put his hand close to hers on the edge of her cushion, and she had immediately moved her hand to take his. They sat now, holding hands, sipping sake. He had leaned to kiss her lightly on the lips, and she had accepted the kiss very soberly, without a smile.

"I could never go back to California," he said to her. "It's a different world out there, and I don't fit into it any more. There's no point in trying to tell your family, your old friends, your old neighbors what all this is, what we live with now . . . they simply can't understand it . . . I can't talk this way to anyone but you. Do you understand what I mean?"

"Looking back," she said softly. "Looking back . . . it seems that everything used to be so simple. Maybe it wasn't, really." She shook her head. "I don't know, I've never had to fight for anything, you know. I don't know if I can—"

"I think you've changed the subject."

"My father . . . and mother . . . have given me everything—"

"Lucky you."

"That's not very perceptive."

"No, it isn't. I'm sorry."

She lifted her white sake cup, smiled and drank. She seemed

to have dismissed the subject. "So . . . any idea who killed Lan?"

He was startled for an instant by what she had called Blaine —"Lan." It was what Martha Kingsley had called him—and the others. It was possible, of course . . . he'd not dismissed the thought that Lynne, too, may have had something intimate with Blaine. She fit his bill . . . she was young, yet very womanly . . . her skirt had ridden up as she sat on the floor on a pillow, and he had to make a conscious effort not to stare at her lovely sleek legs. She had that seriousness and impressionableness that some others had . . . Marya Kalisch and Judith Pringle . . . And she had had opportunity . . . He felt a traitor even thinking it, but it was a thought process his assignment required of him. Nobody was immune from it.

"I don't know, Lynne," he answered her question now.

"I can't believe he's dead," she whispered.

"You cared for him, didn't you?"

"What?" Her head snapped around. "What do you mean?"

"I mean, he was a very close friend, of yours and your family."

Her hard frown softened. "Yes."

"He was always around, since you were a little girl."

She nodded, withdrew her hand from Ron's and poured herself another small cup of sake. The waitress, seeing, hurried in with a fresh flask of the hot rice wine, then in a moment came again with trays of sushi—raw fish—rice and seaweed rolled and sliced.

They ate with chopsticks, and as they did Lynne's mood seemed to lift and she chatted with animation about the Detroit Tigers and the Cincinnati Reds, about a vacation she wanted to take: a sailing cruise in the Caribbean . . . "I can't go, of course. The Secret Service proposes to follow in two PT boats, and a destroyer is to stand by at all times, never more than ten miles away . . ." She smiled briefly. Even though preoccupation and a return to somber introspection seemed not far below the surface, she was not brittle. It was he, in fact, who was preoccupied, though he tried not to let her see it, tried to be attentive to her, to respond to her, to show her a good time. She deserved at least that. She did relax, she even teased him about glancing every few moments at her legs, and pulled her skirt up another inch and asked him if he liked that better.

He said he did, who wouldn't . . . ? And then . . . "Fritz Gimbel was always close to your family too, wasn't he?"

Lynne shrugged, going cool. "There's always been Fritz," she said. "As long as I can remember. I grew up in an establishment, you must understand—not just in a household. My father has always attracted people, hordes of people. The house was always full. In some ways I have more privacy in the White House than I did in our houses in Michigan. Fritz was sort of my father's Figaro, the factotum, moving people out of the way, smoothing things . . . It was inevitable that he would be chief of staff in the White House. He was chief of staff at the company, for the Senate staff, for the campaign staff . . . Fritz is effective. I can't count the things he's done for me, for me personally, I mean, not just for my father."

"Was Blaine around the same way—I mean, as long as you can remember?"

"Yes. There was always Lan. He wasn't part of our establishment. He was a friend, a faculty colleague of my mother's . . ."

"Everyone seems to have liked him in their fashion," Ron said. "I've begun to learn some rather unattractive things about him, but even people who had reason to hold him in contempt seem to have liked him . . . Was it always that way?"

Lynne frowned. "I'll tell you something about Lan . . . there was only one thing in this world that Lan took entirely seriously, and that was Lan. In a sense it was the most attractive thing about him, and in another sense it was the least . . . I remember times when everyone else was absolutely insane with worry and tension —and he'd be sitting in a corner munching a sandwich or sipping wine, relaxed, unconcerned, effective. Maybe it was because he had a sense of history, but he never let a situation overpower him. He had perspective, he knew the worst wouldn't happen, or that we would survive even if it did. He didn't let his emotions overcome his judgment. That was the secret of his success . . . except about himself. When he was the issue, what he wanted, he could be . . . well, ugly about anyone or anything getting in his way. He . . . oh, I've said too much, I'm sorry—"

"Don't be . . . by the way, this is *noritake.*" He held between his chopsticks a slice from a seaweed-wrapped roll of eggs, spinach and mushrooms. "A specialty here."

She took up a slice. "I'm glad we came here," she said.

"About Blaine," Ron said quietly. "You called him your friend. This morning someone told me she doubted he had a friend. I'd like to talk with someone who was really his friend. Do you think your father was his friend?"

"It's difficult for my father to give anyone the time the word 'friend' implies," Lynne said hesitantly. "He and Lan respected each other. I never heard them talk much, though, except about business. I doubt they were close friends, I mean in the personal sense." She shrugged. "Or maybe they were . . . I don't know, Ron . . ."

"Your mother?" Ron asked. "Was she closer to him than your father?"

"What does that mean?" She had gone cool again.

"Nothing. I'm just looking for someone Blaine might have confided in. I know he was upset Tuesday evening. He was nervous. Something was wrong. I wonder if he told anyone what it was."

"Someone he was especially close to," she suggested.

"Yes."

"Well, I can assure you that someone was not my mother," Lynne said with emphasis.

Ron took up another piece of sushi. He would not pursue the question further, but he would not apologize for it either. It was curious to hear her defensive reaction to his suggestion that her mother had been close to Blaine. He put the questions that raised away in the back of his mind, to be looked at later.

Her moods swung. As soon as he changed the subject she took his hand again and squeezed it, smiled and relaxed and returned to the inconsequential banter she had been enjoying before he began asking about Gimbel and Blaine.

"I wish you weren't doing this thing, you know," she said to him over their tea.

He waited.

"The investigation, it's too demanding. And if you fail, well, it could hurt your career—"

"I don't know about that." He took her hand. "Let's not worry about it now, anyway."

"Well . . . I do want you to know, Ron, that, whatever way it turns out, I . . . respect you. Whatever happens, it won't make any difference. None . . ."

His car was a steel blue low-slung Datsun two-seater. He and Lynne had noted with some pleasure on the way to Silver Spring the difficulty the Secret Service men had had keeping up in their carefully nondescript Chevrolet. Now, before leaving Sakura, he told Lester Fitch, head of the detail assigned to them tonight, that he meant to drive through Rock Creek Park, following Beach Drive its whole length. He felt Lynne would enjoy it.

There was an objection in Fitch's silent nod—he was faintly disapproving of Ron's plan to make a long, quiet drive through the park in the middle of the night. As Ron got into the Datsun he smiled at Fitch on the radio in the Chevrolet. He knew what Fitch was saying: that "Hotshoe" (the code name he'd acquired with his appointment as chief investigator) would drive "Kitty" (their code name for Lynne) back to the White House by way of Rock Creek Park and Beach Drive. The detail would follow.

He entered the park directly. By the time Beach Drive passed under the Beltway the Secret Service car had dropped back out of sight. He did not drive fast. The detail had every chance to catch up, but from shortly after the time when he drove into the park Ron did not see the Secret Service Chevrolet in the rear-view mirror.

"Maybe they're trying to be a little accommodating for a change," Lynne said.

In the dark, under the trees with only a wisp of moon above, he could scarcely see her, but he sensed she was relaxed, stretched out, her legs high and extended, her hands clasped behind her head. Except for the Secret Service car following, which would quickly have caught up if he had stopped, he would have pulled off to the side of the road for a few minutes. As it was he could only reach for her hand, and fumbling for it found his fingers caressing the whispery texture of her hose. She said nothing, accepted his touch.

"Damn the Secret Service," he muttered.

"Yes," she whispered.

They had driven some distance in the park, probably out of Maryland and back into the District, when he first noticed headlights behind them, and overtaking rapidly. He supposed it was the Secret Service car, catching up. Of course it could have been someone else, anyone. Then he noticed that the headlights were high. It was a truck, maybe a van. It was coming fast. He edged to the right to let it pass him.

He caught almost no sight of the van, except to see it was light blue. It was noisy, its muffler probably gone. Its headlights were not equally bright; one was dim and yellow. The driver swerved into the left lane. The van came alongside, fast.

The right side of the van crashed into the left front fender of the Datsun, jamming the broken fender into the left front tire, which shrieked and exploded. The bulk of the van kept coming right, shoving the Datsun off the road, totally out of Ron's control. He braked instinctively, wrestled the steering wheel. The Datsun was shoved off the pavement, then off the shoulder of the road, and suddenly it was lurching and skidding down an embankment. The radiator burst. Steam roared loose under the hood. A headlight broke and went out. The windshield shattered. The left front fender ripped loose and rose up like a specter in torn metal. Finally the right side of the car cracked against a tree and the slide stopped in a guttural crunch.

Lynne was screaming . . . Ron hadn't noticed before, but she had been screaming since the van first hit. She was also hurt . . . he tried to snatch off his seat and shoulder belt to help her. She was sitting on the buckle, shoved over by the collapse of the right door, and when he touched her she called out in pain. "My arm is broken—"

"We've got to get out . . ." He was afraid it might catch fire.

He wrenched his belt loose—and hers—in spite of her screams, put his arm under her and tried to pull her across the left seat and out through the one still intact door. She cried out in pain and flailed at him with her left arm. He tried again. Weakened and choking, he was still trying to pull her out of the car when someone pulled him out by the shoulders and thrust his broad shoulders into the car to get Lynne.

It was Fitch. He put her down on the ground a few feet from the car. She stopped screaming and sat there bent forward, clutching her right arm with her left hand. Fitch bent over her, saying something, examining. The one headlight of the Datsun still shone crazily upward into the leaves overhead. Above them on the road an urgent voice was talking crisply about "Hotshoe" and "Kitty"—the other agent of the detail calling for help. Ron collapsed on the ground, heaved for breath and fought to reorient himself.

He was not hurt, only bruised, the wind squeezed out of him when he was thrown around inside his shoulder belt. He was able to stand.

The van had not stopped. "It hit us on purpose," Ron muttered to Fitch.

"Sure," said Fitch.

Ron didn't like the tone of voice. "Well, what the hell do you think?"

"I think you've had a little too much to drink, Mr. Fairbanks, but that's not for me to say, is it?"

"No, and I suggest you don't."

The District police unit that investigated the accident did not say it. Ron gave his report to two District officers, sitting in the front seat of their car. They did not suggest he submit to an alcohol test. They were quick, and when the third Secret Service detail on the scene offered him a ride home, the District officers did not object to his leaving.

An emergency squad wagon arrived and gave first aid to Lynne. The paramedics confirmed that he right arm was broken but said they found no other injuries. They left to take her to Walter Reed. Ron told the Secret Service detail now assigned to him to take him there too.

He was boiling mad, and worried. Someone, clearly, was out to discredit him. Fitch's crack about him having had too much to drink was no accident. None of it was . . .

V

Ronald Fairbanks's Apartment, Sunday, June 17, 7:45 AM

The door buzzer woke him. He'd switched off the telephones—after advising the White House switchboard how to reach him if necessary—and put a Secret Service guard on his apartment door to fend off reporters who had already been clustered around it when he came home at 2:00 AM. Their orders were to buzz for no one short of the President, but now the buzzer was persistent. He rolled painfully off the bed, wincing—surprised, in fact, at how much pain he had. He did not own a robe, slept nude and always had. He wrapped a white towel around his waist and made it to the door.

"It's Miss Keller, from the Justice Department," the man outside the door said. "She says it's important."

Jill had brought a stack of newspapers. "Hey," she said, "you hurt?" He sat down at the table in the kitchen as she put on a pot of coffee. "Seriously. You hurt?"

He shook his head. "Not yet." He was looking at the headlines . . .

PRESIDENT'S DAUGHTER INJURED IN CAR CRASH
Special Investigator Driver
Possibly Intoxicated

Lynne Webster, 22-year-old daughter of President Robert L. Webster, was injured in an automobile accident last night in Washington's Rock Creek Park. Miss Webster was released from Walter Reed Army Medical Center after treatment for a fracture of her right arm and cuts and bruises suffered in the crash of a small Japanese sports car driven by Ronald Y. Fairbanks, 34, Special Counsel to the President, who was this week given special powers to investigate the murder of Secretary of State Lansard Blaine.

The facts surrounding the accident, which occurred in a secluded wooded area on a winding park road, remain obscure. The investigation by Washington police continues. The small car left the road and plunged down an embankment, striking a tree. Fairbanks told police investigators that he was forced off the road by a van that struck his car as it passed him.

The President's daughter and Fairbanks were hurried from the accident scene by Secret Service agents. Fairbanks declined to talk with reporters.

Drinking Suggested

Although the Secret Service agents who had accompanied Ms. Webster and Fairbanks to a Silver Spring restaurant followed them in a Secret Service car and were first on the scene after the accident also declined to talk to reporters, one witness at the scene told this reporter that Fairbanks appeared to have been drinking heavily. Inquiries at the Japanese restaurant where the couple had dinner resulted in somewhat confused insistence that Fairbanks had been served nothing but sake, a Japanese rice wine. The witness at the scene said that Fairbanks smelled of alcohol and that his speech was slurred. But Police officer James St. John, who took the accident report, said he did not detect any sign of excessive drinking by Fairbanks and had seen no reason to give him a drunkometer test.

Secluded Road

No explanation has been offered as to why Fairbanks chose to return to the White House from Silver Spring by driving through Rock Creek Park. The long dark road may have, some speculated, provided a romantic interlude for Fairbanks and the President's daughter, whose names have often been linked. Washington gossip has had it for more than a year that Fairbanks might become the President's son-in-law.

"They're all the same," Jill said. "Some of them aren't as fair as that one."

She was right. The story that had gone out on the wire included the statement that a witness said he had been drinking but did not include the statement by the police officer that he had detected no sign of it. Out of town that was the way the story would read, at least at first.

He was a tangle of sore muscles. Every move he made hurt. Some bruises had appeared overnight: on his hips where the seat belt had restrained him and prevented his going against the windshield, on his legs where the steering wheel had hit him, and on his arms. A cut across the back of his hand that had gone almost unnoticed had bled overnight—he'd find the blood on his sheets—and produced a smeared scab. Jill saw him wince when he moved. She served him coffee and offered to scramble some eggs.

"Thanks for coming. I really appreciate it . . ."

He remained at the table, dressed in the towel looped around his hips. She had come hurriedly, dressed in sand-colored slacks and a white blouse, wearing no makeup. "Gabe called me," she said. "He heard about you on the radio, at five this morning."

"What's he doing up at five in the morning?"

"I didn't ask."

"Am I paranoid to think I was deliberately run off the road?"

"Who's your phantom witness?" she asked. "That's what I want to know. Who gave some reporter the story you smelled of booze, words slurred?"

He rubbed his forehead with the tips of his fingers. "I know who did that," he said. "I've no doubt about it."

"Who?"

"Lester Fitch, the head of the Secret Service detail that was supposed to be following us—"

"*Supposed* to be following . . . ?"

"Supposed to be, but dropped back. I wasn't driving fast. Lynne and I wondered if they'd dropped back deliberately, to give us the sense of privacy . . . Now I wonder, more than wonder, if they didn't drop back to give the van a chance to run us off the road and make me look like a damned drunk driver."

Jill pushed the eggs aside on the counter and turned to face him, hands on hips. "Lord, man—"

"It makes some kind of sense, if you think about it." His head ached, he was not altogether awake even yet. "Blaine *was* killed by someone in the White House. Let's not forget that. If we're getting close to someone, why so farfetched that someone wants to discredit the investigation? Or at least try to scare me off."

She shook her head. "You're accusing Fitch?"

"No, not of killing Blaine—"

"Then someone would have to have had enough authority, or enough influence over Fitch . . ."

"Gimbel," Ron said.

"That's a guess."

"It fits, though."

"Have you said this to anyone but me?"

"I just got up."

"Well, don't. I think maybe you had your brains a little scrambled last night. Before you make an accusation like that you'd better have a ton of hard evidence to back it up. Ron, you're the lawyer—"

"I don't have any hard evidence to back *anything,*" he muttered. "So I'm beginning to speculate just like any other layman. I have another thought—"

"I'm not sure I even want to hear it."

"Based on Lynne's reaction to something I said, I'm beginning to think Catherine Webster had an affair with Blaine."

Special Investigation Office, The West Wing, Sunday, June 17, 11:00 AM

Ron sat behind his desk. He was stiff, had had to ease himself into his chair. Gabe Haddad smiled, having already heard him joke grimly about his aches and bruises, but Walter Locke, the FBI agent, frowned and looked away.

Lying on Ron's desk was a note from the President. It was handwritten in the familiar hasty scrawl. "Carry on," it said. "Our confidence in you remains all that it was. RLW."

"We were going to have a minute-by-minute of Blaine's last day," Ron said. "What progress?"

"It has gaps in it," said Locke. "We don't know where he was all day—"

"How much do we know?"

Locke pulled a paper from a flat leather folder. "He left his Watergate apartment at 7:20. He was picked up by his limousine and driven to the State Department. He had breakfast with some members of the Senate Foreign Relations Committee—a champagne breakfast."

"Blaine knew how to live," Ron said, and didn't smile when he said it.

"So do two or three of the members of the Senate Foreign Relations Committee," Gabe said.

Locke went on. "He spent the morning after the breakfast in his office. We have a list of his appointments and telephone calls. His chauffeur drove him to the Madison Hotel at 1:30. His secretary, Mary Burdine, says he had an appointment for lunch but doesn't know with whom. No one at the hotel recalls his having been there. The chauffeur picked him up at 3:30 and drove him to his apartment. He picked him up there at eight and drove him to the White House. He was there until he was killed."

"Where was he in the White House?"

"With Eiseman, for half an hour or so, then with Gimbel for a while. He spent some time in the Cabinet Room making telephone calls. He was in the men's room at least twice. Eventually he went up to the Yellow Oval Room, which is where he was when the President arrived."

"The autopsy report says he had an ejaculation within the last eight hours before his death," Ron said. "The Madison . . . He could have let his chauffeur drop him off, and he could have taken a cab and gone anywhere. More likely, though, he had a lady with him in his apartment between four and eight, when the chauffeur picked him up. If so, where did he go when he was supposed to be having lunch at the Madison Hotel? And who was the lady?"

"And where did he get the dextroamphetamine?" Gabe asked. "You remember it was found in his stomach. His doctor didn't prescribe it, didn't even know he was taking it."

"We haven't been able to locate a doctor who prescribed it or a pharmacy that filled the prescription," Locke said.

"How about his supply?" Ron asked. "Did you find a bottle of the pills in his apartment or office?"

"No, and we looked," Locke said. "He didn't have any on his person or in his briefcase either."

"It's an upper, right?" Ron said. "Mood lifter. Did he need it? In the Yellow Oval Room that night I noticed how nervous he was. Where's the cause and effect here? Had he taken dextroamphetamine because he was upset, or was he upset because he had taken dextroamphetamine?"

"Whose fingerprints did you find in his apartment?" Ron asked.

"Blaine's. Judith Pringle's. Marya Kalisch's. Martha Kingsley's. Gus Meridian's . . ."

"Gus was his administrative assistant at the State Department," Ron told Gabe.

"The chauffeur's," Locke went on. "The maid who cleaned up the apartment every day, hers were there too. A man had been in to work on the dishwasher . . . Nothing, in short, we couldn't account for."

"Maybe someone came in after he was dead and cleaned up the place," Gabe suggested. "I mean, got rid of his uppers."

Ron shook his head. "Marya Kalisch slept in the apartment that night."

"She didn't know he was dead when she left the apartment in the morning, or so she says," Locke pointed out.

"I've asked around a little and have come up with something you may find interesting," Gabe said. "I asked some military types who, if anybody, teaches killing with a loop of fine wire. It seems some military units do. Some others used to. It may only be a coincidence, but the technique was taught for years and drilled into the members of the First Marine Ranger Battalion."

"Where's the maybe coincidence in that?"

"Fritz Gimbel," Gabe said, "served two years in that outfit."

The White House, Sunday, June 17, 9:45 PM

Ron went back to the White House at nine. The President had asked him to be available after the dinner being given that evening for the Prime Minister of Australia. It was an unusual state dinner, being given on a Sunday evening; but the Prime Minister was in Washington only on Sunday and was flying Monday morning to London for the opening of a Commonwealth Conference. The President very much wanted to entertain him, having been himself entertained at a memorable dinner in Australia only four months before. When Ron arrived at his office in the West Wing he found a telephone message telling him to go up to the private residence and wait for the President there.

Lynne was sitting in the west hall. It was she who had sent down the telephone message. "Sit down," she said. "Let me order you a whiskey, you look as if you could use one."

She had a cast on her arm, a shallow red scrape covered her right cheek. She was wearing a pair of faded blue jeans and a white cotton T-shirt lettered in blue: FIRST DAUGHTER. She picked up a telephone and, without his having responded to her suggestion, told the butler to bring in a glass of white wine and an Old Bushmills on the rocks.

"Do you believe everything you read in the newspapers?" he asked wryly. A stack of newspapers lay on the floor beside her chair, and it was plain she had been reading the accounts of their accident.

"I called three reporters this afternoon," she said. "Mother suggested I do it. I told them you were *not* drunk."

"Thank you," he said. "I had to face a gaggle of them this afternoon."

"Have you seen a doctor?"

"Doctor Sekulve"—the President's personal physician—"suggested a session in the steam room and a light rubdown. I accepted the suggestion, went home and took a nap late this afternoon . . . You're the one who got the worst of it—"

"It wasn't an accident, was it, Ron?"

"I doubt it. It *could* have been a drunk, but I'm afraid it was a deliberate attempt to—"

"To *kill* us?"

"No. If they'd wanted to do that they would have done it. We were helpless."

"Where was that damn Fitch? Mother really gave it to him this morning. He said you drove so fast he couldn't keep up with you. I called him a liar to his face."

"What did he say to that?"

"He was very apologetic, but I thought it was an act, it was too smooth. I think he dropped back and made it possible for that van to ram us."

"It's quite a situation. Using the powers your father gave me in the executive order I've now put the FBI to work investigating the Secret Service. That's a hell of a note. The Secret Service protects me from the world, but who protects me from the Secret Service?"

She showed him some of the newspapers that had come in that evening, including early editions of Monday morning papers. The story that he'd been drunk the previous night made the headlines of two of them. One columnist had picked up the reporter's story that Ron had ordered the Secret Service car to drop back so he and Lynne could have privacy, that they'd been parked at the side of the road, in the dark, when the van came around the curve and hit them . . .

The butler brought their drinks. He'd also, Ron was glad to see, put some cheese and crackers on the tray. He'd eaten almost nothing all day.

Lynne tossed a newspaper across the room. "Nuts. Let's talk about something else." She kicked off her shoes and propped her bare feet on the ottoman in front of her chair, then began to talk about a movie that had opened the previous week to rave reviews.

Ron, who had been in the private quarters many times, idly noted the furniture the Websters had brought from their Michigan home, to surround themselves with what was comfortable and familiar. They liked to live, he realized, in something of a clutter —their sittingroom in the west hall was littered with untidy heaps of magazines and newspapers—and they did not receive visitors in their private rooms. That Ron was received there conferred a status on him that very few in the White House enjoyed. Fritz Gimbel came there. Blaine had come there. Ron had begun to be invited there after he began to have frequent dates with Lynne.

Both the president and his wife were clearly enjoying the ceremonial duties of their office. When they came to the west hall a little after ten-fifteen they were visibly up, smiling and chatty. The President wore a tuxedo, Catherine Webster wore a raspberry-colored silk gown. It had been prearranged, apparently, that Lynne would go to her sittingroom when the President came to the west hall; she immediately got up, got a kiss from her mother and from the President, kissed Ron on the cheek and left. The President called the butler and ordered coffee and brandy. He sat down. Catherine sat beside him on a couch. Ron faced them from an overstuffed chair.

"Neither of us for a moment believe you'd had too much to drink last night," the President began. "I'm sorry to ask you to come here on a Sunday evening, but Catherine and I wanted to see you together, to assure you on that personally. We can cope with the lousy stories that are going around, and I think we should just put the accident thing behind us."

"I appreciate your saying that."

"It's not so easy as that," Catherine Webster said rather sharply. "Ron, I join Bob, of course, in telling you we continue to have complete confidence in you, both in your job and your friendship with Lynne. But I'm not so ready to put what Bob calls 'the accident thing' behind us. I'm not so sure it was an accident—"

"Catherine . . ." the President protested gently.

"Bob," she said firmly, "Lynne was hurt last night. She *could* have been killed, so could Ron. The Secret Service failed to protect them. They were rammed by a truck and run off the road. Ron was not drunk, but immediately the stories began to circulate that he was. It's perfectly obvious that the whole thing was arranged, and it comes very close to home. At the least, someone is trying to discredit Ron, have him removed from the investigation."

The President shook his head. "The news media will always jump on a story like this, and any little suggestion—by anyone—of excessive drinking or whatever else will be picked up and exaggerated and repeated *ad nauseam,* just because the President's family is involved. We're public property. Public opinion loves to build us up into demigods, then tear us down. Every President and every President's family for two hundred years has had to live with that. It's an American game, and Americans love to play it. It also sells news—"

"But who's been planting the stories?" Catherine demanded. "Lan was a womanizer for twenty years, and he pretty much managed to keep it quiet. The day after his death we begin to read in the newspapers and hear on the news broadcasts about all the little girls he slept with. Ron was *not* drunk last night, but this morning the papers say he was. Where'd they get the idea? Who planted the story? Bob, you appointed Ron to investigate Blaine's

death. You did it because you have confidence in him. It appears it's in someone's interest to undermine that confidence, to discredit him before the public. And as to the stories about Blaine . . . maybe it's in someone's interest to divert attention from the real issue, to divert our attention to a sideshow—"

"But if we're not diverted, what's the difference? My attention's not diverted. Is yours, Ron?"

"No, sir."

"Well . . ."

The butler entered with the coffee, and Catherine stopped, took the tray of coffee and brandy and a plate of cookies. She poured coffee and brandy for the three of them.

"Bob," she repeated wearily, "Lynne was hurt last night. We're lucky it wasn't worse. Maybe it was an accident, I don't think so. At least you have to admit the strong possibility that it was not an accident. If it wasn't, then somebody is hitting awfully close to us, and I'm not ashamed to say I'm frightened. I think it's time to quit playing games with this investigation and tell Ron the truth about our old friend Lansard Blaine."

Ron could not conceal his surprise as he put down his coffeecup.

"I think," the President said quietly, "we have given Ron all the authority he needs to conduct this investigation, and I think he has all the relevant facts—"

"No, he hasn't," she said flatly.

The President frowned. "Well . . ."

"I won't tell him," Catherine said. "It has to be your decision."

"Catherine, I'd say you have made my decision for me. After what you've already said, how can I not tell Ron?"

Catherine shrugged, looked away from the President and sipped the Courvoisier from her snifter.

"Ron," said the President, "bluntly said, maybe *I* had a motive to kill Blaine. Before I tell you what that reason was, I want you to summarize for me—and for Catherine, who hasn't heard it—what you've found out about Blaine. Maybe you've found out more since you last reported to me. Anyway, whatever it is . . ."

Ron put his cup and brandy snifter on the table by his chair. The President sat leaning forward on the couch, his hands clasped between his knees. Catherine Webster sat straight up, staring hard at Ron.

"Short and not so sweet," Ron said, "Blaine took bribes. He was influenced in the conduct of his office by payoffs he received from foreign governments and representatives of foreign economic interests—and maybe by payoffs from American interests too . . . I haven't found out about that yet. He spent a great deal more money than he earned. Even so, I suspect there's a Swiss numbered account with a very large amount of money in it. When it's all traced out, it may be a major scandal. Or maybe, since he's dead, it doesn't have to be traced. Personally, I hope we don't find he was killed because one of these deals of his. But I'm afraid we will, and it will all come out . . ."

"I'm not surprised," Catherine said quietly.

"He betrayed us, simple as that," the President said, his voice tight.

"And in more ways than one," Catherine said. "You must tell Ron now."

It was a painful moment. The President and his wife for once did not hide their intense emotions, which made Ron acutely uncomfortable. They apparently felt compelled to tell him something neither of them really wanted him to know. The situation compelled it . . .

The President sighed, nodded. "When I began to develop my ideas about the multi-lateral trade agreements—this was before I ran for President, when I was still in the Senate—Blaine made some halfhearted arguments against those ideas, all based on his old liberal adherence to the notion of absolute free trade, and then he conceded I was right. He conceded grudgingly maybe, but he conceded. And he helped me convert a loose body of ideas into a specific program. He was a part of it, Ron—I mean, a part of my program, one of the *authors* of it. He played a role in some of the early negotiations. He went along. If he didn't really believe in what we were doing, at the very least he went along. Then, maybe a year ago, he began to talk against me. Privately, of course. In meetings. More often with me alone. He turned around and became an outspoken opponent within the Administration.

"I didn't know why. I suppose his old liberal conscience hurt. Maybe he got some criticism from the academic community. Anyway, I was willing to concede that his opposition was honest. Then it changed. He stopped reasoning with me and became emotional. He argued with me, vehemently. It was always in private, and as time went by he became downright irrational. He badgered me about it, every chance he had, every time we were alone. It was—"

Catherine interrupted. "He began to talk about exemptions from the agreements. The exemptions he wanted didn't make any sense. We had to suspect some motive other than reason and honest judgment. Looking back, it's perfectly obvious. But you couldn't believe it. The idea of the Secretary of State being influenced by . . . money, or whatever. We couldn't believe it. Maybe we were too naive."

The President drank his brandy as Catherine talked, and when she stopped he shook his head and sighed again. "About ten days before Blaine was killed—in other words shortly before Catherine and I went to Europe—there was an ugly scene between Blaine and myself. Ron, I don't think we need to go into the details. I will tell you it was extremely painful. After it was over, it was impossible for him to continue to serve in my Administration in any position of trust and confidence. And he knew it. When Ted O'Malley of CBS asked about rumors that Blaine was going to resign, he was onto something. Blaine *was* going to resign, he was on his way out—"

"Tell Ron *all* of it, Bob," Catherine said. "He probably knows most of what you've just said."

A quick nod. "What happened was that . . . well, there's no other way to put it but to tell you that Blaine tried to blackmail *us.*" The President glanced at his wife. "In our background, Catherine's and mine, there is something we would not want revealed. It has *nothing* to do with my qualifications to be President. It does not involve any crime or anything of that nature . . . but it would be extremely painful for us if it were revealed. Lansard Blaine had been our close personal friend for a very long time, and he knew about this thing. He threatened to tell it . . . to influence me to drop the multi-lateral trade agreements" —the President said it with grim anger— "he threatened to tell this thing that would hurt us so personally. It was done in a fit of temper, I suppose, and the next day he apologized and promised not to mention the matter again, but our confidence in him was completely, permanently destroyed. Neither of us would ever have trusted him again. He understood that. He offered to resign and I accepted his resignation immediately. Then he asked me for a little time to put a good face on it. He thought he could arrange a faculty appointment—maybe a chair in history—at some university if he had a few weeks to explore it. I agreed to give him a few weeks. But not more. He had to go."

From now on, Ron realized, the investigation took a new turn, more dangerous for him, more dangerous for the President. "How many people knew about this?"

"Besides Catherine and myself—and now you," the President

said, "I guess it's just Fritz Gimbel and the Attorney General. Fritz and me and the Attorney General . . . we discussed it—"

"And Lynne," said his wife. "We talked about it over dinner, and Lynne heard. In fact, we considered not telling her, but we decided to. She had to know why we were so upset. Anyway, Blaine was a special friend of hers and she had to know why he was leaving and why we weren't friends any more. Naturally it upset her."

"Yes," the President said, "it was a cruel thing to do, I wish we hadn't." He glanced at Catherine, as though to remind her of his original feelings.

Ron got up to leave, thoroughly embarrassed now by such a personal exchange.

VI

Office of the Attorney General, Monday, June 18, 8:45 AM

Ron lifted his coffee cup from the tray on the Attorney General's desk. They were having breakfast in the Attorney General's office. Attorney General Charles Sherer had eaten little of the scrambled eggs, toast and bacon on his tray. Now he leaned back in his tall leather chair, a cup of coffee in one hand, a cigarette in the other, and regarded Ron with a wry smile.

"I know it's a tough damn question," Ron said as he sipped from his cup. "I don't expect an answer, just a reaction."

The Attorney General was sixty-two, one of the oldest members of the Webster Administration and one of the most experienced. He had been a deputy assistant attorney general as long ago as the Johnson Administration; he had been special counsel in the Carter White House; and in the years between his tours of duty with the government he had practiced law with the Washington firm of Wiley & Salmon. He was an old Washington hand, and he maintained—at least in Ron's judgment—a degree of separation from the Webster Administration. Like Ron, he withheld something of himself. Ron trusted him and over the years had come to him for advice a number of times.

Attorney General Sherer reached now to the big ashtray on his desk and ground out his cigarette. "I suppose she did," he said. "Sometime or other . . ."

Ron had just asked him if he thought Catherine Webster had possibly had an affair with Lansard Blaine, and, more important, if *that* was what Blaine had threatened to reveal to embarrass the President. "But it hasn't been recently, not since they've been in the White House. At least I don't think so."

Ron thought of how Catherine Webster had said she felt someone was creating a diversion with the publicity about Blaine's social life, and how that would seem to have argued against her as a suspect. But it might also have been a clever diversion of her own . . . especially if she retained strong feelings about Blaine.

. . . No, the Attorney General was saying, "I suspect it was something more damaging than that . . . I think they should tell you—"

"Lynne . . . ?"

The Attorney General shrugged. "Could be." He paused for a moment. "The day it happened, the day Blaine threatened blackmail, I was called to the Oval Office. When I got there the President was with Gimbel, and the two of them were as angry as I have ever seen two men. They were so angry, Ron, it makes them suspects, yes, either one of them, even the President . . . especially the President . . . was capable of killing Blaine . . . at least that afternoon. They didn't tell me what it was Blaine had threatened, only that he had threatened to publicize something that would be personally devastating to the Websters. They wanted to talk about getting rid of Blaine, how to get rid of him. They wanted to know if we could hold a prosecution over his head to keep him quiet."

"Prosecution for what?"

"Malfeasance in office. They said they knew something about him—"

"He took bribes," Ron said.

"Yes. They told me. They suspected it, they thought evidence could be found."

Ron shook his head. "Then why in God's name hadn't he fired him?"

The Attorney General shrugged. "After a couple of days the President called and told me Blaine had offered to resign. I assumed he had fought fire with fire—had threatened to prosecute him for taking bribes unless he kept his mouth shut and got out."

"The President told me Blaine had a change of heart and offered his resignation."

"Well, maybe . . ."

"Do you really think the President was involved in his death?"

"Do you? You're the official investigator."

Ron shook his head. "But I think Gimbel could have been."

The Attorney General, a ruddy-faced man whose fierce black eyebrows sometimes all but hid the upper rims of his eyeglasses, threw up his hands. "Despite what I've just said, I find it difficult to believe either of them did it . . . Bob Webster is a well-organized personality. He's smart. He's in control of himself. If he had killed Blaine—it's really a farfetched notion—he'd have done it differently, and somewhere else. Fritz Gimbel is easy to underestimate. But he's surely too smart to kill a rat for his master and leave the carcass on his master's doorstep."

"Dammit, I'm still betting he's involved some way," Ron said.

"Blaine was corrupt, you've identified one man who was paying him bribes. There's your lead, in my judgment. Maybe it does come back to Gimbel some way. *Maybe* it even comes back to the President. But there's your lead. Put the pressure on that fellow Jeremy Johnson. Put it on the others, if you can find them. That's my advice to you."

Ron heard it, nodded, and at the same time wondered if perhaps the Attorney General, like himself, just couldn't face the possibility of the unacceptable . . . that someone on the White House staff . . . *in* the White House . . . was somehow responsible . . .

Special Investigation Office, The White House, Monday, June 18, 10:00 AM

Jill Keller was in Ron's office. Walter Locke, the FBI man, sat beside her on the couch reviewing once more Blaine's telephone log. He'd identified several more of the names that initially had escaped identification.

"But nothing on Philippe Grand," he was saying. "I'm betting it's a code name."

"Which would make it all the more interesting," Ron said.

"Yes. Inoguchi Osanaga . . . he's interesting too. He covers himself too well. All of us leave a trail—bills, checks, tax returns, medical records, credit applications, correspondence . . . we leave a trail of paper behind us—perfectly innocent, usually, but a record that tells who we are and where we go and what we do. It's usually nothing that needs to be covered, we don't worry about it. But not Osanaga. He does business in cash. He even pays his apartment rent with cash. He gets no mail but ads. His trail is too clean."

"Not much of a reason to suspect someone," Jill put in.

"Pick him up and bring him in," Ron said.

"He'll squawk, he's a heavyweight."

"Treat him with elaborate courtesy," Ron said.

Locke nodded. "I'll make a call."

"Next," said Jill. "I think we'd better take a look at this." She handed Ron a newspaper. "Have you seen the morning's offering from New York?"

THE PLAYBOY BLAINE
$$$?
By Barbara Dash

While Secretary of State Lansard Blaine was alive, he managed somehow—probably with the cooperation of a lot of us in the news business—to keep quiet that he was a high liver, devoted to the good life in many forms. If we knew how many young women passed through his life, we helped him maintain his privacy; after all, the day has long since passed when there was anything unusual in even a top government official enjoying the company of a variety of playmates. If we saw that he lived well, we smiled and shrugged.

Perhaps we were wrong. Now that the Secretary is dead, facts have begun to emerge which suggest that Blaine spent money far beyond what he earned as Secretary of State or what he could have earned and accumulated as a professor of diplomatic history.

Item: In the Secretary of State's office at the State Department a Louise Nevelson wood sculpture hangs on the wall. It was purchased by Blaine with personal, not government, funds. The price? The gallery where he bought it in New York reluctantly disclosed to this reporter that he paid $57,000 for it in April of last year.

Item: In the late Secretary's Watergate apartment hangs a painting by Symbari, one of the artist's "Crazy Horse" series. Blaine acquired it within the last six months. We have not yet learned where he bought it, or for how much, but art experts tell us its market value six months ago exceeded $20,000.

"Damn," Ron said. "What else?" He scanned the article. The writer went into Blaine's furniture, the wines in his rack, his clothes, his tabs at expensive Washington restaurants, his resort vacations . . . his lifestyle. She concluded that all this could not have been supported by his salary and other visible earnings such as the royalties on his books. So where did he get the money to live "like a sheik"?

"We don't have much time, Ron," Jill said. "There's already competition for the evidence. Our investigation is going to be smothered in a hundred unofficial ones. From now on it's going to be tougher and tougher to get anybody to talk, and whoever we're after will have a blueprint of what to expect and how to protect themselves from it . . ."

Ron looked at Locke. "Get me Osanaga," he said.

Special Investigation Office, The Justice Department, Monday, June 18, 1:30 PM

Inoguchi Osanaga was tall for a Japanese. He sat facing Ron across the desk in the shabby Justice Department office, where Ron had told the FBI to bring him. From the outset of the interview it was apparent to Ron that he had not frightened Osanaga by having the FBI pick him up and bring him to the Justice Department. Osanaga was angry, curt. He did not withhold answers but he volunteered nothing.

"Did you know Blaine? Do you deny you ever talked to him?"

"I do not," Osanaga said impassively.

"In what capacity did you talk to him?"

"As a journalist, interviewing him for my newspaper."

"Did you call him?"

"Yes."

"Did he call you?"
"Yes."
"Often?"
"Yes."
Perhaps fifty years old, Osanaga showed gray at the temples, his face was smooth and flat, his small black eyes communicated nothing. It was difficult to imagine him laughing.
"What was the chief topic of your interviews with the Secretary of State?"
"The multi-lateral trade agreements. They will have a profound influence on the economy of my country—"
"You wrote articles based on your interviews with Blaine?"
"Yes."
"Can you provide me copies of those articles?"
"Of course."
"Did you ever give Blaine a gift?"
"On a number of occasions, after he had been particularly courteous to me, returning my calls, giving me information, I sent the Secretary a bottle of plum wine."
Ron could not help smiling. "Did you ever buy him dinner?"
"Yes."
"Other entertainment?"
"No."
"Did you ever give him money?"
"No."
Ron picked up a pencil and for a moment tapped it on the yellow legal pad that lay before him on the scarred old desk, then dropped it, regretting he had shown Osanaga any sign of frustration. "Mr. Osanaga," he said slowly, "the United States government is under no illusions about who you are and why you are in this country. You are not a journalist. You are the confidential representative of certain large Japanese corporations, and your

function in the United States is to lobby for their interests, to influence the U.S. government to adopt policies advantageous to the companies you represent. Specifically, you would like to block the multi-lateral trade agreements that would exclude the products of your clients from the U.S. market. You tried to influence the Secretary of State to oppose the President. You try to influence members of the Senate to vote against the treaties when they come up for ratification. *That's* why you had repeated meetings with Blaine, not to interview him for *Honshu Shinbum.* We know this."

"I had supposed you did."

"Did you happen to read the Barbara Dash column this morning?"

Osanaga nodded.

"We know where he got the money."

Osanaga nodded again. "Indeed?"

"So I ask you again, did you give Blaine money?"

"Mr. Fairbanks, if you are suggesting I made an improper gift to a high official of your government, you are in effect accusing me of a crime. I shall have to consult legal counsel."

"Mr. Osanaga—"

Ron was interrupted by a tap on the office door. It opened, and Gabe Haddad gestured that he should come outside. Ron excused himself and went out.

"Telephone," said Gabe. "Senator Finlay wants to talk to you."

Senator Walter Finlay, Republican from Indiana, was a member of the Senate Foreign Relations Committee and a bitterly outspoken critic of President Webster's multi-lateral trade agreements.

"H'lo, Ron," said the Senator. (First name, like an overanxious insurance salesman: the old political game. Ron had met the man only once.) "Y' feelin' okay after that accident?"

"Yes, Senator, thanks. Just a few bruises."

"Well, you take care of yourself. Listen, Ron, I understand you had the FBI pick up Inoguchi Osanaga this morning. Is that right?"

"I just want to ask him a few questions. I'm talking with him now."

"I don't see the connection, Ron. Surely he's not suspected of having anything to do with Blaine's murder—"

"Not really"—he tried to sound off-handed—"I just need some information he may have."

"I see . . . well, I just wanted to put in a good word for the man, Ron. I've gotten to know him a little. I'd say he's a pretty straight fellow. You know, you can scare the devil out of a fellow like that, bringin' him in, questioning him. He doesn't know our way of doing things, of course. I just wanted to put in a word for him."

"He's all right, senator, and I can assure you he's not scared."

"You gotta remember, Ron—you being fairly new at this and all—that you can embarrass our government pretty bad if you're not very careful, hauling in a citizen of another country like that. I hope you're being *very* careful. You know, too, there's some question about how much power you've really got under that Executive Order. I mean, how much authority the President can give that way. I wouldn't want you to get your tail in a crack, Ron."

"I'll remember the advice, senator. I appreciate your calling."

"Okay, son . . . and you be sure you don't have any hidden injuries from that accident. I'd get myself X-rayed if I were you."

When Ron sat down again behind the desk in his temporary office he was still unhappy about Osanaga . . . the man had revealed nothing new, but at least picking him up had smoked out Finlay. The Secretary may have been on the side of his clients, worked hard to earn his pay, but in the end he was getting panicky

. . . and who really trusts a man who takes bribes? Sooner or later he might turn on you . . . blackmail . . . The net wasn't closing, though, it was widening . . .

"Mr. Osanaga. You will persist, I take it, in your denial that you paid Blaine money?"

Osanaga nodded. "If you have evidence that I did, I assume you will present it."

"And of course you know nothing about Blaine's murder."

"I was at dinner with two members of Congress at the time the newspapers say the Secretary of State was murdered. Indeed, Mr. Fairbanks, I have never had the honor of being inside the White House."

"And you have no idea who might have killed him, or why?"

"No. I have no idea. *None at all.*"

"Finlay . . ." Ron said to Gabe Haddad and Jill Keller. They had brought him a ham salad sandwich, a Coke, and an apple, which he now sat munching, "That old son of a bitch—"

"If Osanaga wasn't paying Blaine, he has for sure been paying Finlay," put in Gabe. "A member of the Senate Foreign Relations Committee . . . it fits."

"Be careful," Jill said. "There is, after all, some honest opposition to the trade agreements."

"Not in the person of Senator Walter Finlay," Ron said. "Incidentally, has either of you that list of the friends of Martha Kingsley?"

"I've got it," Gabe said, reaching into his open briefcase. He handed the list to Ron. "The Senator is on the list."

The list was the one the FBI had compiled of the men who'd been seen in the company of Martha Kingsley. "I thought I remembered Finlay on here . . . Finlay and Blaine . . ."

"The fascinating Mrs. Kingsley looks like an important link," Gabe said.

Ron nodded. "And here's an old friend of mine. I didn't pay much attention before—it doesn't make sense. Paul-Victor Chamillart. I think I should talk to friend Paul . . ."

Le Bagatell, Monday, June 18, 9:00 PM

"Mon ami! Comment ça va?" Ron laughed. He hadn't seen Paul-Victor Chamillart for two years, but Chamillart had not changed. Preceded by his great Gallic nose, his short, fat, smelly French cigarette dangling in the corner of his mouth, Chamillart ambled carelessly into the restaurant, straight past Ron, overlooking him and his outstretched hand.

"Ah, Ron-ald, good to see you."

Chamillart was a lawyer at the French Embassy. During the days when he was practicing law in Washington Ron had lived in the same apartment building with Chamillart. They'd become friends, had played handball together, gone to a few plays, gallery openings, had eaten together often in restaurants Chamillart always criticized with the fervor of an offended gourmet. They saw each other less frequently after each moved out of the building, and since Ron had been at the White House it had been difficult for him to find the time for the long restaurant evenings Chamillart especially loved.

Their table was waiting. Paul-Victor ordered a half bottle of champagne as an *apéritif.*

"Is it true?" Chamillart asked. He swallowed his words in a deep, growling French accent. "Will you marry the daughter of the President?"

Ron laughed, shook his head. "Not soon, anyway."

"Perhaps never, then," said Chamillart. "If it were a true infatuation, you would not say 'not soon.' You would say soon, soon, immediately!"

"What about you, Paul? A bachelor forever?"

Chamillart turned down the corners of his mouth, laughed, and shrugged. "I was much interested in a young woman, an American . . . a tennis player. However—"

"I saw something about that in the papers."

"Yes, but, Ron-ald, a tennis player! Ah, in the end, her executions of love were all in her game. And in tennis, love is only acceptable for the *other* person."

Chamillart laughed delightedly at his own joke. He was a well-educated man, deeply immersed in the artistic and literary history of his country. He was proud of French culture and quick to notice anything French that was appreciated and adopted in America. At the same time he openly resented anything un-French that Americans persisted in calling "French"—salad dressing, rotation pool, deep-fried potatoes ("ugh, that gummy orange mess you call French dress-ing, it is a libel on my country").

"Paul," Ron said after they'd finished their champagne and agreed on their dinner. "I need to ask you a couple of questions."

Chamillart lifted his brows. "In your official capacity as the investigator into the death of Blaine?"

"Well . . . unofficially."

"I didn't kill him."

Ron laughed. "And you don't know who did. But you may be able to help me."

"I am afraid, my good friend, you are going to need help . . . and much of it . . . I was distressed to learn you had become the chief investigator—"

"It seems a lot of my friends were."

"He is using you, my friend."

"He?"

"The Presi-dent. Are you certain he wants you to find out who killed the Secretary of State?"

Ron almost did a double-take. Then: "Yes, Paul, I'm sure—"

"Ah, but when we find out who killed Blaine, then what will we know that the President does not want us to know?"

"What do you have in mind?"

Chamillart shrugged.

"What had you heard about Blaine? I mean, before he died. Did you know, when the President didn't, that Blaine was, as we say, corruptible?"

"We say it too, old friend . . . Corruptible? No. I did not know, I doubt my government knew. I hear the talk *now,* but we did not know before."

Their talk was interrupted by the headwaiter, Jacques, who came to take their order. Ron let Chamillart settle the menu with Jacques.

"Well . . ." Chamillart said when the waiter had left, "what questions, *Monsieur l'Investigateur?*"

"Two. First, did you ever hear the name Philippe Grand?"

"Certainly. Many times."

"Good. Who is he?"

"He could be fifty people, a hundred. The name is hardly unusual. There was an old café singer in Paris—"

"Do you know anyone specifically, today, named Philippe Grand?"

Chamillart shook his head. "Why? Who is he supposed to be?"

"Someone who called Blaine on the telephone many times during the last few months. Blaine always returned his calls. We don't know who he is. We'd like to know. Blaine's secretary says

Grand spoke with a French accent."

"A French accent? What is that?" Chamillart allowed a smile.

"Look, old friend, we need to find out why Blaine got and returned so many calls to a man we can't identify. The man left his name repeatedly with Blaine's secretary—Philippe Grand. So why can't we find a Philippe Grand?"

"I will put the question to our security officer in the morning," Chamillart said. "We will ask Paris. I'll be able to tell you by tomorrow afternoon if we know anything about your man."

"I'd appreciate that."

"But don't forget, they speak a sort of French in Canada. Your Philippe Grand could be a *Quebecois.*"

"I'll check that too."

"Ah. Then, what is the second question."

Ron smiled. "The second question involves your relationship with a certain young woman—"

"Ahh!" Chamillart grinned and kissed the tips of his fingers. "The wo-man in the case; and who is the woman?"

"Martha Koczinski. Or Martha Kingsley, depending on how recently you knew her."

Chamillart's grin instantly disappeared. "Ah, Martha . . . the lovely, intriguing Martha." He nodded. "Of course. So she is the woman in your case—?"

"I'm not sure what her involvement is, but she's in it some way. I need to know all I can about her—"

"So why do you ask me?"

"The FBI has a file on Martha Kingsley. She's been involved —or has been suspected of being involved—in certain leaks of confidential information. The FBI file includes a list of men known to have been her—shall we say friends? Your name is on the list."

"Not prominently, I hope—"

"Not prominently enough to spoil your dinner. I was surprised, though, to find your name on the list . . . Did you pay her?"

"In her own coin," said Chamillart. He was subdued. "She wished to be invited to certain parties, to be introduced to certain people. We provided each other a *quid pro quo.*" He smiled faintly. "For my part I did what I was qualified to do for her. And for hers, she did what she was eminently qualified to do for me."

"And when she had all she wanted from you she broke off the relationship—?"

"Oh, *no!* It was *I* who broke off the relationship."

Ron smiled. "Sorry . . ."

Chamillart looked at Ron for a moment. "You misunderstand, my friend. It is not me you underestimate with your suggestion, it is *her.*"

"She calls herself a prostitute," Ron said. "Not me."

"Maybe she would like you to think that is all she is. I assure you, she is more."

"She had a relationship with Blaine—"

Chamillart frowned. "She *was,* then, somehow involved in his death. I think you may be sure of it."

"Oh?"

Chamillart sighed. "A tale of woe, I will tell you . . . But how shall I explain? Perhaps to begin with by reminding you that while it is not true that all cats are gray in the dark, it is a fact that a woman cannot hold a man's attention long by what she does in bed." He shrugged. "Nor can a man hold a woman's attention long by what *he* does, for that matter. If the charming Martha wants to call herself a prostitute, very well, but she is a great deal more than that. Ron-ald, would you believe that I genuinely cherished my nights with her, not so much for what she did—which most any woman can duplicate—but for what she *said?* I enjoyed her *company,* her conversation, my friend. Her understanding, her capacity to amuse. No . . . more than to amuse—to *stimulate.* Do you understand?"

Ron nodded, waited.

"Do you remember the details of the N'Djamena affair?"

"I remember," Ron said. Chamillart had referred to an incident two years before when a Pan American 747 on a flight from Capetown to Rome had experienced mechanical troubles and been forced to land at N'Djamena in the Republic of Chad. The Chad government had previously announced that any aircraft or airline crew member that took part in any flight to or from the white Republic of South Africa was barred from landing in Chad. The Chad government sent the passengers on their way but held the airplane and its crew—the crew to pay fines of $5,000 or to serve six-month jail sentences for their violation of Chad law by landing at N'Djamena, the 747 against a fine of $10,000,000 imposed on Pan American. The American *chargé d'affaires* at N'Djamena had not been able to negotiate a settlement, and the United States had secretly asked France to intervene on its behalf . . . "You bailed us out of that one," Ron said.

Chamillart nodded. "You sent me a note, expressing your appreciation."

The waiter had arrived with plates of tiny scallops and mushrooms in a clear sauce, and their conversation stopped while the waiter served the dish and the white wine Chamillart had ordered to go with it.

"Were you ever in Chad?" he asked Ron. "I wonder what they eat there."

"McDonald's Burgers?"

"Probably . . . Anyway, about N'Djamena. Your Secretary of State—it was Blaine, of course—called our embassy in the middle of the evening. It was a Friday. By chance it was the birthday of Madame Gravier and we were celebrating the occasion with a small private dinner at the embassy. After dinner Ambassador Meline telephoned the Foreign Minister in Paris. We woke him in the middle of the night—it was, indeed, four in the morning in Paris—and communicated to him the urgent request of Secretary Blaine. The Foreign Minister was annoyed to have been wakened at that hour; he also recognized that the matter would not be simple, that our government would not be able to secure the release of the Americans and their airplane merely by asking. In fact, as you may not know, we applied pressure to the government of Chad by suggesting we might experience difficulty in delivering certain anti-insurgency weapons they had contracted to buy from us. The Foreign Minister was petulant. He remarked that it was strange how quickly Secretary Blaine came to him for help, immediately after refusing to cooperate in the matter of Martine Nanterre. His petulance was momentary, of the hour. He would never, in fact, have allowed *l'affaire Nanterre* to stand in the way of France's doing what we could for the United States in the N'Djamena matter. At the moment, however, being wakened at four in the morning, he linked the two. Do you know what I mean . . . *l'affaire Nanterre?*"

Ron knew . . . Martine Nanterre was a French actress who had been arrested and jailed in Florida some years before for possession of a large cache of heroin and cocaine. She had jumped bail and returned to France, and the French government, consistent with its law prohibiting the extradition of a French citizen, refused to return her to the United States. An arrest warrant remained outstanding for her, however, and later, when she was performing on the stage in London, the United States asked the British to arrest her and hold her for extradition to the United States. She was forced to give up her London play and return to France, which produced complaints in the French press that the United States was harassing a French citizen, hurting her career.

Foreign Minister Thiers had, only a few weeks before the N'Djamena affair, quietly asked the government of the United States to drop the charges against Martine Nanterre. Secretary of State Blaine had refused . . .

Chamillart held a bit of mushroom on his fork, letting it drip sauce onto his plate before he leaned forward and took it into his mouth. "Now back to Martha Kingsley," he muttered as he savored the morsel. "I left the embassy before midnight and took a cab to Martha's apartment. She was waiting for me, with a bottle of champagne chilled—my champagne. I provide it by the case. It was a memorable night, Ron-ald. A most memorable night. She inspired me to talk about things I had not talked about for years. Things from my childhood . . . I described my family's summer holidays on the Brittany coast, and she seemed to enjoy every word of it. She also told stories of her own. It was a memorable night . . ."

Chamillart put down his fork. "And during that night, Ron-ald, I committed a grave indiscretion. It was the kind of indiscretion that terminates foreign-service careers. I tell you in confidence, of course."

"Of course," Ron said. "I guarantee it."

"I told her what the Foreign Minister said. Influenced perhaps by too many glasses of excellent wine, influenced certainly by her infectious enthusiasm for good conversation, I wanted to tell her something at once amusing and confidential, something only I could tell. So I told her how we awakened the Foreign Minister before dawn and how, most grumpy, he had joined the matter of Martine Nanterre to the matter of the Pan American 747. She appreciated the ironies of the story. The next day I was to learn how much she appreciated it."

"Who did she tell? Blaine?"

"Not Blaine. Blaine was in Tokyo."

"Then who?"

"I do not know," said Chamillart. He picked up his fork and speared a morsel of scallop. "I left her apartment about nine Saturday morning, after a delightful breakfast. By noon—*by noon,* my friend—Ambassador Meline received a call from Alfred Eiseman at the White House, advising him that the government of the United States was dropping all charges against Martine Nanterre. I need hardly tell you that I never saw Martha Kingsley again. But I also need hardly tell you that someone in a most important position in your government did talk to Madame Kingsley . . . and the talk was about Secretary Blaine and *l'affaire Nanterre* . . . I told you the lady was extraordinary. Clearly her connections go beyond, above, your own Secretary of State . . ."

Special Investigation Office, The White House, Tuesday, June 19, 10:00 AM

The President sat on the couch in Ron's office, apparently relaxed, his legs crossed and one arm laid across the back of the couch. Jill had offered to leave when he came in unannounced, but he had only motioned her to scoot down the couch and make room for him as he sat beside her to talk with her and Ron.

"I like your word consortium," he said to Ron. "There *is* a consortium of interests determined to block the trade agreements. They have so much at stake, they are entirely capable of trying to corrupt any cabinet officer, of even killing him. In Japan they are trying to bring down the government to prevent Japan's adhering to the agreements. Japanese manufacturers have so much at stake that they might well turn to assassination if they fail by political means. In the Netherlands the opponents of the agreements have accused the government of internal corruption, hoping to bring it down before it commits the country to the new trade arrangements that would limit their exports to the U.S. Here in the United States . . ." He stopped, shook his head. "It's difficult to believe, but I can see no other convincing motive for Lansard's murder."

"It may be too easy a conclusion, Mr. President," Jill said. "And there's a contradiction in it. Why would the consortium want to murder the only highly placed member of your Administration who opposed the agreements? I'd think they'd want him alive."

"Maybe," the President said. "But remember this . . . that what we are calling the consortium includes some pretty ugly people. Maybe Blaine *promised* them, assured them he could kill the agreements, and when they paid him a great deal of money and he could not deliver . . . maybe they concluded he had welshed on them, that he was, simply and inelegantly, shaking them down and had never intended to kill the agreements—"

"There's also the possibility," Ron said, expressing for the first time some of his earlier thoughts, "that someone was afraid he would talk, or threaten to talk. Of course if he did he would have been the first one in deep trouble, but maybe someone in the consortium was also afraid Blaine might simply confess, under pressure, that he had received bribes, and tell who had paid him . . ."

"The point to remember," Webster said, "is that the consortium consists of people who have, literally, billions at stake. That's enough to move the kind of people they are to do almost anything . . ."

Ron nodded, then: Changing the subject a bit, "Are you worried about a congressional investigation?"

"I am hoping," the President said, "that you will have concluded the investigation before a congressional investigation can get off the ground."

The previous afternoon Senator Kyle Fleming had spoken on the floor of the Senate, calling for an independent investigation either by a senatorial committee or by a special prosecutor sanctioned by Congress . . . "The truth is," the senator had said, "the President has appointed as head of his investigation an inexperienced member of his own White House staff, a young lawyer beholden to him who, in fact, may one day soon—as repeated rumor would have it—become the President's son-in-law. Is it appropriate, Mr. President, for a member of the President's personal staff and a prospective son-in-law to conduct this sensitive investigation? Is it appropriate for this young man to hold authority greater than that of the Director of the Federal Bureau of Investigation? Is it appropriate for this young man to hold special, unprecedented powers . . . ?"

And so on. Several Republican senators had spoken in support of Senator Fleming. One of them complained that nearly a week had passed since the death of Blaine and nothing, apparently, had been accomplished by the special investigator. Another senator suggested that Ronald Fairbanks should be called before a committee to report on what his investigation had produced.

"We can't promise quick results, Mr. President," Ron said. "We've got a lot of suggestive material . . . we know far more today than we knew this time last week, but I can't tell you we're about to solve the case—"

"Well, like they say, the heat's on, and it's going to get worse . . . we don't have much more time—"

"I'm worried about what's coming out about the way Blaine spent money—"

"That he was taking bribes," the President said quietly. He sighed, shook his head. "Ron . . . Jill . . . I'm going to have to live with that. *We* have to live with it. It may destroy this administration. It may even destroy the trade agreements. Whoever killed Blaine may have accomplished what he couldn't accomplish for them by accepting their bribes. So . . ." The President got up from the couch. "Let the chips fall where they may. Find out the truth for me. Whatever it is. Whoever . . ."

For a long moment after the President left the room Ron and Jill sat staring at the door he had carefully, quietly closed behind him.

"We're in trouble," Jill said finally. "He is . . . and you . . . and me."

Ron nodded.

Two major newspapers, one in New York, one in Los Angeles, one the previous evening, one that morning had published editorials expressing no confidence in Ronald Fairbanks as chief investigator into the death of Lansard Blaine. He was not, they said, qualified for the job. He was making no visible progress. What's more, said one of them, it was now apparent that Blaine's death was not an isolated event but rather the dramatic event that had begun to expose deep corruption in the Webster Administration.

The Dash article of Monday morning had been followed on this morning by another, reporting more details of the personal finances of the late Secretary of State. He had had, Barbara Dash now reported, an inexplicable habit, developed only since he became Secretary of State, for paying bills with cash—he ran up accounts with stores but came in, or sent his chauffeur in, to pay the bills with cash in large denominations. A wire story said that Blaine had reported an annual income of less than one hundred thousand dollars in each of the past five years—hardly enough to pay for his art collection, his wardrobe, his wine cellar, his vacations, his gifts to women . . .

"It's just beginning," Ron said. "It's going to break . . . Whatever *he* says, they'll say he put the investigation in the hands of a bunch of amateurs to cover up, delay . . . but I don't think he's sacrificing us, I just can't believe that, Jill—"

"He's a convincing man," she said noncommittally.

"Well, we can't just quit, walk out."

"No."

The telephone buzzed. He picked it up. "All right, in a minute." He said to Jill, "There's a man here to see me. Look . . . I can get you out, you and Gabe. I can send you back to Justice—"

"*No,* damn it."

He smiled, a graveyard smile. "Okay, kid . . . but if you change your mind—"

"I won't," and she went out to send in the man waiting to see him.

It was Burke Kincaid, security officer from the Canadian Embassy. A crisp, quick, middle-aged man, he sat in the chair beside Ron's desk, and briskly opened a small leather briefcase.

"You sent us an inquiry about one Philippe Grand," he said.

"Yes," Ron said, surprised. He'd called the inquiry to the embassy only early this morning. "The name mean anything to you?"

"It does, and we're curious that an inquiry should come from the office investigating the murder of Lansard Blaine. I hope there's no connection."

"Who *is* Philippe Grand?"

"I wish we knew," the Canadian said. "It's a name used by one or more operatives of the Quebec liberation movement. Probably more than one. Whenever there's mischief, it's attributed to Philippe Grand . . . a bomber, a sniper, a saboteur. They paint his name on walls. If he's done half what they claim for him we could hang him . . . Why have you inquired?"

"During the four months before his death Lansard Blaine had a number of telephone calls at the State Department from a man who called himself Philippe Grand. Blaine returned those calls."

"Your Secretary of State had conversations with a Quebec terrorist?" Kincaid was indignant.

"He had conversations with someone named Philippe Grand who spoke with a French accent. We're checking all the names on his telephone log. This is one of them we have no explanation for."

"The only explanations that come to mind are ones I should very much not want to hear."

"Look, since Blaine is dead and I have no information other than the name Philippe Grand on a telephone log—plus the recollection of a secretary that she heard a French accent on the telephone—I'm afraid the explanation will have to come from you," Ron said.

"I should like," said Kincaid, "to have some assurance that Blaine's contacts with the Quebec liberation movement did not have the sanction of official U.S. policy—"

"I've no authority to give you that assurance. I think it's apparent, though, if you've been following what's come out since Blaine's death, that he was involved in a great many things that didn't have the sanction of U.S. policy."

"Will your government disavow him?"

"I don't know. Frankly I don't think it's necessary."

"I've brought here," Kincaid said, taking a document from his briefcase, "a summary of what we know about Philippe Grand. If you learn anything that might help us track him down we should be very grateful to hear it."

"Quebec liberation movement!" Gabe Haddad was looking at the report Kincaid had given Ron. "For God's sake, what was Blaine doing?"

"Complicating our investigation," said Ron glumly . . . "as far as I'm concerned it's just someone else who might have killed him. Playing cozy with fanatics can be dangerous stuff . . ."

"I had a call this morning from Barbara Lund," Gabe said. "You know, the nude dancer? Jeremy Johnson called her yesterday, wanted to know if we'd talked to her and if so what she told us. He told her she was stupid to talk to us and she wouldn't talk to us any more if she knew what's good for her. I feel like shaking him up a little—"

Ron shook his head. "We have worse problems, time is running out."

"I know."

"I offered Jill the chance to go back to Justice."

"She didn't take it," Gabe said, again looking at the paper from Kincaid—or pretending to.

"Did she tell you?"

"No. I can guess what she said. I know what kind of woman she is. I hope you appreciate her."

He paused, said quietly, "I do . . . she's capable, tough—"

"Not what I mean."

"What *do* you mean?"

Gabe glanced down at the Kincaid paper again. "She'll stick with you, you've made an impression on her."

"Meaning . . . ?"

"Meaning is obvious, for God's sake."

Ron nodded, changed the subject. "I make you the same offer I made Jill. We look like we're falling on our faces. If you want out, I won't blame you—"

Gabe shook his head. "I'll stick," he said. "I'm a sucker for lost causes."

Ron had a one o'clock appointment for lunch. He worked until twelve at his desk, making calls about the names on the Blaine telephone logs. In a week the FBI hadn't been able to identify four more names—George Vogel, Sandra McGraw, Allison Keller, and William Furst. The usual sources had produced nothing, and Ron's calls on hunches produced nothing. He spoke to the President's press secretary and promised either to submit to questioning at a news conference the next day or issue a statement about the progress of the investigation. He reviewed a report from an FBI field agent in Las Vegas, sent in response to an order from

Locke, saying he had reason to suspect Lansard Blaine had money on deposit with two casinos even though he'd never been to Las Vegas and had never gambled there. The evidence behind the agent's suspicion was not hard, and Ron put the report aside. An effort to find out whether or not Blaine had kept number accounts in Zurich had run up against a wall. Very blank.

He locked his files and desk. He was ready to leave for his lunch date when the telephone buzzed. Lynne was outside and wanted to see him.

"I've been reading the papers, watching television," she said quietly, unhappily. She sat on his couch, wearing a faded red blouse, a sleeve of which had been split to let the cast on her arm through. "They're not treating you very well."

"It's to be expected—"

"No. When they said you were drunk Saturday night, that was bad enough. Now they're saying you're incompetent to conduct this investigation, even that you're covering up something for my father."

"We had to understand, Lynne, from the moment Blaine was killed that things would get very, very tough." He stood facing her, leaning back against the front of his desk. "I didn't have to accept this job. When I did I knew the possible consequences—"

"They don't have to be personal," she said, half whispering. "The political attacks, they don't have to be so *personal* . . ."

He smiled. "You should be used to them by now."

She shook her head. "Not the personal things . . . I only hope . . . when it's all over, you won't wish you'd never heard of us—my family . . . me . . ."

He bent forward and kissed her. "I doubt very much I'll ever wish that."

The Supreme Court of the United States, Tuesday, June 19, 1:00 PM

He was on time, even though he'd had to break away from Lynne too abruptly—he'd not told her where he was going. It was the Justice, though, who was a few minutes late, and so he had a moment to talk with Elizabeth Delsey, the Judge's secretary; and when word passed around that he was in Justice Friederich's office and waiting for him, others drifted in to see him—pages, secretaries, two of the library staff . . . they all remembered him, a former law clerk to the judge. It was like a family . . .

It was almost ten years now since he'd come to the Court to clerk for Justice Friederich. To be chosen by him was a special distinction. In the tradition of Felix Frankfurter, Friederich chose no one but the best and expected nothing but the best from them. That they should spend a part of their careers in the public service was part of that tradition. In addition to a Special Counsel to the President, Justice Friederich's ex-clerks included a former Attorney General of the United States, the current Deputy Attorney General, a Securities and Exchange Commissioner, the Ambassador to the United Nations, a Judge of the United States Court of Appeals, two Judges of United States District Courts, the Chief Justice of the Supreme Court of North Carolina, a former United States Senator and the Mayor of San Francisco. None of them ever failed at least to telephone Justice Friederich when they came to Washington or, if they lived there, to call on him once or twice a year. He remained their mentor, their sponsor.

From that first day ten years ago the Supreme Court never failed to intrigue Ron Fairbanks. He was fascinated by the vested power of the Court, the subdued tensions among the justices, and the self-conscious traditions in which the Court enveloped itself to conceal both power and tension. His only defined—and secret—ambition was to become a Supreme Court judge himself, though it was so lofty an ambition he had never dared mention it to anyone . . .

"Ron . . . " Justice Friederich said warmly, shaking his hand. He, too, was a politician; he'd been a district attorney in upstate New York, then a New York Court of Appeals judge and a judge of the United States Court of Appeals for the Second Circuit before he was appointed to the Supreme Court of the United States thirteen years previously. But he was a politician of a rare stripe . . . he communicated a genuine warmth, Ron could *feel* he was really glad to see him. Judge Friederich was a tall man, six-feet-three, with gray hair around the edges of his spotted bald head. He wore horn-rim spectacles and favored bow ties. "Sit down, be comfortable. A whisky before lunch? You take Scotch, as I recall."

Their lunch was to be served in the Justice's office. Ron said he'd like the Scotch and soda, then sat down in the fat brown-leather couch where he'd sat so many times, years ago, while he reviewed with the judge his research into the complexities of some case pending before the Court.

"Got yourself a real mess, haven't you?" Friederich settled into the huge leather armchair that faced the couch across a big, low table.

"Yes, sir."

"He asked you to take it on?"

"Yes."

"Well, you couldn't have refused. He's in trouble himself. Deep trouble. And you can't be a member of a president's official family and refuse your share of the trouble when it comes."

"Given time, we can wind up this thing, but it takes time—"

"Given time you could bail out the ocean with a bucket. Well, do you want to talk about it?"

"I'd like to, yes."

"It won't be coming before this Court?"

"I don't think so."

After a discreet rap on the door Elizabeth Delsey entered and served their Scotches, told them lunch would be ready in fifteen minutes.

"Are you sure Webster's not making you the goat? Do you trust him?"

"Yes . . . I do, but I also feel he hasn't told me everything I need to know, and I'm damn troubled by that . . . "

"Well, if it's any comfort to you, it's my estimate of the man that he's as honest as you can be and be President of the United States today. I wouldn't have suggested you join his Administration if I didn't think so—"

"Blaine threatened him," Ron broke in. "Blaine threatened to make public something that's intensely painful to Webster, and his wife. I've no idea what it is. He insists it's personal and has nothing to do with his conduct of the presidency—"

"*Everything* in his life has to do with his conduct of the presidency."

Ron nodded, but as he watched the judge, sipping his Scotch he wondered if in his successive judgeships he'd not withdrawn a bit from the real world, if it were not a little too easy for him to pronounce his judgments. The world didn't intrude much into this room of leather chairs, leather-bound books, old wood, thick carpets; if it had, it had left no visible sign.

"You're telling me, Ron, that *he* had a motive?"

"I am."

"Do you really think he had anything to do with it?"

Ron shook his head. "Maybe I'm just naive—"

"No," Friederich said thoughtfully, "I don't think so. Between you and me, and strictly off the record, I think Robert Webster is potentially a great President. His notion of the multi-lateral trade agreements may be a return to mercantilism, but it represents about the only fresh thought in international economics in fifty years. I know he didn't originate the idea but he had the sense to consider and adopt it, and for that he deserves credit—"

"I just can't think he'd kill a man this way. It's that basic for me—"

"I agree"—he took another sip of Scotch—"nothing so crude as a piece of wire, and in the White House itself . . . Seriously, did I ever tell you, Ron, how I met him?"

"No, sir."

"We were on a program together. He was a senator. I spoke, then he did. We were seated together at the dinner that followed. His wife was there—Catherine. She's a psychiatrist, as you doubtless know . . . she was a professor of psychiatric medicine at the University of Michigan at the time. I admire a man who's not embarrassed to openly display affection for his wife, and when I saw he was holding her hand under the dinner table, I began to like him. After dinner they asked me to have a drink in their suite and I went up with them. There were some people in and out, but after a while we were alone and sat and talked. They'd had enough to drink, both of them, to be fairly open, and they began to tell me about their children . . . Bob, Junior, you know, is a successful lawyer on Wall Street. Sam's a marine biologist. Lynne was still in high school then, but they told me how well she was doing. They came to a sort of self-conscious break, then looked at me, obviously expecting me to say something about *my* children. I only have one child, as you know, and of course I had to tell them that my son was retarded. A lovable thirty-five-year-old child. Catherine Webster began to cry."

Ron stared into his glass, not knowing what to say.

"An exchange like that tends to make people friends sooner than they'd expect."

"Yes . . . sir, do you have any idea what Blaine was talking about when he threatened to reveal something from the Websters' personal lives?"

"No, but it's hard to imagine that people who've lived in the public eye as long as they have could have too many skeletons in their closet."

Ron sipped his Scotch. "Well, it's obviously something that troubles them pretty deeply . . . "

Lunch served, Friederich asked Ron about the confirmation hearings soon to begin on the President's appointment of Judge Roscoe Runyon to the Sixth Circuit Court of Appeals, and over lunch they talked about that appointment and the senatorial opposition to it. He'd confided to Ron before that he hoped President Webster would appoint Judge Runyon to the next vacant seat on the Supreme Court. Although Justice Friederich did not expect ever to be chief justice, he was flattered to hear the present Court called "the Friederich Court." If Runyon could join him, his group of pragmatic intellectuals would be in a solid position to dominate the Supreme Court. Ron also knew Runyon's chances weren't too good. The President admired Friederich but he wasn't sure he wanted to give him the majority swing in the Supreme Court. The Senate opposition to Runyon's Sixth Circuit appointment was not real and would go away when the time came to vote. Ron suspected it had been quietly arranged by Fritz Gimbel, probably at the President's suggestion, to make it easier to pass over Judge Runyon when a Supreme Court seat did become vacant.

It was only after lunch that Friederich led the conversation back to Ron's murder investigation . . . "What you call a consortium is real, I'm sure. I'm sure it exists, and I'm sure Blaine was involved in it some way. Indeed, he may have been its victim. But it seems to me you're losing something. I think perhaps you've misplaced your emphasis—"

"How?"

"What in your judgment, Ron, is the most significant single fact about the murder of Blaine?"

Ron smiled. The judge was reverting to his favorite conversational technique—the Socratic dialogue. "What's the most significant fact in *your* judgment, sir?"

Friederich shrugged. "That Blaine was murdered inside the White House."

"I can't disagree with that—"

"So the killer must have been—"

"A White House insider," Ron said, finishing the sentence as he knew the Justice expected him to do.

"So?"

"So whoever did it covered it very well. I can't clearly identify a suspect—except Fritz Gimbel, and my suspicion of him may be only a prejudice on my part. To find a suspect, to build a case against a suspect, I need a motive. It's primer stuff, but only when I know *why* Blaine was killed will I be able to get close to *who* killed him—"

"And your motive lies in the so-called consortium and in Blaine's corruption—"

"I haven't found any other."

"All right, let's assume that . . . but he was killed *inside the White House.* You need the link between the consortium outside and the killer inside."

Ron nodded, half-smiled. "The good old missing link. The anthropologists haven't found it after years of hunting. I hope to God I have better luck . . . "

TWO

I

But he thought he might know the link. No doubt it was impetuous to rush into a confrontation, he should telephone his office, tell Jill or Gabe where he was going and why. But for the first time in this investigation he let himself be moved by an instinct, a *feeling* that maybe he was about to break the case . . . He didn't want anyone to tell him to wait, to consider alternatives. Maybe he could provoke a break . . .

He took a cab. He did not stop to telephone. He overtipped the driver instead of waiting for change. He poked impatiently at the doorbell, making successive, demanding rings.

When Martha Kingsley opened the door she was already irritated. "Well! Mr. Investigator. Why didn't you just smash the door in?"

"May I come in?"

"Do I have a choice?" She was standing in the doorway, leaning on the doorframe, wearing cut-off blue jeans, complete with frayed edges, and a white T-shirt. She was barefoot, as she'd been the first time he saw her. Reluctantly she now stepped out of the doorway and with a toss of her head indicated he could follow her into the apartment.

Her packing appeared to be finished. Boxes were stacked high all around the rooms, labeled so that he could see some were going into storage, some to Paris. She had been eating off of two stacked cartons. Now she gathered the scattered newspapers and magazines off her couch to make a place for him to sit.

"When are you leaving?"

"Thursday, two days."

"Then you have two days to tell me what you didn't tell me Saturday morning."

She sat at the far end of the short, pale-yellow couch, facing him. "Since Saturday morning I've been questioned once by you and twice by the FBI. It's getting more than a little tiresome—"

"It stops when I find out what I want to know."

"Frankly, you're something of an amateur . . . these characters from the Bureau were much tougher than you, and they asked better questions. In any case, I told them everything I'm going to tell. You're wasting my time, and yours."

"Where's your husband?"

"He'll be here tomorrow, we're flying to Paris together—"

"Whether you are or not depends on how much you cooperate—"

"Bull." She got up from the couch, her face flushed. "I really think it's past time. Now please leave."

Ron shook his head.

She drew a deep breath. "Look, I read the papers too . . . you talk a big deal, you can do this and that. The *fact* is, you're falling on your face. My God, you got drunk and damn near killed the President's daughter. That was Saturday night, wasn't it? The day before you were here. You're about to get a vote of no-confidence on the Hill—"

"Mrs. Kingsley, it's no big deal to stop you going to Paris. Your husband is not qualified for his assignment and was given it only as a personal favor to Blaine. That's on record in his file at the Navy. The Secretary of the Navy is already nervous about it. A call from me . . . all I'd have to do is suggest the assignment be rescinded . . . "

She turned her back to him, walked between two stacks of

boxes to a window, then leaned wearily against the window frame. "Do your damndest," she said. "I don't *have* to go to Paris."

"My damndest is a little more than that, Mrs. Kingsley. I can get a warrant and have you held in jail as a material witness."

She turned to face him, her back still touching the window frame. He could see her only between the stacks of boxes, which made a curious optical illusion that she was farther from him than she was. She was staring at him, debating with herself, and he recalled what Paul-Victor Chamillart had said about her . . . She *was* beautiful, no question about it. Conventional wisdom had it that an admitted prostitute should look coarse, at least worn, used. She didn't. She looked younger than her years. She looked ingenuous and vulnerable—which she wasn't.

"We've been arguing," she said quietly, "about whether or not I will answer your questions. So far you haven't even asked one."

All right, so he'd won. At least for the moment. "As far as I am concerned," he said, "you can go to Paris. I probably won't even need you as a witness. But I think you know some of the things I need to know."

She sighed, came between the boxes and sat down again on the couch. "Just what do you think I know?" she asked wearily.

"What did Blaine tell you about the President?"

She frowned. "What do you mean? Half his talk was about the President."

"What did he say about his relationship with the President—his special, personal relationship?"

"Well, he always said he had a unique personal relationship with the President based on years of friendship. He said he was closer to the President than Gimbel was—"

"Was he jealous of Gimbel?"

She shrugged. "He didn't like Gimbel."

"What did he tell you about the President's wife?"

She shook her head. "Nothing, nothing much . . . she was his friend too." She kept a straight face.

"Look . . . I *know* Blaine told you more than that about Catherine Webster—"

"What do you want me to say, that he told me he had an affair with her? Well, I can't tell you that. He didn't say that."

"But . . . ?"

"What do you want? He told me she sometimes used to drink too much . . . she was restless . . . with being the wife of a corporation president, with being the wife of a senator . . . she'd been a professor herself . . . a professional woman, just like me . . . " She said that with a straight face too.

Ron let it go. Then . . . "I guess I'd better explain something" —she was evading him, being cute, he'd try a small bluff—"after I was here Saturday morning and we had our little chat you called the White House and reported to someone. You told him I was here, and you told him what I asked you."

"You're crazy," she said, but there was a sharp edge in her voice. A defensive edge?

"From time to time over the last couple of years," he said, encouraged, "people have planted bits of misinformation with you, to see if they would show up at the White House. They always have. Some people aren't as stupid as you think."

She was clearly frightened now.

He pressed. "So please no more games, Mrs. Kingsley. You don't, for example, know how much I already know."

She said nothing, then sighed, shook her head.

"Now—please tell me what he told you about Catherine Webster."

"I swear to you, he never told me he had an affair with Catherine Webster—"

"What about Lynne?" He hated the question, and himself at the moment.

"No."

"You told me Blaine confided in you. Well, let's try this another way. *What* did he confide in you?"

She pressed her lips together hard. "Let's have a drink, Mr. Fairbanks. Scotch okay?"

He said it was and went with her to the kitchen, where everything was packed now but some paper cups and paper plates. Two half-empty bottles stood on the counter: one gin, one Scotch. She poured Scotch over two rocks for him, gin over rocks for herself. They went back to the couch in the livingroom.

"You said I don't have to be a witness . . . "

"I doubt your testimony would carry much weight no matter what you said," he told her bluntly.

"Thanks." She lifted her cup and swallowed her bitterness with the gin. "All right, I know how he got the money all the papers are asking about. People gave it to him, people paid him . . . he did favors and got paid for them. He also said the same thing you just did, now that I think of it—that my testimony couldn't hurt him, and he could afford to tell me anything. He was a peculiarly cynical man. I don't think he had a conscience . . . if he did, he'd long since anesthetized it, or at least seemed to have."

"Who gave him money, Mrs. Kingsley?"

She shrugged. "More than one. When General Ortiz was killed in Santo Domingo our government gave his nephew political asylum. That nephew was no student. Ortiz's money came out of Santo Domingo through that nephew by arrangements he'd made in Miami and Las Vegas. They brought ten million dollars into the United States, most of it in dollars. Blaine was paid twenty thousand for his help—"

"What did he do, exactly?"

"He didn't say, *exactly.* It had to do with entry permits, visas. It had to do with Santo Domingan embassy people and their diplomatic immunity. It was complicated."

"Go on."

She shook her head. "What else do you want to know?"

"I'm going to run some names by you," Ron said. "I want to know what Blaine said about each of them."

She shrugged. "Fire away."

"Philippe Grand."

She shook her head. "He never mentioned that name."

"Inoguchi Osanaga."

She shook her head again. "Never mentioned Osanaga either."

"Do you know him?"

"Sure. Osanaga is a bag man. He's the payoff man when Japanese companies buy anything over here."

"Jeremy Johnson."

She smiled. "Blaine and Osanaga were in one league. Johnson is in another one entirely."

"Senator Walter Finlay."

She smiled again. "Finlay plays Osanaga's game, but he belongs in Jeremy Johnson's league."

"All right. What game were Blaine and Osanaga playing?"

"The big one," she said. "To kill the trade agreements. Blaine promised he could kill them. If you want my theory about his death, he was killed because he couldn't stop Webster from going to Paris and signing those preliminary agreements . . . aren't you impressed? Lan taught me a lot about his work, I could probably be an undersecretary . . . " This time she allowed herself a smile. "He'd taken a lot of money. Some very important—and tough—people had put their confidence in him."

"Who, besides Osanaga and Johnson?"

"Schleicher of Nord Deutschland . . . Fantalone of IIG. There were others whose names I don't know."

"But he was killed in the White House. Who inside the White House?"

She shook her head, hard. "I wouldn't know, I haven't a clue."

Nor, Ron thought, did he . . . He stared into his Scotch. "I guess I asked you this before," he said blandly, "but when did you last see Blaine?"

"You did and I told you . . . two or three weeks before his death. The FBI got me to be more specific . . . it was two weeks before his death. I spent the night with him in his apartment. I never saw him after that."

"Did you and Blaine have a falling-out of some sort?"

"No."

"But you never saw him after that night?"

"It wasn't unusual for me not to see him for two weeks or more."

Ron decided to try another bluff, a very small one. "Did he tell you about his . . . emotional scene with the President?"

"Yes, that's why he wanted me that night. He was upset, very upset."

It had worked. If she had said Blaine had not told her about his scene with the President, he couldn't have contradicted her . . . "He came to you the day he'd had the scene with the President. Right?"

"Well . . . he called me from the White House. His voice was breaking. I couldn't tell if he was angry or what. He asked me to go to his apartment. I had a key. He came home about ten o'clock. I was waiting for him."

"Was this the kind of appointment he paid for?"

Her face went tight. "Yes. He paid me five hundred dollars, for the night . . . Would you like to hear the details? Is that a part of the investigation?"

"No, but I want the details of what he said."

She sipped at her gin, and as she did Ron thought he could almost read her thought . . . maybe she should stop now, refuse to say any more . . . If she had a few minutes to think she would probably realize he didn't know much, really, and she could lie to him with impunity . . . he couldn't risk letting her have time to think—

"I was in his apartment waiting for him," she was saying now quietly. "I had some champagne on ice. He unlocked the door and stalked into the apartment. He said he was out, an ex-Secretary of State. It turned out, of course, that that was an exaggeration, but he said he had to resign. He said he'd lost his temper and had said something to the President. I sort of laughed. I thought maybe he'd called him a son of a bitch or something like that, but he said it was worse than that and wasn't at all funny. He kept prowling around the room, muttering to himself. I tried to calm him down. I got him to take some champagne. He hadn't eaten so I made him some sandwiches. I . . . I did something for him . . . you understand. It calmed him down. But then he was depressed, said he was in deep trouble—"

"What kind of trouble?"

"He said he'd lost the President's friendship, that he really did have to resign. He said he didn't know what he would do, he couldn't go back to a university campus after he'd been Secretary of State—"

"Did he describe the scene with the President? Did he tell you *what* he'd said that had cost him the President's friendship?"

"Not then, he didn't . . . later."

"Go on."

She looked hard at Ron, appraising him. "I encouraged him to tell me," she said. "Do you understand why?"

"Someone would pay you for the story."

"Well, put it this way . . . I thought I might find out something that could be . . . valuable." Her expression didn't change. "He told me everything later, after we were in bed—"

"What?"

"A lot of it you already know. The multi-lateral trade agreements, he was supposed to change the President's mind. He apparently had told people he could do it, and he believed he could—"

"But he couldn't," said Ron.

"I said he *believed* he could . . . after all, he said, he'd taught the President everything he knew about foreign policy and international economics. It was well understood in informed circles, he said, that President Webster's foreign policy was really *his* foreign policy. He'd established an outstanding record in his three years as Secretary of State . . . he was very high on that, he talked about it a lot."

Blaine was, Ron reminded himself, indeed a highly successful Secretary of State. He no doubt would have had his Nobel Prize . . .

"He thought he could turn the President around," she was saying. "After all, *he* was the expert on international affairs, and if he told the President he had changed his mind, had decided the trade agreements weren't a good idea after all, he thought Webster would go along . . . He'd been really shocked to find the President so stubborn on the subject, shocked that he had such strong convictions in this area . . . "

"Was he being threatened by the people who paid him?"

"He never said he was."

"Go ahead . . . what happened?"

"That evening, early that evening just before he called me, he'd had a real bitter fight with Webster. It had broken down into name-calling, he told the President the multi-lateral trade agreements were going to produce economic catastrophe. The President asked him why he hadn't said that at the beginning, three years earlier when the policy was being developed and the first steps taken toward negotiating the agreements. Lan said—"

"What did Blaine *really* think about the agreements? Was he for them or against them, personally?"

"You know, I don't think he really cared all that much . . . trade and economics, he said, had never really grabbed him the way diplomatic wheeling and dealing did. Anyway, when the President asked him why he had changed his mind and suddenly become such an opponent of the agreements, Lan didn't have a good answer. He said something like he'd studied the thing more thoroughly than he had at first. The President laughed, said that wasn't the reason. That's when things began to heat up."

"Were they alone?"

"Oh, no, I should have told you. Mrs. Webster was there. Catherine . . . this exchange was upstairs, not in the office."

"What did she say?"

"Nothing until later. I'm coming to that. When the President said he didn't buy Lan's reason for changing his mind, Lan got sore, asked what the President was suggesting and the President told him flat out he had reason to believe Lan was accepting money and favors and such from people against the agreements. He challenged him to deny it, Lan said he wouldn't dignify an accusation like that by denying it . . . This was when Mrs. Webster spoke up. She told Lan she couldn't believe he would betray them like this. He said she had tears in her eyes when she said it, and I can tell you, cynic or not, he had some in his when he told me all this . . . "

"They'd been friends for a long time," Ron said quietly.

"Yes . . . well, the President used the same kind of words his wife had used. He said Lan had betrayed them, betrayed their friendship. He called him a cheat and a liar. If you knew Lansard Blaine, you'd know something was about to blow at that point . . . He had a very strong sense of his personal dignity, and being faced with the truth made the humiliation even worse. So he struck back—"

"What did he say to them?"

"He told the Websters *they* were fine people to call him a liar when they'd been living with a lie for more than twenty years. He said they'd been glad enough for him to lie when *he* had lied for *them.* If they wanted to call him a liar, then he would return the favor . . . if they wanted to disgrace him and drive him out of office, fine—he could do the same to them and they damn well knew it . . . if they wanted to destroy him and bankrupt him by telling the whole world that he had no influence on the foreign policy of the United States, fine—but he had some weapons to protect himself with and he would use them . . . You understand I'm trying to give you the best idea I can about what happened from what he said. That's all I know—"

"Except you've left out the most important thing—"

She nodded. "What it was that Lan knew about the Websters, *their* lie, *their* secret. Well . . . sorry, Mr. Fairbanks, Lan didn't tell me."

"I don't believe you."

Once again she got up from the couch and walked between the stacks of boxes to stand at the window and stare out at nothing. "Whatever he said to me, he said it while he and I were in bed. If I say he didn't tell me, he didn't tell me. And you can't prove he did."

Ron sighed. "God, do we have to go through this again? I don't like to threaten you—"

"Then don't." She turned around and faced him. "Don't tell me you're going to put me in jail as a witness. Anyway, it just occurred to me that you're not going to."

"Really? Why not?"

She took a step toward him. "Lan was on the ragged edge when he came home that night," she said. "I sympathized, rubbed his back, held him . . . And he talked. And talked. And talked. He told me the Websters' secret. It's a personal thing. It has nothing whatsoever to do with your investigation. It's really sad, I feel sorry for the Websters. And so did Lan. In fact, that was what bothered him most: that he'd threatened to tell their secret, something so personal that would hurt them so much if it got out. But he did tell me—the scarlet woman in the case. Can you beat it? Just like in the movies. Anyway, now I figure he wouldn't mind if I used it to protect myself. If I go to jail . . . in fact if I don't go to Paris day after tomorrow, I'm going to let out the secret of President and Mrs. Webster. I *promise* you."

"All right," Ron said. He was furious, but managed to control himself. "Let's drop it for now. One more question . . . and I'm going to have an answer to this one. So save your threats . . . Who's your White House phone pal? Who did you call after I left here Saturday morning? I know it has to be one of three people."

She was smiling. "I do have a friend at the White House," she said, "and he's a perfect gentleman."

"*Who?*"

"I guess I can tell you. What's the difference?" She nodded. "He's a damn sight bigger man than you—"

"*Who,* damn you . . . ?"

"Fritz Gimbel."

II

Martha Kingsley—Deep Throat. Gimbel . . . her contact was Gimbel. She had called Gimbel to report what Paul-Victor Chamillart had told her about the French foreign minister and Martine Nanterre. God knew what else she had learned and reported over the years from all the men she'd gotten to confide in her or who had done it on their own. Gimbel, the cold, deadly and so loyally efficient administrator, had a private intelligence operation in a call girl's bed. She had called Gimbel as soon as she'd left Blaine's Watergate apartment. She had called Gimbel the previous Saturday to report that Ron had questioned her. She would likely call him now. She was on the telephone at this very moment, almost certainly, while he was cabbing back to the White House, and by the time he got there Gimbel would know every detail of their conversation.

Gimbel. It had been his instinct from the beginning to suspect Gimbel. Gimbel could go where he wanted in the White House. No one would question him any more than they would question the President. He knew how to kill with a loop of wire . . . he had learned it in the marines. He was the President's man. Everyone took orders from him. He could have called off the Secret Service detail the previous Saturday night, making it possible for the van to run Ron's Datsun off the road. He could have planted the story that Ron was drunk. He could have planted all the stories about Blaine's women too . . . he knew about them . . .

But his motive, why would he kill Blaine . . . Was *he* the

executioner for the disgruntled consortium? Not likely. But the alternative was nearly unthinkable . . . that he had killed a blackmailer to keep him quiet . . . and if he'd done that, then who was he protecting . . . ? The President? Catherine Webster? Did the President *know?* Not necessarily . . . But Blaine was murdered in the White House. Wouldn't it have been smarter to get him outside? Maybe not, if Gimbel—working, say, *with* the President's knowledge—had to do it alone, without involving anyone else . . . and it was decided that doing it on the President's very doorstep, literally, was the surest way of diverting suspicion from him, from anyone in his official family . . .

It would be a long summer evening. A red sun was still high above the Potomac when the cab stopped at the Executive Office Gate and Ron checked into the Executive Office Wing. As he walked toward his office he wondered if the gate guard was on the telephone advising Fritz Gimbel that Ron Fairbanks was back. . . .

Both Jill and Gabe Haddad were in his office waiting for him. They had called the Supreme Court, knew he had left there and had become anxious about him, not knowing where he was. He called the switchboard—immediately, after no more than a quick word of greeting to Jill and Gabe—and learned that Honey Taylor was still in the White House. He spoke to her and told her he had to speak to the President. She said she would be calling upstairs in a few minutes to give the President several messages and she would give him this one.

He turned to Jill and Gabe, told them what he had learned and what conclusions he drew from it. Jill did not agree that the murderer was, inevitably, Gimbel . . . "Anyway," she said, "I've warned you already—it would be a bad error to accuse that man unless you have overpowering evidence. He's tough, he has the President's confidence, in a showdown between you and him you'd come off second, face it . . . You can't bring down the President's hatchet man on the word of a Martha Kingsley . . . "

Gabe spoke cautiously. "Ron, I can see how Martha Kingsley is a link between Blaine and Gimbel . . . she slept with Blaine, reported everything he said to Gimbel. But where's the connection between Gimbel and what we've been calling the consortium to defeat the multi-lateral trade agreements? Or have we given up the idea that the consortium is somehow behind the murder?"

"Martha Kingsley links Gimbel to the consortium too," Ron said. "The connection is Osanaga. He fronts as a Japanese journalist. You and I didn't know he was really something else. The FBI didn't know either. It was the CIA that had the file on Osanaga and told us he's actually a lobbyist, an influence buyer. *But Martha Kingsley knew.* When I mentioned Osanaga to her, she called him the bag man for certain Japanese companies. And remember, when I had the FBI bring Osanaga to the Justice Department office for questioning Senator Finlay was on the phone to me almost before we got Osanaga in there—telling me to take it easy on his good buddy Osanaga. The FBI file on Martha Kingsley lists Finlay among her intimate friends. She knew Blaine took money from the consortium and promised them he could kill the trade agreements. If she knew, Gimbel knew. If Gimbel knew Blaine took a bribe from the consortium and Gimbel still didn't blow the whistle on Blaine, then—"

"Not necessarily," Jill interrupted. "The fact that he didn't blow the whistle doesn't prove he too was bribing Blaine."

"We don't even know that he didn't blow the whistle," Ron said. "A private whistle—"

"Yes, strictly private to the President . . . "

Ron nodded. "So when the President accused Blaine of dishonesty and provoked the blowup between them, maybe he wasn't guessing, maybe he *knew.*"

"And then," Gabe said, "Blaine threatened to reveal the Websters' big secret . . . It comes back to that . . . was Blaine killed to protect that secret? Maybe the consortium's scheme to defeat the trade agreements was only the spark that led to the very personal motive for killing Blaine."

Ron was spinning the dial of the combination lock on his file cabinet. "Suddenly some really damned unpleasant thoughts come to mind."

"You're not exactly alone in them," Jill said.

Ron tugged on one of the heavy drawers of the cabinet, which finally slid forward. "Forgive me, Jill . . . Gabe, tomorrow you may decide to certify me . . . " He pulled from under some hanging file folders a .25 caliber Browning automatic. He showed it to them for a moment, then pushed it uneasily, like a dangerous live thing, into the waistband of his trousers on his left hip. He buttoned his jacket over it. He looked at them. "You guys figure I'm nuts?"

"An hour ago I'd have said yes," Jill told him. "Now . . . "

Ron sat down behind his desk. "Martha Kingsley talked too much. Your intrepid leader got her off balance by convincing her he knew a damn sight more than he did. It played pretty well, if I do say so myself. But she also talked too quickly. I thought about it on the way back in the cab. Why would she open up and tell so much, so easily? Well . . . she knew she would call Gimbel and report everything that was said. Maybe she decided she could throw out any information she wanted to because—"

"No," Gabe said firmly. "It's too much, I can't believe it—"

"They ran Ron's car off the road Saturday night," Jill said. "What he knows now is a whole lot more dangerous to them than what he knew Saturday—"

Gabe shook his head. "I'm sorry, but I can't help think we're getting a bit melodramatic. There has to be some other explanation, some logical explanation—"

"We're too civilized, is what we are," Jill said. "Here we sit—three smart lawyers who don't think in terms of doing violence on people, who look always for the rational solution. But let's not lose sight of a basic, Gabe—we're investigating a murder—"

"I'll tell you what I want to—" Ron began, and was interrupted by a buzz on his telephone.

The President. He had gotten Ron's message and was asking if it was really necessary for Ron to see him this evening. Ron said it was and that he thought Mrs. Webster should be on hand too. To convince, he told the President he thought he had a good idea who had killed Blaine. The President promptly said he would see him in half an hour and hung up.

"I think you're being a little premature, Ron," Jill said. "Are you really going to meet the Websters and accuse their long-time friend Gimbel of murder?"

"Or are you going to accuse the President himself?" Gabe put in.

"I don't know," Ron said. "I'm going to put what I know in front of them. Maybe then they'll tell me what they've obviously held back."

"Eight to five that when you come back down here tonight you'll be an ex-chief investigator," Gabe said. "And probably an ex-counsel."

"I didn't ask for the job."

"Are you going to tote that pistol upstairs in the White House?" Jill asked.

Ron looked sheepish but didn't say otherwise. "Something else, you two, I want you to take some record of what we've found and think out of the White House. At the least, take a dictaphone tape. I'm going to make a tape now. I'll make two. Be sure you get them out of here. Take some of the files. Go separately—"

"Ron—" Jill began to protest.

"Maybe I'm crazy," Ron said sharply. "I know that. But do what I ask anyway. *Now,* please."

The President kept a small private office in a room across the hall from his bedroom—a small room other First Families had used as a guest room. It was furnished with a desk that had once been in the Oval Office—Ron forgot which President had used it there—and President Webster's high-back leather chair from the Senate. There were two overstuffed armchairs and a couch, all upholstered in a nubby, cream-white material. There were few books on the bookshelves; most of the space was taken up by family photographs, including pictures of the President's parents and grandparents. It was the President's private untidy office . . . stacks of file folders and briefing books covered the desk. With the elaborate telephone on the desk he could pick up any of twenty lines, and by pressing a button could dial any of forty numbers held in the instrument's electronic memory.

Ron had often met with the President in this office, had sometimes found him here in faded blue jeans and a cashmere sweater, once in white tennis shorts. The office was never photographed. Outsiders never were allowed here. Ron had often seen Gimbel here and occasionally Blaine. Members of the President's personal staff were brought here from time to time, but except for Blaine no cabinet member ever came here and no member of Congress had ever seen this office.

The light in the room was dull gray when Ron came in. The sun in the west did not shine on this room's one window, and the President and Catherine Webster were sitting in the gloom talking quietly when Ron arrived. It was Catherine who got up and switched on the lamp on the President's desk, and the light shining through the top of the lampshade fell on a painting Ron had always wondered about—uncharacteristic of this President, he would have supposed, and out of place among the other furnishings of the room: a nude of a young girl, by Edvard Munch. Ron had never had the nerve to ask if the painting was on loan or owned by the Websters. It symbolized for him a contradiction in this President's character.

There had apparently been an early dinner, probably with guests since the President was still dressed in a dark gray suit, white shirt, and tie, and Catherine wore a dark blue knit blouse and a full white, green and blue skirt. Both of them, in Ron's experience, were likely to be more casually dressed in the middle hours of a summer evening.

The President opened with, "You say you think you know who killed Blaine?"

"I can't prove it," Ron said, "but everything I know so far seems to point to one man."

The President sat down on the couch beside Catherine, pointed to one of the armchairs for Ron. "Go ahead."

"Before I tell you what, who, I suspect, let me tell you why I suspect it. Otherwise it's *very* hard to believe."

The President nodded.

Ron glanced apprehensively at Catherine, then back to the President. "I've tried to stay away from it as much as possible, Mr. President, but every way I turn I keep coming back to that . . . confrontation between you and Blaine when he, as I understand it, threatened to reveal some personal secret of yours . . . I've of course accepted your word that that could have nothing to do with Blaine's death, but still, it keeps coming up—"

"Blaine wasn't killed on account of that," Webster said flatly.

He scowled and looked away from Ron. "If he had, I'm the one who would have killed him—"

Catherine broke in. "How does it keep coming up, Ron?" She glanced at the President, apparently annoyed by his obvious impatience. "Who brings it up?"

Ron was watching the President, who was still staring angrily at the wall.

The President, apparently sensing that Ron was hesitating, glanced around. "Go *on,*" he said.

Ron took a deep breath. "Blaine was killed in the White House. Here, and by someone who had access to the second floor. We also know that Blaine had been bribed by several people over the years, mostly over things of no great importance. But lately he'd taken a good deal of money, more than ever before, and he'd promised the people who paid him that he could kill the multilateral trade agreements. Failing that, he'd promised, he at least could get exemptions from the restrictions for the people who were paying him . . . exemptions for Japanese cars, for example. So—"

"So he was killed by some greedy murderous people who were paying him," the President interrupted. "That has *nothing* to do with our personal lives—"

"I'm sorry, sir, but there's sort of a link."

"Let Ron talk, Bob," Catherine put in.

"We've called the group of people involved in bribing Blaine a consortium," Ron said. "He took their money and couldn't deliver. But I'm not so sure they would kill him for that. It would, they might figure, be against their interests to kill the only prominent member of this Administration who was opposed to the agreements. Of course, they might have been afraid Blaine would crack under pressure from you and compromise them—which would mean disgrace and perhaps jail sentences here or at home

. . . Anyway, if they were behind it they still had to do it through someone inside the White House. Blaine wasn't killed by a Japanese influence buyer or a British gambler. He was killed by someone with free access to the second floor of the White House."

"Yes . . . ?"

"There's a link," Ron said quietly. "One person who links the consortium to the White House insider. A woman. Blaine was involved with her too."

"Another one of Lan's women," Catherine said glumly.

"Her name is Martha Kingsley. She calls herself a prostitute, but I'd use another word . . . she's a courtesan in the old sense. She is *very* knowledgeable. She knows her way around Washington. She knows, in fact, too much, things I've had to work very hard to find out. The FBI links her to Senator Walter Finlay. Finlay is a hired hand of the consortium—"

"No surprise there," said the President.

"One of her . . . clients was Lansard Blaine. I realize Blaine was an intelligent man, brilliant, with some marks of greatness. But it means he had a side he didn't control too well . . . he could drink too much, sometimes talked too much to Martha Kingsley. Unfortunately for him, confidences were . . . are her stock in trade. She sells the information she gets . . . she was selling it regularly to someone here, in the White House . . . "

"And you know who?" Catherine said.

"In a moment . . . Blaine told her about the favors, bribes, he was taking. She reported that to her contact here at the White House. Her contact has known for months that Blaine was being paid to scotch the trade agreements. I have to ask you a question, Mr. President. Did anyone ever report to you that Blaine was being paid to argue you out of the trade-agreement program?"

"I suspected it—"

"But did anyone *tell* you?"

The President shook his head.

"On the night when you had the blowup with Blaine, he was very upset. He went to Martha Kingsley for consolation, spent the night with her. And he told her—I'm sorry to tell you this—what he had threatened you with. She knows your secret . . . "

The President reached quickly for Catherine's hand, shook his head and looked closely at her. She lowered her head for a moment, then drew a deep breath and looked up at him.

Ron watched them for a moment, then turned away. His impulse was to leave the room, to give them their privacy; but to get up now and leave would be awkward and perhaps hurtful. He heard them speaking very quietly and was glad he couldn't make out what they said. He tried to be absolutely still, wished he could make himself invisible.

Finally, after a minute or so, the President told him to go on. "But tell us who it is. No more prologues."

"Mr. President," Ron said quietly, "Mrs. Webster, after every conversation with Blaine, Martha Kingsley called the White House and reported to Fritz Gimbel—"

"Fritz . . . yes, you suspect Fritz . . . you have from the beginning—did from the beginning."

Ron was determined not to be intimidated. "If you can tell me, Mr. President," he said, "that Gimbel reported to *you* what Martha Kingsley reported to him, then my suspicions become a lot less valid."

The President looked hard at him.

"Bob . . . " Catherine whispered.

The President shook his head . . . "It doesn't prove . . . Fritz wouldn't necessarily report something to me he'd been told by a prostitute . . . anyway, how do you know she told him anything? Who says she did?"

"She does—"

"So we're to accept her word? Suppose I call him in here and he denies it?"

"I would appreciate it if you wouldn't, sir. Not yet . . . Mr. President, it's my job to report to you what the evidence indicates. I admitted I couldn't *prove* my case . . . yet."

"You've talked to this woman?" Catherine Webster asked.

"Yes, twice. Saturday morning and this afternoon. After the first meeting she called Gimbel and reported what I'd asked her—"

"According to *her,*" the President said.

Ron nodded. "According to her."

Catherine said, "Are you sure Lan told her . . . ?"

"She told me he did."

"But she didn't tell you what?"

"No."

Catherine reached for her husband's hand, then looked at Ron. "Do you feel you must know the story to finish the investigation?"

"I'm not sure. There are other reasons for suspecting Gimbel. I think he arranged my automobile accident Saturday night, but I'm not certain why. Is he in the pay of the consortium too? Even if he is, why would they kill Blaine in the White House? Why not at his home or somewhere else? So what other motive? Maybe—to be entirely frank—to protect your secret. It all keeps coming back to that . . . Gimbel is one of the very few who knows Blaine threatened you. Even the Attorney General, who knows Blaine threatened you, doesn't know what he threatened to tell. Is it something important enough, damaging enough, Mrs. Webster, for Gimbel to have killed Blaine to prevent him telling . . . ?"

"We are *not* going to tell you," the President said bluntly. "If we have to deal with this woman—pay her, or whatever—we will do that. But I tell you it has nothing to do with the murder of

Lansard Blaine. And Fritz did not kill Blaine. I just don't believe it."

Catherine shook her head while the President was talking. "I think you're making a mistake, Bob."

Ignoring her, he said to Ron, "Blaine made his threat in a burst of temper. I admit I took it seriously at the time but . . . I *told* you this . . . he came to us and apologized and said of course he wouldn't reveal a personal matter. He said he was deeply ashamed even to have mentioned the notion . . . He promised to keep our confidence, just as he had for more than twenty years. We felt we could trust him to keep it in the future, in spite of his momentary tantrum. He offered me his resignation then, and I accepted it. He asked for time, I gave it. The incident was closed. And Fritz heard it all. If Fritz ever thought of killing Blaine to keep him from telling our secret, that motive evaporated." The President shook his head. "No. It's your damn *consortium* that killed Blaine. And you haven't linked Fritz to that."

"Martha Kingsley links him to it," Ron said.

The President was about to say something in rebuttal when the telephone buzzed. He went to his desk and picked it up . . . "I'll have him call you," he said after listening for a moment. "As soon as he can." He turned to Ron. "Your office. But let's finish this. As I hope I've made clear, I'm not ready to accept your accusation of Fritz—you don't really have very much to back it up, and it doesn't make any sense to me . . ."

"I'm sorry, sir, but the investigation still seems to focus on him—"

"We're about to lose control of the *investigation,*" the President said impatiently. "It's ready to break out in all directions—"

"Do you want my resignation?"

The President shook his head. "You have an impossible job, Ron. I knew it might be, and so did you . . . God, I guess it *might* be Fritz. To be honest, we've thought of it too . . . and if Fritz did have anything to do with it it will bring down the Administration. Blaine . . . then Fritz . . . everything we've worked for . . . Find me somebody else, Ron. God, let it be somebody else . . . "

Ron, stunned by this naked show of emotion by a President admitting his vulnerability, asking for help, putting himself and his presidency in his hands, Ron tried to get out something reassuring, and was abruptly stopped by the President's next words.

"If Fritz did it, we can't protect him, no matter his good motive . . . we can't cover it up . . . " And then, as if grasping at straws, the President said very quietly, "But you said you didn't have evidence, only a strong suspicion—"

"Ron," Catherine broke in, "why don't you check in with your office? The call may have been important . . . "

The President sat on the couch, hunched forward with his folded arms resting on his knees while Ron went to his desk and picked up the telephone. Catherine caressed the President's back.

Ron called the switchboard. The operator said the call was from the FBI agent Walter Locke, and she would connect him. He was at FBI headquarters.

"Mr. Fairbanks? I'm sorry to interrupt. They said you were with the President, but I think you ought to know what's happened."

"It's all right, go ahead."

"We have standing orders with the metropolitan police. They have a list of people. They're to notify us immediately if anything happens involving any of those people. We had a call about an hour ago. One of the people on that list is Martha Kingsley. The woman is dead, Mr. Fairbanks. She's been murdered."

IV

The President's face was an alarming, unnatural high pink. His voice was unsteady. "It hasn't anything to do with . . . "—he glanced at Catherine—"I mean, a woman like that . . . plenty of people could have had reason . . . "

Ron, still standing beside the desk, rested his hand on the telephone he had just returned to its cradle. If the President's face were conspicuously red, he imagined his own was white. Catherine Webster had covered her face with her hands. Was she crying? He couldn't tell.

Ron spoke first. "The police think she might have been raped. Locke went to the apartment and saw the body before it was taken away. She'd been beaten and strangled, and she was naked. It could have been a rape-killing . . . might have nothing to do with this at all."

"Coincidence . . . " the President said weakly.

"It could be . . . "

Catherine looked up. "Both of you know better."

"Even if it was a complete stranger," the President said, "her life, and the people in it, will become news . . . including her customers . . . and maybe that she and Fritz were . . . friends. Complete security with someone like her would be near-impossible . . . *someone* else must know about the contacts between Fritz and her . . . "

"Except for ourselves," Catherine said woodenly, "no one has known about our personal matter except Lan, and Fritz, and then, apparently, this young woman. Lan is dead, and now she's dead—"

"What are you suggesting?" the President said, knowing only too well what it was, and not wanting to face it.

"It's another of Ron's links, Bob. What did the two have in common? Not much, except that both of them knew our secret—"

"And Gimbel knew they knew it," Ron finished for her.

"Doesn't *prove* anything," the President muttered.

"Coincidence again?" asked Catherine.

The President looked thoughtfully at Catherine. "You never liked Fritz." He said it with regret in his voice.

"That's right, Bob . . . I admit it, I just don't trust men who can be so *devoted* . . . "

"Assuming I even understand you, who *should* I have trusted? Lan Blaine?"

"Right now you had better trust Ron . . . and, Bob, if you won't tell him the whole story, I will—"

"I said before it isn't necessary, has nothing to do with—"

"Bob . . . someone is going around killing the people who know. It *might* be a coincidence but it's irrational to persist in thinking so. Ron is entitled to know. You made him investigator and put him in an impossible position. He has something at stake too. You have to trust him. Besides, please remember that Lynne cares for him, he may even be a member of the family someday . . . "

The President looked up at Ron, who still stood by the desk with his hand still on the telephone. The President inclined his head toward the chair where Ron had been sitting before. Ron sat down. The President rubbed his mouth with a fist.

"Ron . . . I'm afraid Catherine is right. You have to know."

"Perhaps I should tell him?"

Robert Webster shook his head . . . "I called Blaine a liar, told him I couldn't trust him, that he'd lost his integrity. Which not surprisingly made him furious. He all but screamed at me. 'I'll tell the world what integrity means to Bob Webster,' he said. 'I'll tell the world what it means to Catherine Webster.' He said he *would* tell, unless I accepted some exemptions from the trade agreements. He said—and it was pretty chilling, I can tell you, to hear him—that he would tell what he knew about Catherine and me . . . Ron, I *could* have killed him, and for sure I can't honestly tell you I'm sorry he's dead . . . " It was apparent he had to struggle to speak. He was still flushed, shook his head and took a deep breath.

"Bob . . . " Catherine said, "*I* can tell it, it's *my* story anyway—"

The President shrugged miserably.

Catherine turned on the couch to face Ron. The President was between them, and she leaned forward a little, to see past him to speak directly to Ron. She put her hand on the President's hand . . . "We lived, as you know, in Ann Arbor. Bob's business was in Detroit, and I taught at the University of Michigan. This was twenty-two years ago . . . twenty-*three.* I was—what?—thirty-one? The boys were home. Bob was building his business, we certainly had no thought of ever going into politics. We had a comfortable little circle. Lan was on the faculty. I met him there. He was, I suppose, more my kind of person than Bob's. I liked Lan, I made him our friend. He was at the house often. He knew the boys. Fritz Gimbel was around too, and the contrast between them then was even greater than later. Fritz—Bob doesn't like me to say this—was Bob's factotum . . . He worked at the company and made himself so ingratiating, so useful, you just couldn't run him off. So he was around too. Anyway, there were the two of them . . . There were stories around that Lan and I were lovers. Well, we *were not.* Never. I suppose in this investigation you've come across suggestions to the contrary. I'm telling you it never happened. Bob knows it never happened . . . "

Ron, feeling increasingly uncomfortable in the face of such personal exchanges, could only listen and nod rather dumbly.

"My field is psychiatry, as you know," she went on. "I'm a psychiatrist, not a psychologist. I have my M.D. I taught, and I also practiced. Some of my patients were students. I saw them at home. We had a big house and I had room for a study where I saw my patients. Bob's business kept him away a good deal. Many nights he worked late, he traveled some. We have always loved each other, but we have lived independently, each having a career, interests, friends . . . As you know, I didn't give up my career to be an adjunct to his until he was elected President . . . All right, I'm setting the scene, in a roundabout way, for what happened . . . "

Ron nodded automatically, his attention fixed not only on the story she was telling but on her effort at self-control. Her tone was calm, cool, but the tension beneath was palpable; so far she'd managed to overpower it. She was, by any standards, a handsome woman, poised and polished.

The President, too, was watching her closely.

"As I said, there were Bob's friends, and my friends, and our friends, although inevitably the friends became intermixed some. One of Bob's friends was a man named Oakes, George Oakes . . .

"George Oakes was a business acquaintance of Bob Webster, and Bob arranged for the Oakeses and the Websters to meet for dinner. George and Betty Oakes were some ten years older than the Websters, but they became friends and saw a good deal of each other. They were at each others' houses, went out to dinner, to shows. One year they even took a vacation together in Jamaica . . . "

"Our boys were still young," Catherine was saying. "Bob, Junior, was in high school at that time, and Sam was in elementary school. The Oakeses had a son . . . Stan. He was graduating from high school about the same time we met the Oakeses and was a student at the university during this time when we were such friends with his parents. Uh . . . Stan was a handsome, personable, warm-hearted kid, you couldn't help liking him . . . but he had a problem—"

Catherine stopped abruptly, looked at her husband and whispered something to him that Ron could not hear. The President, *sotto voce,* said something back, perhaps, Ron guessed, that she didn't have to go on.

"George pretty much dominated his son," the President said, taking up the story with obvious reluctance. "I'm not the psychiatrist in this family but I always thought that that had a bit to do with what was wrong with Stan. He was plain afraid of his old man, could never do enough to suit him. The boy was bright, all right, but never bright enough to suit George, who'd scrambled his way up at General Motors and had ambitions to go even higher and saw life generally as a constant fight to do more, earn more, get recognized more—and in the process never to be satisfied. I have to say this for him, though . . . he was as hard on himself as he was on Stan."

"He was a severely flawed man," Catherine said. "We didn't know it then, he was pleasant enough to be around and a psychiatrist isn't always too perceptive out of the office . . . everyone needs time off . . . "

Was she apologizing, Ron thought? It seemed so. Strange . . .

"His wife had her problems too," the President said. "You

know, people like that pass through your life, you sort of fall in with them because on the surface they're pleasant enough, you have some apparent, surfacey things in common . . . "

"We had to keep Lan Blaine away from the house when the Oakeses were there," Catherine said, rather abruptly taking back the story. "He would cut little slices off George—conversationally, I mean—and either George was too self-absorbed to notice or too much the gentleman to fight back." She sighed, and her face colored. "Anyway, as we said, their son Stan had an emotional problem. He needed help, that was plain. One night at dinner George and Betty proposed that I take Stan on as a patient. I declined, I said our personal relationship precluded my taking their son as a patient. They brought it up several times after that, literally begged me to take their son on as a patient. They argued that I owed it as a friend, and besides if Stan were *my* patient, it could be considered just friendly counseling or some such, and I suspect they rationalized on their own behalf that they wouldn't have to admit, to themselves or anybody, that their son needed and was getting psychiatric treatment . . . Well, I felt for the boy. You could see he was living in some kind of hell, but still, I felt I couldn't mix a personal and professional relationship. Then one night we got a call . . .

"George asked the Websters to come to their house. He sounded scared to death. He said Stan had tried to kill himself. The police were all over the place. The emergency squad had taken him away, pumped phenobarbital out of him and barely managed to save him. George and Betty Oakes, having denied the truth so long, were unable to cope. They just couldn't understand how . . .

"So . . . against my better judgment," Catherine said, "I did take on Stanley Oakes as a patient."

She stared hard at Ron for a moment, as if trying to guess how he would react to the rest of the story and trying to decide how to tell it. Clearly, Ron thought, it was deeply painful for her to go on.

"Catherine," the President said, "how about I go out and make us some drinks?"

She nodded gratefully.

The President put his hand first on her shoulder, then on Ron's as he went by them out of the room.

"Mrs. Webster, I'm really sorry to put you through this, maybe the President is right, maybe it *isn't* necessary—"

She smiled weakly, shook her head. "No, I've gone this far, it wouldn't be right to stop now . . . Well, Stan's suicide attempt was kept quiet. I persuaded him to go on with his classes at the university. He was doing well in spite of his emotional problem. He would go to classes until the middle of the afternoon, and about three he would come to our house. I would meet with him in my little home office . . . Ron, I don't know how much you've studied psychology so let me put it this way . . . Stan Oakes was emotionally *empty.* Never mind the technical term for it . . . He was convinced that no one loved him. That sounds like a sob story, except when it's not, it's a terrible thing. This is what this boy literally believed. He *felt*—and that's what counts—that he had never received any love, and so he believed he was unworthy of it, that he didn't deserve it. And he couldn't give what he didn't feel worthy to receive. He was a boy without a shred of self-esteem. The sessions were painful. He would break down and cry. His parents had taught him it was not manly to cry, that his father never cried. With me he at least was able to risk crying. It wasn't easy for him . . . Do you see where this is leading?"

Ron shook his head.

"No, of course you don't . . . why should you? . . . Well, I made the mistake of a lifetime," she said bleakly. "And not just a professional lifetime . . . He felt he couldn't give, or receive, love. I, his doctor and counselor, proved to him he was wrong. I'm not defending it, although I suppose I could . . . It was unprofessional. It was disloyal to my husband and children"—she did not look back at the President—"it was, God knows, stupid, at best, bad judgment. And it didn't even help him, although he said otherwise. He had never been allowed anything much before, by girls his age. I . . . introduced him . . . and he was shrewd enough to think of the best way to encourage me to continue . . . He pretended it helped him, and he was very convincing.

"I know, I know, I should have seen through all this, but psychiatrists are human too, they're vulnerable almost by definition. Still, no question, I was a fool. Even when I told myself that my instinct had been wrong, my judgment bad, I still went on with him . . . he would come to the house for his appointment, and almost every day . . . in my office . . . for a month . . . "

She had closed her eyes. "Oh yes, I wanted to stop. But now I was compromised . . . he demanded that I go on. I lost control . . . I was afraid he'd become hysterical and go screaming to his parents, maybe to others . . . Even so, I at least began to . . . well . . . extricate myself from the situation. I stopped seeing him on a daily basis. He would call and say he had to see me, that he was feeling very depressed. I couldn't be sure when he was lying . . . it's not so easy to tell as you might think, and remember, he'd tried to commit suicide . . . I would tell him he could come to see me, but only to talk. He would come, and too often he got what he wanted . . . He would beg, he . . . he would threaten suicide, and he was suicidal . . . The sessions were exhausting . . . each one was a war . . . But at least gradually I was weaning him away, I felt . . . the last time was ten days after the time before . . . And then, I found I was pregnant." She looked directly at Ron, who could not face her.

"I told Bob," she said. "It was—to put it mildly—the most difficult thing I've ever done in my life. Bob Webster is a finer man than you can imagine . . . he was shaken at first . . . who wouldn't be? . . . but then he told me that we would just announce that we were having another baby. We would raise the child. He would be its father and we would never tell Stan Oakes that he had had anything to do with it. Yes . . . we talked about my having an abortion, but decided against it. It was illegal at the time, and in any case we were opposed to it in principle. Bob reminded me that no one but ourselves would ever know the baby was not his . . . and it wasn't his, if you're wondering . . . we weren't doing much together at that time. Too preoccupied with our separate worlds. No question, the child was Stan Oakes'."

Ron opened his mouth and formed a word. It did not come. He tried again. "Lynne?" He could barely get it out.

Catherine Webster nodded.

"Does she know?"

"Yes."

"And Blaine knew? And Gimbel?"

She nodded again. "There's more, and if you can believe it, it gets worse . . . "

Ron remembered what Martha Kingsley had said, that even she pitied the Websters. The cynical call girl, hearing the story only from Blaine, had pitied the President of the United States and the First Lady. No wonder . . .

Catherine straightened, took a deep breath. "Things went all right for a while. I was three months pregnant and we hadn't told anyone as yet. Bob assured me he would love the child. I did the same. I kept Stan Oakes away from me. Bob helped. I could tell Stan that Bob was home. And he was. Stan would call and beg for a session but I kept him away. I didn't see him at all for more than two weeks. George and Betty asked me why I wasn't seeing their son any more, and I said something also unprofessional . . . that Stan had improved enough to cut down on his therapy. I should have told them to get him another doctor, even to a hospital if necessary, but, to be frank, I was afraid he would tell them, or another psychiatrist, what I had done. I could have lost my license. I *should* have lost it . . .

"Finally there was the night Bob and I were having a small dinner party. It was an unusual party, just Lan Blaine and Fritz Gimbel were there. Fritz, because we were celebrating some contract Weber Corporation had just won. Lan, because he was almost always there. I had drunk a good deal of wine. I felt almost relaxed, for a change . . . "

The telephone was ringing. The maid answered and told Catherine that a patient was calling, he said it was an emergency and he sounded scary. Catherine, of course, knew immediately who it was. And, all unreasonably she told herself, she felt a tremendous anger, resentment. Damn it . . . this was the first time in months she'd felt almost human . . . she tried to suppress her feelings, but they were dangerously close to the surface . . . Stan was crying. He said he'd lost her love, that she was the only person who had ever cared anything for him and now he had lost her . . . He *had* to see her, he said. He demanded she leave the house that minute and meet him somewhere, anywhere. She told him she couldn't do that, and that she was not going to see him at her home anymore, only at her office at the university. And with the door open. He knew what that meant, of course . . . He sobbed and groaned and carried on as he'd done before. He told her he would kill himself if she didn't go on with him . . . it was all he lived for . . . She was the only person who'd ever loved him, the only person he'd ever been able to love. Catherine, fighting to regain her composure, told him he would find other women who would love him, now that he had learned how to love . . . No, he said, he hadn't learned, he'd only lost his love. And *on* and *on* . . .

"Well," she said, "I finally lost patience, became sharp with him. I told him to try to control himself and stop acting like an idiot. I actually used that word. I was no longer the doctor talking to a patient, I was a woman in her own home reacting to an infuriating, terrifying, personal situation . . . I'm not excusing it, just explaining, as best I can . . . I talked to him just the way his father had. It was, of course, the worst thing I could have done.

"Finally I hung up on him. I went back to the dinner table, told Bob who had called and said I had told him never to call me again. Bob handed me a glass of wine, and, God help us, we drank a toast to that. Neither Lan nor Fritz understood, of course. Not then . . . An hour later we got another call. This time it was from George Oakes . . . Stan was dead. He had shot himself."

She was weeping quietly now, and went to the President's desk and pulled a handful of tissues from a drawer to wipe her eyes.

When the President returned, she was sitting slumped, holding tissues to her face, quietly sobbing.

Ron looked up at the President, who stood just inside the door with a tray of glasses. "I'm so sorry," he half-whispered. "I'm sorry I insisted that you tell me—"

"Did she tell you about the note?" the President asked as he put the tray on the coffee table.

"No."

"I didn't get to it." Catherine's voice was barely audible.

"All right," the President said. "Might as well get it all out now . . . There was a suicide note." He handed a Scotch and soda to Catherine, then one to Ron. "When we got the call saying the young man had shot himself, Catherine was, of course, terribly upset—"

"I was *hysterical,*" she said. "The great psychiatrist . . . "

The President shook his head, went on. "The Oakeses were on the telephone begging us to come over, to help them, deal with the police . . . Catherine was crying. I went to the Oakeses' house and Fritz Gimbel went with me. Lan Blaine stayed with Catherine. When Fritz and I got to the house the police hadn't yet been called. Fritz and I went upstairs, to look at the body. I found the note. It said too much, and I put it in my pocket. Later, at home, I burned it."

"That was the night when Lan learned everything," Catherine said. "I told him everything that night. He was sympathetic, he was more than a casual friend—"

"She wanted to give up her license to practice psychiatry," the President cut in. "She wanted to resign from the faculty. Lan had at least talked her out of those notions before I got back. He had a special knack for getting to people in a crisis, propping them up. Well, we were grateful to him. We damn well had to be—"

"George and Betty Oakes vaguely blamed me for their son's death," Catherine was saying, "but, of course, they didn't know how much I *really* was to blame. All they could criticize me for was cutting down on the number of Stan's appointments. God . . . As you can imagine, we saw less and less of them after Stan's death."

They sat there together now, not the President and First Lady, just a man and woman who had relived an awful tragedy in their lives. They looked as they felt . . . exhausted, drained. And Ron felt the same way.

"You said you told Lynne all this?"

"Not all of it," Catherine said dully. "Not as much as you have just heard. She knows who her father was. She knows that he killed himself. We told her the story, gradually, once we felt she was old enough to understand. We thought she had to know, we were afraid someday she would find out from somebody else first.

Better that we tell her. But we've never told anyone else."

Catherine held her glass in both hands and stared into it as though hoping it would yield up, finally, her forgiveness. Then abruptly she looked up and went on . . . "When Lan threatened Bob—I mean, threatened to go public with what he knew—we told Lynne about it. That was probably a mistake, but we've always been honest with her, and it's worked out pretty well. We're a very close family now . . . "

"I thought I'd noticed that she was upset," Ron said. "I mean, before Blaine died."

"That's what I could never have forgiven him," said the President. "The pain he was ready to cause that innocent girl . . . It outweighed all his friendship. *All* of it . . . "

"There isn't much political damage in the story," Ron said. "Mostly personal. In a lot of people's minds, I suspect you'd be bigger people, not smaller, for what you did. I mean afterward . . . "

"Maybe," Webster said. "But I did destroy the suicide note . . . "

Ron nodded, and for a moment sat silent, staring at his shoes. "Mr. President . . . Mrs. Webster," he said slowly, "I'm sorry, but I still think Fritz Gimbel is the most likely suspect. His motive may have been personal, or political, or some of both. It may be he's involved with the consortium too, though I can't identify the specific connection. But the coincidences are just too many. Too much points at him. And, nothing points to anyone else. Frankly I can't think where else to look. Except for Fritz Gimbel. This thing is dead stuck."

The President thought for a moment, then: "There may at least be a simple way to prove he didn't kill Martha Kingsley."

"How?"

"Check with the Secret Service. People have to check in and

check out of the West Wing, you know that. What time was she killed? If Fritz was in the West Wing at that time, then he at least didn't kill her himself. He *might* have sent somebody, but he didn't do it himself."

"Well, I left her apartment a little before five. The FBI called me here shortly after eight, and the man said the call to the FBI had come an hour before. That puts it between five and seven."

"Fritz rarely leaves the West Wing before eight or nine." The President got up and went to the telephone. Frowning, he chose a line and pushed the button. The line was answered immediately. "This is the President," he said. "Is Mr. Gimbel still in the West Wing? No. Well, what time did he leave? I see. Thank you."

"What time, Bob?" Her voice had reverted to the near-whisper.

The President did not look at her as he said, "Five-fourteen."

V

Along with his underlying competence and acumen, Robert Webster had a sense of the dramatic. He'd found out long ago that a confrontation could help strike through complexities to clarify and reduce a problem to a hard solution. Tonight his emotions were strung tight. The evening had generated a sense of doom for him, an unaccustomed pessimism for the dynamic Midwesterner. Worse, he felt defensive, partly for himself, more for his wife. Which made him angry.

He called Fritz Gimbel—the switchboard found him at home—and ordered him to come to the White House. He summoned the Attorney General. He would take charge, settle right now, once and for all, the question of Gimbel's innocence or guilt.

Although he generally disdained them, he would use the trappings of the presidency. He led Catherine and Ron through the corridors of the White House into the West Wing, to the Oval Office. Lights in the Oval Office in the middle of the night, the spreading word that the President was there . . . all alerted the media and the duty officers in a score of offices. Abruptly, shortly before midnight, the White House came tensely to life.

The Attorney General arrived before Gimbel. The President, taking him aside in the Oval Office, briefed him quickly, quietly. At the same time Ron was on the telephone to FBI headquarters, asking that Walter Locke report to the White House as soon as possible, then directed the switchboard to locate and summon Les Fitch, the man who had headed the Secret Service detail assigned to Lynne on Saturday night. He also called Jill Keller's apartment and Gabe Haddad's home, but no one answered at either number.

Ron sat on one of the couches, watching the President talking quietly at a window with the Attorney General. Catherine Webster stood at another window, staring out at the lights of the city in the summer's night sky. It occurred to Ron that this might be the last time he would see this room. If Gimbel survived the confrontation the President had arranged, Ron's resignation would be expected—not just as investigator but as Special Counsel to the President as well. No one had said so, but it was clearly understood. Even if he were right and Gimbel confessed to Blaine's murder, his tenure here was probably foreshortened. Assuming the Webster Administration survived—which would by no means be certain—he would almost surely be eased out—kill the messenger of bad tidings . . . Another unspoken understanding had been, from the first, that he find some graceful way for the President not to be involved in whatever happened . . . and he had not found that way. To the contrary, by rushing headlong to Martha Kingsley this afternoon he had probably, in a sense, at least provoked her death, and he'd brought the focus of the investigation directly back to the President himself. It had not exactly been a subtle preference . . . he'd win no thanks no matter how this turned out. Between a rock and a hard place . . . Jill Keller had been right about that.

He'd lost control of the investigation as the days passed and he failed to score a clear breakthrough. He wished, though, that he could have had another day or two of digging instead of this midnight round-up. The investigation had turned in on itself. Now it involved only a few people close to the President; men like Osanaga, Johnson, Grand and others, who might well be important to it, were abruptly outside, all but forgotten.

The telephone buzzed. The President picked it up, listened, spoke curtly. "Fritz is here."

Fritz Gimbel came in. He stopped just inside the door and peered through his round, steel-rimmed spectacles at the assembled group—the President, just sitting down beside Catherine on one of the couches, the Attorney General, sitting beside Ron on the other. The points of Gimbel's blue eyes were the only color in his pallid face; the gray of his hair seemed, somehow, to blend with the gray of his loose-hanging gray-checked suit. He was a small man, no more than five-feet-six, with the misleading air of a bemused accountant. It was difficult to believe that this insignificant-looking man was the terror of the White House staff: indeed, a feared and hated man. He ambled across the room and sat down in an armchair facing the group on the two couches. He glanced at each person in turn, said nothing.

The President spoke first. "Have you guessed what this is about, Fritz?"

Gimbel nodded. "I expect so."

"I'm sorry to subject you to this. If we're wrong, there will never be any apology strong or deep enough to make up for it. You're of course entitled to refuse to say anything. I have one question, maybe just one. If you answer it, maybe it's all we need to know.

Gimbel glanced at Ron. His eyes were very cold. He nodded curtly.

"You left the West Wing at five-fourteen," the President said. "I need to know where you were between then and seven o'clock. And can you come up with witnesses?"

Gimbel's lips were white, rigid, his pallid face stayed fixed in its original hostile mask. He said nothing.

"Fritz?" the President said.

"I went home."

"When you got there did you call the White House switchboard and tell them where you could be found?"

"No."

"You always do."

"I didn't today. Didn't feel well, didn't want any calls—"

"And no one saw you, no one saw you enter your building."

"No, not that I know of."

The President looked at Ron. "Ron," he said curtly.

Ron picked it up. "You received a telephone call from a woman about five o'clock," he said . . . it was a guess but an informed guess . . . all right, a bluff, actually. "Her name would be on your secretary's telephone log. Who was she?"

"Donna Kemper."

Donna Kemper. Of course . . . Martha Kingsley would have been told to use a pseudonym when she called Gimbel at the White House, where a record was kept of every incoming call. "Who's Donna Kemper?"

"A friend."

"We can identify her and interview her. In fact if you'll give us her number we can call her now—"

Gimbel turned to the President. "Bob . . . " Never before had Ron heard anyone but Catherine Webster call the President by his first name. " . . . how much of this do I have to tolerate?"

"You can settle it damn easily, Fritz." He was clearly appealing to Gimbel to do just that.

Gimbel looked at Ron. "I will not allow you to disturb Donna Kemper in the middle of the night—"

"Walter Locke is here," Ron said to the President. "I'll give him the name. The FBI can make a quick check to see who she is, or if there really is such a person—"

"A five o'clock telephone call, where I was from five to seven, what does all this have to do with anything—?"

"Martha Kingsley," Ron interrupted him, "was killed between five and seven. "If you weren't involved you can easily prove it by letting us call your friend Donna Kemper. Except you can't let us call her, can you? You can't because Donna Kemper is the name Martha Kingsley used when she called you at five o'clock—"

"I don't have to prove anything to you—"

"Mr. President," Ron said—he glanced at Gimbel, then fixed his eyes on the President—"let's at least find out if there's a Donna Kemper in the telephone book. Let's find out if the FBI can identify such a person."

The President looked to Catherine, as if to see if she could save him from the misery of this confrontation. Then he looked at the Attorney General. Catherine was staring at the floor and did not look up. The Attorney General stared back at the President through the curling smoke of his cigarette, showing no intention to intervene. The President sighed heavily. "Call the FBI."

Ron picked up the telephone on the end table, told the switchboard to find Locke, who was in the West Wing, and send him to the Oval Office. The operator told him Les Fitch had also arrived, and Ron told her to send him in.

Gimbel sat stiffly erect during this telephone call. To Ron he seemed caged . . . he couldn't get up and stalk out, he couldn't withstand interrogation. A facade seemed to be breaking up as he sat there.

Locke and Fitch had been waiting just outside, and when there was an immediate rap on the door Ron went to it, separated Locke and Fitch, told Locke what he wanted and led Fitch into the room.

"Mr. President," Ron said, "I think we can settle another matter. You know Les Fitch. He was head of the Secret Service detail that was assigned to protect Lynne Saturday night. He's going to tell us what really happened."

Fitch, ordinarily a self-possessed man, was stunned. Here he was facing the President, Catherine Webster, Gimbel, the Attorney General, and Ron Fairbanks all at once—in the Oval Office, at midnight. "Uh . . . just what is it you want to know—?"

"Please just answer the question," the President said in a flat, weary voice without looking up at Fitch.

"We already know a good deal," Ron told Fitch, "but we'd like your contribution. Just tell us what happened Saturday night."

"Well . . . it's of course not true that you were drinking too much, Mr. Fairbanks. I . . . I wasn't the source of that story." He paused, hoping that he had told them what they wanted to hear. "I . . . just somehow lost you, Mr. Fairbanks. We try to be courteous, to combine security with courtesy . . . that's the ticket . . . I guess I overdid the courtesy . . . I'm sorry . . . "

"Who told you to drop back?" he asked. "Who told you to leave Lynne and me without Secret Service protection for ten or fifteen minutes?"

Fitch shook his head. "I—"

"Fitch, you're talking bull and you know it. I'd say you were in a bag of trouble."

"Mr. Gimbel?" Fitch snapped.

Gimbel did not react. During the exchange between Ron and Fitch he'd sat motionless, staring straight ahead. He'd shown no sign that he was even aware Fitch was in the room. He continued to stare ahead.

"What am I supposed to say, Mr. Gimbel?" Fitch demanded. "They're asking questions you promised wouldn't be asked . . . "

Gimbel looked up at him, shrugged.

"Well, at least that settles that," Ron said.

"No, it doesn't," Catherine put in, and swung around on the couch to face Fitch directly. "Who ordered you to do what? I want to know exactly what your orders were."

Fitch's defiance collapsed. "Mrs. Webster—"

"Wait a minute," she said. "I want Lynne to hear this." She picked up the telephone.

"No, Catherine," the President's voice was more a plea than an order. "Lynne needn't—"

"She's going to hear plenty second-hand. I want her to hear how they left her unprotected, let somebody break her arm . . . maybe trying to do worse." She spoke to the White House operator on the line.

"Catherine . . ." Gimbel said, shaking his head. "Please . . . "

"Let Fitch tell us," she said firmly. "Go ahead, Fitch. *Who* ordered you to do *what?*"

"Catherine," Gimbel protested. *"No,* don't do this . . . please . . . leave Lynne out of it . . . "

"Fitch. Enough of this. Tell us."

The Secret Service man gave up. "All right . . . I was ordered to drop back," he said. He swallowed hard. "Mr. Gimbel ordered me to drop back and leave a gap between my detail and the Datsun Mr. Fairbanks was driving. The other men in the detail didn't know. I pretended I was having trouble with my Chevy. I lost the Datsun just after it entered the park. I was supposed to give somebody five minutes time to . . . interfere with the Datsun—"

"Interfere." Catherine stood up. "Fritz, my God, you actually tried to kill Lynne—"

"No." Gimbel shouted it. "No, Catherine, for God's sake. *She* wasn't supposed to be hurt, not even a little. The man who hit them is an expert. He was to run them off the road, scare Fair-

banks, make him out to look like a drunken driver. She wasn't supposed to be hurt, I guarantee you . . . I knew she always wore her belt in the car, she was *not* to be hurt . . . There was not to be *any* chance of it—"

Catherine stood looking at him, shaking her head. Gimbel stared at her, whispered something inaudible, then put his hands to his face.

"You valued her . . . and her life . . . very very little, Fritz, if you could do what you did," the President said.

Gimbel spoke through his hands in a voice now clearly breaking.

"No . . . wrong . . . my God, I *love* that little girl, I couldn't possibly hurt her . . . I watched her grow up, you know that . . . She's always been so lovely, so innocent—"

"And the daughter you never had," Catherine said coldly. "I've heard you say it more than once."

Gimbel nodded. He uncovered his face, pulled off his glasses and dabbed at his eyes with his fingertips. "So I *couldn't* hurt her . . . just the opposite—"

Ron broke in. "You wanted to discredit me because I'd been to see Martha Kingsley. I was getting too close to you."

Gimbel only glanced up at Ron. He did not respond.

"I interviewed Martha Kingsley again this afternoon," Ron went on. "As soon as I left her she called you. She told you what I had asked. She told you how much she had told me. She told you . . . just a minute. Fitch, you can leave."

The Secret Service man left the Oval Office, shoulders slack, red-faced.

Ron spoke directly to Gimbel. "Blaine had told Martha Kingsley all about Mrs. Webster and Stanley Oakes and Lynne. She knew it all. This afternoon she told me she did. And when she called you, she told *you* she knew. Didn't she?"

Gimbel appeared to sag inside his over-large suit. He sighed and nodded, and he turned to the President.

"Sir, over the last year and a half I've paid Martha Kingsley some twenty-five thousand dollars out of the reptile fund—"

"What the hell is the reptile fund?" the Attorney General asked.

Webster explained. "It's the fund we use for bribing snakes."

Gimbel went on, ignoring the interruption. "Blaine in many ways was a fool. He ate too much, he drank too much, he even talked too much, and for a man in his position . . . well, not all of the young women he condescended to sleep with were the little idiots he thought they were." Gimbel looked at Ron. "Marya Kalisch, who was in his apartment when he was being killed, reported back to Eiseman the things Blaine confided in her. But in Martha Kingsley he met a woman every bit as smart—street smart, anyway—as Blaine. She knew how to work him. She'd played the game before. She was interested in money. I paid her, she reported Blaine's conversations to me. I've known for a long time he was taking outright bribes."

"Why didn't you tell me?" the President said.

"Was I to accuse your Secretary of State, your brilliant, witty friend, on the word of a prostitute?"

The President shook his head. "I didn't know we dealt with—"

"There are a lot of things you don't know," Gimbel said. "They're my job. The dirtier the better . . . "

Ron wanted to bring things back on course. "Blaine told Martha Kingsley about Stanley Oakes," he repeated.

"Is someone going to tell me who Stanley Oakes is?" the Attorney General said.

"Isn't that right, Gimbel?" Ron said, avoiding the question. "She knew about Oakes . . . and all the rest of it."

Gimbel nodded. "Blaine was a damn fool." He bit off the

words. "When she called me this afternoon she said, 'Don't worry, I didn't tell Fairbanks the big secret." I asked her what secret. 'The one about Lynne,' she said. 'Don't worry,' she said, 'I won't tell it. It's the kind of thing I don't tell.' Of course I knew better. She would tell it the first time she saw enough advantage in telling. She would sell the story to the highest bidder. If she didn't tell Fairbanks here, it was only because he wasn't important enough. He didn't shape up as the highest bidder." He said that last with a certain amount of relish, despite his circumstances.

"You didn't know before this afternoon that Blaine had told her?" Ron said, not believing it.

Gimbel shook his head. "Blaine spent the night with her the same day he threatened Bob, tried to blackmail him. He told her then, but she didn't tell me that. She told me all about that night but not that he'd told her about Oakes."

Ron looked for a moment at the President, then spoke again to Gimbel. "I say you killed Martha Kingsley. If she talked, the whole story would come back around, and it would be obvious who killed Blaine."

Gimbel stared thoughtfully for a moment at Ron. Then, abruptly, he shrugged and turned up the palms of his hands.

Catherine Webster was quietly sobbing, holding tight to her husband's hand.

The President stared downward. "I guess this is the end of my presidency . . . my Chief of Staff involved in . . . "

The Attorney General seemed not to have heard the President. "Fritz, will you sign a confession?" he asked Gimbel.

Gimbel looked at him, appearing not to have understood the question. Again he shrugged.

"Well, we—" the Attorney General began, and stopped.

Lynne had just come in. She had knocked once, then walked in. She was wearing a pair of faded blue jeans and her FIRST

DAUGHTER T-shirt, and a black sling for her broken arm.

"Tell her to go back upstairs," Gimbel said intensely to Catherine. His eyes seemed especially naked without the spectacles that always covered them. "Don't let her—"

Lynne glanced around the Oval Office, walked over to the couch where her mother sat. "What's going on?" She sat down beside her mother in the space Catherine and the President had made for her. She looked at Ron. "Actually, I think I know . . . "

"Lynne . . . " said the President quietly, "we are talking about Lan, about who killed him . . . Fritz has admitted he arranged the automobile accident you and Ron had Saturday night. Also"—the President stiffened and spoke crisply—"also, Fritz has admitted he killed a woman named Martha Kingsley, he did it late this afternoon—"

"Fritz . . . " Lynne was up from the couch. "My God . . . who is Martha Kingsley? Why did you have to . . . what's that have to do with Lan? Why somebody else . . . ?"

Gimbel's face was a mask of anguish.

"Lynne . . . " The President stood to face his daughter. "What are you saying? What do you *know?* You said 'somebody else'? Did you know that Fritz killed Blaine too—?"

"He's *right,* Lynne," Gimbel said quickly, and nodded urgently at her. "Don't say anything more . . . it's true . . . *I* killed Blaine . . . for good reason—"

She shook her head, spoke with a weird calm. "No . . . *I* killed Lan. I had to do it . . . and I did." She looked from her mother to the President, and finally to Ron. "I killed him," she whispered. And repeated, "I killed him."

The President held his daughter in his arms, an island of humanity, abruptly cut off from all trapping of office, from all others except themselves. Lynne finally was able to look away . . . to Ron, who looked as stricken as the Webster family. He looked away, at Gimbel, sitting there hunched over, his hands covering his face.

"Listen to me," Gimbel was saying to Ron, and including the Attorney General. He spoke now in a weak, throaty voice, held his spectacles in his left hand and with his right rubbed his eyes. "It's absolutely true, what you said. I did kill Martha Kingsley . . . I didn't realize until she called at five o'clock that Blaine had told her *everything* . . . enought to *destroy* Bob, and Catherine . . . and Lynne . . . enough to destroy this Administration, and me with it . . . She knew all about Lynne, that Blaine took bribes . . . and I knew she'd use what she knew, use it to her best advantage, as soon as she found out what that was . . . I'd thought before about doing it . . . today I *had* to. There was no more time once I found out what she knew . . . except I moved too fast to try to cover myself . . . well, it doesn't matter—"

"You face a murder charge," the Attorney General said. "Aggravated murder. I'm sorry, Fritz, there's no way around it—"

"I know," Gimbel said, and shrugged. "It's end of the line . . . but it doesn't need to be for her . . . " and looked for the first time directly at Lynne. "No one outside this room knows what she's done, or has heard her say it . . . As you say, there's no way out for me now, so what difference if I go to jail for one murder or two? I confess to both of them, and an innocent girl . . . yes, damn it, *innocent* in the real sense, will be spared what she doesn't deserve anyway . . . "

"Oh, Fritz . . . " Catherine began, tears in her eyes, but the Attorney General broke in.

"I can't go along with that, Fritz . . . none of us can . . . we'd all be accessories to Blaine's killing . . . " He shook his head vehemently. "Frankly I find it very hard . . . hell, almost impossible . . . to accept Lynne's confession, but now there's nothing for it except to have it go through the legal process . . . I'm sorry . . . but—"

"You're right, of course," Webster said. "Fritz, we're grateful for the . . . gesture, but it's no good, it can't be done and it would be wrong . . . "

"Look here," the Attorney General said, "Lynne says she did it but a court may find differently. Ron, does it seem plausible from the facts you've uncovered—?"

But before Ron could answer him, Lynne broke away from her parents and spoke up, going over to Ron and touching him briefly on the shoulder, his face, as she began to speak. *"Please,* don't make a mockery of what I did. I appreciate what everybody is trying to do for me, but I have no regrets over what I did. My God, you have to understand, I really *had* to do it . . . Ron, by now you know what Lan Blaine really was, or you know some of it. But there's more . . . " And she turned to look at her father. "Remember, dad, when I used to call him Uncle Lan . . . ? He was our very best friend, the one we loved and trusted the best. He brought me presents from the time I was a little girl. He kept our secret, right from the first . . . you told me he knew when you first told me about it . . . you said we could always trust him. You, too, mother . . . Well, it's not so surprising, I guess I fell in love with him . . . One night during the campaign—I never told either of you this, and it's obvious he never told you—I think it was somewhere in Kentucky . . . Louisville, that was it, I got his key, said I wanted to talk, got into his bed before he got there . . . I offered myself to him that night . . . and he was so incredibly kind . . . He told me I was a beautiful girl, and if I were anybody else . . . well, nothing really happened. He was kind and gentle and that was it . . . So you see, again he seemed to be showing we could trust him . . . God knows, I trusted him even more after that night, though maybe I was just a little surprised that—anyway, you see now what he was really doing. Just putting us off-guard, putting *me* off-guard, just waiting for the chance to use what he knew to make the most of it . . . "

She looked a little wild now as she spoke . . . "When the time came to profit from our friendship, from mine, he didn't care what he did or how much it could hurt . . . "

"Lynne," Ron said very quietly, still not wanting to believe it, hoping against reason that somehow it was a temporary delusion or *something* . . . "how was Blaine killed, I mean do you know . . . ?"

She looked directly at him. "Thank you, Ron, I know what you're trying to do, but it's no good, just like the Attorney General said a minute ago. Yes, I know because I *did* it . . . I'd read somewhere, I don't remember, about how if you pulled a wire tight, pulled hard enough"—she held up her hand—"no, don't stop me, let me get it all out . . . well, I got a guitar string and wrapped it around a roller and . . . Lan liked to have me rub his shoulders, and I *used* to like doing it, so it didn't seem unusual when I walked up behind him, he just went on talking into that telephone . . . "

The silence was like thunder. Finally the Attorney General nodded to Gimbel. "And you?"

"I happened to walk in, I wanted to talk to Blaine about something. I was too late. I took the wire and roller out of her hands and told her to go to her room and not to say a word. Afterward I disposed of the . . . You know the rest."

Abruptly Lynne, who had seemed so strong in telling what she'd done, broke into tears, long terrible shudders wracked her body, she began to sway as though she would fall before her father could rush over to hold her . . . And now she looked around the room, to her father, her mother, and finally to Ron. And she was more like a little girl, strangely reverted, looking bewildered, looking for understanding . . .

"This is the way she was right afterward . . . when I found her that night," Gimbel said. "I'm not sure, at one level at least, that she understands what she really did—"

"Then maybe that's the defense," Ron said quickly, looking to the Attorney General and the President.

The President frowned, began to shake his head.

"Oh, I don't mean a literal insanity plea," Ron hurried on, reading the President's thoughts. "More that Blaine had involved her, manipulated her, got her into such an emotional state that she did what she did without understanding, when she did it, that it was wrong. There are plenty of precedents for that . . . "

Catherine looked to her husband, then the Attorney General.

"Well," he said, "we'd have to establish that the emotional impact of what he did or threatened—or what Lynne honestly thought he did or threatened—was so strong that she was deprived of her normal perception of right and wrong. It wouldn't be easy, but it's certainly not unreasonable . . . A sympathetic jury would be a help and—"

"She'd have one," Ron put in quickly. "How could they be otherwise—?"

"If," Catherine said, "they had all the facts. *All* of them."

Lynne was shaking her head now, a bit more composed. *"No,* that's what Lan was going to do, tell everything, ruin everything, don't you see? . . . oh, daddy, it would be terrible for you, ruin your chances for reelection . . . "

"I'll survive, honey. I've had it, we don't need it any more—"

"Forgive me, Mr. President." The Attorney General seemed almost angry. "I don't see that at all."

"Neither do I, sir," Ron put in.

"Well, my own handpicked Secretary-of-State and longtime

friend turned out to be a liar and a cheat and a thief working against the interests of this country—"

"And," Gimbel said morosely, "your Chief of Staff has killed a woman—"

"But none of that is *his* fault or responsibility," Ron said, and spoke now directly to the President. "Sir, you had no idea what Fritz was doing. When the investigation began to point to him, you immediately confronted him . . . As for Blaine, you picked him for the right reasons and he performed well in many areas. When you began to suspect him of what he was doing, you immediately asked for his resignation. Except for tearing up a suicide note twenty years ago, what have you done wrong?"

Catherine tightened her arm around her daughter and looked directly at the President. "It does seem a poor time, Bob, to talk about quitting. It's never been your way . . . "

He took a deep breath, tried to break a smile. He kissed his daughter and his wife. "All right, we'll do what we have to do . . . we'll go this one together, just like we always have with all the others . . . all of it, all the way. We've been a family a long time. It's never been easy. But we've made it this far . . . " He stopped for a moment, as though gathering up his resources from the furthest depths of himself. "I say we go on. *No matter what. . . .* "

Ron, wrung out, went back to his office. He was still carrying the pistol he had taken from his filing cabinet earlier in the evening and wanted to put the thing back before he left the White House.

He unlocked his office door. It was not dark inside. The lamp burned on his desk.

On his couch, stretched out asleep, was Jill Keller. He nudged her, and she woke up.

"It's all over," he said. And he told her everything.

"Oh, my God, Ron . . . Lynne . . . ?"

"The President thought he had to resign but I think he's been persuaded otherwise . . . You know, they're quite a family, the Websters. I mean *all* of them . . . " He looked at her, undid his tie. "Well, I guess it's over, at least our part in it . . . "

She got up from the couch, took his arm. "Then, sir, I suggest you take the girl home and let her buy you a drink. Some things end, some others begin . . . You get my drift, counselor?"

"I do," he said, and he did.